Also by Elinor Lipman

ISABEL'S BED

THE WAY MEN ACT

THEN SHE FOUND ME

INTO LOVE AND OUT AGAIN

THE INN AT

LAKE DEVINE

THE INN AT

Lake Devine

A NOVEL

ELINOR LIPMAN

Random House New York

Copyright © 1998 by Elinor Lipman

All rights reserved under International and Pan-American Copyright Conventions. Published in the United States by Random House, Inc., New York, and simultaneously in Canada by Random House of Canada Limited, Toronto.

Library of Congress Cataloging-in-Publication Data

Lipman, Elinor.
The Inn at Lake Devine / Elinor Lipman
p. cm.
ISBN 0-679-45693-7
I. Title.
PS3562.I577I48   1998
813'.54—dc21   97-1307

Random House website address: www.randomhouse.com

Printed in the United States of America on acid-free paper

24689753

First Edition

Book design by Lilly Langotsky

FOR MY SISTER,

DEBORAH LIPMAN SLOBODNIK,

AND IN REMEMBRANCE OF WILLIAM AUSTIN

AND VACATIONS PAST

PART

ne

ONE

It was not complicated, and, as my mother pointed out, not even personal: They had a hotel; they didn't want Jews; we were Jews.

We were nothing to them, a name on an envelope, when it began in 1962 as a response to a blind inquiry my mother had sent out in multiples. We'd been to Cape Cod and Cape Ann, to Old Orchard, Salisbury, and Hampton beaches, to Winnipesaukee and the Finger Lakes. That year she wrote to Vermont, which someone had told her was heaven. She found a lake on the map that was neither too big nor too small, and not too far north. The Vermont Chamber of Commerce listed some twenty accommodations on Lake Devine. She sent the same letter to a dozen cottage colonies and inns inquiring about rates and availability. The others answered with printed rate cards and cordial notes. But one reply was different, typed on textured white stationery below a green pointillist etching of a lakeside hotel. Croquet on the lawn, the Vermont vacation guide had said; rowboats, sundown concerts on Saturday nights; a lifeguard, a dock, a raft, a slide. The Inn's letter said, "Dear Mrs. Marx: Thank you for your inquiry. Our two-bedroom cabins rent at the weekly rate of sixty-five (U.S.) dollars. We do have a few openings during the period you requested. The Inn at Lake Devine is a family-owned resort, which has been in continuous operation since 1922. Our guests who feel most comfortable here, and return year after year, are Gentiles. Very truly yours, (Mrs.) Ingrid Berry, Reservations Manager."

I hadn't known up to that moment that I had a surname that was recognizably Jewish, or that people named Marx would be unwelcome somewhere in the United States because of it.

I asked if these were Nazis. My mother sighed. I had been wed to the subject since reading, without her permission, *The Diary of a Young Girl*—specifically obsessed by where we, who had no attic, could hide that would be soundproof, and who among our Gentile acquaintances would bring us food under penalty of death.

My mother explained: There were people, unfortunately—for reasons it was hard to explain or understand—who weren't Nazis but didn't like Jews. Not that she wanted me to worry, because this was America, not Germany, not Amsterdam. We were safe here, remember? The letter was ignorant, and very bad manners. Someone should give this Mrs. Berry a piece of their mind.

I said, "Can we go?"

"You don't go where you're not wanted," my mother said. "Anyone who could write such a letter doesn't deserve our business." She took it back and stuffed it in its envelope with no particular archival care. Two days later, I removed it from the dining-room sideboard to a safer place—my sweater drawer. It fascinated me, the letter's marriage of good manners and anti-Semitism. Why bother to answer Jews at all if you don't want them at your hotel?

I tried to picture this Ingrid Berry who had signed neatly in blue ballpoint—the nerve of her insincere "Very truly yours." Was she old? Young? Married? Was Ingrid a German name? Did she get pleasure from insulting the people she banned from her hotel? And why didn't my parents respond to this slap in the face? "If you paid us a million dollars, we wouldn't come to your stupid hotel," I thought we should say. "If you had a baseball team, would you tell Sandy Koufax he couldn't pitch for you? Would you let Danny

Kaye rent a room? Tony Curtis? Albert Einstein? Milton Berle? Jesus Christ?"

My mother didn't show the letter to my father, because she knew that he, like me, would want to jump in the truck and fix the problem. And so I produced it for him with the same flourish my mother had staged for me. "Good God!" he said, struggling with one hand to put on his reading glasses.

I asked him if people who didn't rent rooms to Jews knew about the concentration camps.

"Everybody knows by now, honey."

I asked if he thought they had seen *The Diary of Anne Frank*.

"Probably not," he said. Then, "You know what I think we should do? Let's write back and tell her we want one of her stupid cabins."

I said, "I don't think they have cabins. It looks like a hotel."

He embroidered a little drama—not too seriously, but enough to get my mother's goat: We'd go as the Gentiles! Ed and Audrey Gentile. He'd known a man named Gentile in the navy from somewhere like Delaware or Pennsylvania. It was a real name. People truly had that for a name.

My mother said, "You'll have to drag me there."

"You don't want to see what a place like this is like?"

"And lie for the whole time we're there?"

"About what?"

"Church," said my mother. "You can bet the whole place empties out to go to church on Sundays."

"The Gentile family doesn't go to church when they're on vacation," my father said. "We go regularly on the other fifty weeks, but we pray in the cabin when we're on vacation."

"People will know," she said.

He thought they wouldn't. He was tall, taller than most Christians I knew, while my mother was a redhead no bigger than Gidget. And his two daughters looked like any two little American girls. "Except," my father said, smiling broadly, "nicer and smarter."

"And how would you make your point? Announce as you leave that we were the Eddie Marx family? Jews?"

"We wouldn't even have to tell them," said my father. "We could come and go and just know we fooled them."

Of course we didn't go. My mother found a place to rent on the opposite shore of Lake Devine—not a resort, but a heated cottage on a dirt road of private camps, listed with the Chamber of Commerce. We went there for two summers and found it, if not heaven, then very nice. The air smelled like bayberry. Indian paintbrush, a wildflower we didn't have at home, dotted every field. We swam and fished from a rowboat without an anchor, caught only ugly black-horned pouts we couldn't eat, and took a day trip to Fort Ticonderoga. The best miniature-golf course I'd ever played was a five-minute car ride away. The local dairy, which offered not only milk but cheddar cheese, made home deliveries even to the summer population.

My older sister and I often rowed past the Inn at Lake Devine, and studied it as best we could from offshore. It had a very green lawn, broad and sloping to the water, a white flagpole, and a chalky string of buoys marking off its swimming area. Closer to us, a raft covered with teenagers floated on shiny black oil drums. My sister and I had only each other for company, and a dock with no wading area, but here there were kids our age from what had to be a dozen families, swimming and diving as well as if they were on teams.

The following winter, having studied it and envied its postcard perfection, I put a long-thought-out plan into effect as a thirteenth-birthday present to myself. With a deerskin purse full of coins, I went to a pay phone. I called the Inn at Lake Devine and asked for Mrs. Berry. Amazingly, the party said, "This is she."

I read from my notes: "I was wondering if you had a cottage available for the entire month of July?"

"With whom am I speaking?" she asked.

"Miss Edgerly," I said, having elected the name of a Massachusetts man recently tried for murdering his wife in a particularly hideous fashion.

Mrs. Berry asked the caller's age, and I said fifteen; yes, I knew I was young to be making inquiries about accommodations, but my mother was recently deceased and my father was spending long hours in court.

She said, "We do have two lovely cottages with sleeping porches."

"Are they really, really nice?" I asked.

"They're in great demand," she said. "Electric stove, baseboard heat, stall shower, picnic table—"

"Is it private? Because my father's kind of famous. He really needs an escape."

"We're quiet and peaceful here," said the Berry woman. "It's a perfect hideaway vacation."

"Can you save it for us?"

"Do you want to inquire about our rates first?"

I told her that my father, *Mr. Edgerly*, had instructed me to get the best accommodations available no matter what the cost.

"We require a deposit," said Mrs. Berry. "Do you have a pencil?"

I took my time, pretending to record every syllable. "My father will send you a cashier's check first thing tomorrow," I said, adopting the disbursement method repeated daily on *The Millionaire*.

"You are a very smart young lady," said Mrs. Berry.

The next morning on my way to school, I anonymously mailed Mrs. Berry an old *Globe* clipping, its three-column headline blaring, EDGERLY TRIAL ENTERS 6TH WEEK; JURY SEES "GRUESOME" PHOTOS, to make the point vividly to Mrs. Berry that her system— rooms open to any Gentile who dials her number—was unfair. I enclosed another clipping from my archives (LIZ AND EDDIE/SAY I DO'S/BEFORE RABBI)—this one from *Photoplay*—which spoke respectfully, even warmly, about Liz Taylor's conversion. The wedding shot showed them under a *chupa*, the new Mrs. Fisher in a flowered headband and Eddie in a somber dark suit and white satin yarmulke. Honored guests included their best friends, famous and beautiful Hollywood Jews.

In 1964, I would send Mrs. Berry a copy of the new Civil Rights Act. I wrote, "U.S. House of Representatives, Washington, D.C.," in the upper-left-hand corner of the envelope, and typed a letter that said, "Dear Hotel Owners, It isn't only Colored people who are helped by this law. Jewish people and others you have excluded in the recent past must now be welcome at your accommodations. It is the Law of the Land."

Who knew if I'd ever exchange another letter with a documented anti-Semite? Just in case no one ever insulted me again—in this land of religious freedom and ironclad civil rights—I employed the big gun I was saving for future transgressors: "P.S.," I typed and underlined: "In spite of everything I still believe that people are really good at heart."

$\mathcal{T}$ w o

$\mathcal{W}$e lived on Irving Circle, a cul-de-sac in Newton, Mass-achusetts, famous for its esprit de corps and its near-perfect record of all girls and no boys. The houses were built in the mid-1950s by one man, who named the street after Irving Berlin and added a breezeway, a cupola, a picture window to give each identical ranch house its own character. All had one-car garages, hot-top drive-ways, lampposts in a lantern motif, and italic house numbers in hammered wrought-iron. It wasn't the grandness of the street that made real estate agents bring a certain kind of family to it—it was modest, in fact, and cookie-cutterish—but the democracy: No one's house was better than anyone else's. All the buyers were vet-erans, new homeowners, and, as the developer bragged at the clos-ings, good people who would cut the other guy's grass if he was on vacation.

For a long time, we did that and more. We walked into one an-other's kitchens without knocking, opened refrigerators without asking, trick-or-treated as a gang. All you had to do was look at the group photo, updated annually at the Memorial Day block party—dads in the back row with long-handled utensils behind wives holding cake plates behind children sitting cross-legged in cotton sunsuits—to see what we had. *Life* magazine could have snapped

us with a wide-angle lens and captioned us AN AMERICAN NEIGH-
BORHOOD BEFORE HOUSES NEEDED ALARMS.

My parents were Audrey and Eddie Marx, no famous love story,
mismatched from their first date, but decent people who stayed
married to each other. He was a fruit man and she was a number
of things: a pixie-haired redhead, size 4, who cleaned our immaculate house in short shorts, and introduced the neighborhood
women to iodine in baby oil as a tanning agent. Her interior deco-
ration was thought to be advanced: shellacked *Gourmet* covers as
kitchen wallpaper, and an oil painting in the living room that no
one understood.

Our neighbors were the Donabedians, the Iacovellos, the Nagys,
the McKemmies, the Forestalls, and the Loftuses, representing
enough cultures and religions to substantiate Newton's unwritten
boast of being one third each Catholic, Protestant, and Jewish.

Mr. and Mrs. Loftus, the other Jewish family on Irving Circle,
built the last house on the street in 1959, the same year we lost the
handsome and adventurous McKemmies temporarily to California. The spring before, after a Disneyland vacation, they returned
with the news that they were moving there. It had been a scouting
trip, we learned; California promised wonderful opportunities for
McKemmie Storms and Screens. Four or five months later, they
were back. Kathy McKemmie told us that Whitey and Judy from
Leave It to Beaver had been in her class, as well as Tonto's daughter. They had had Thanksgiving dinner in a restaurant, and almost
every yard had a swimming pool. I heard a neighbor say, over
drinks in aluminum tumblers, "No need for storm windows out
west, Al?" and Mr. McKemmie had said, "Margaret missed her family."

Soon afterward, a moving van pulled up to the newly built Loftus house, and the circle was complete. Pammy and I watched the
contents unload, and guessed by the tasseled bike handles and the
white provincial bedroom suite that we were getting more girls.

When my mother dropped in that afternoon with her two-toned pistachio bundt cake, Mrs. Loftus invited my parents for dinner on the spot. My mother said, "Absolutely out of the question; you've just moved in and couldn't possibly entertain." Mrs. Loftus said, holding the pink-and-green cake aloft, "We've got dessert. I'll broil some steaks and bake some potatoes."

And that was that. She came home and reported as much as she was able to observe without asking rude questions: The girls were Marla and Shelley (I was between them in age); the house was completely unpacked and set up, down to pictures on the walls and the spoon rest on the stove. There was a mustard-and-brown dining room (hated) and cuckoo-clock kitchen wallpaper (loved). Both girls were adopted, which explained their straight blond hair.

For a few happy days, I was courted by both sisters, who wanted nothing to do with each other. Marla soon recognized my low social standing on the street—defined by my braces and glasses and twenty-inch bike—and worked her way into the clump of girls a year older (Claudia Forestall, Marybeth McKemmie, my sister, Pammy) who took the public bus to the junior high and dressed alike. Our mothers took us two younger girls to lunch in department stores, pretending we were better friends than we were. That's how it was on Irving Circle and how I was raised: You made the best out of what was within reach, which meant friendships engineered by parents and by the happenstance of housing. I stayed with it because we both had queenly older sisters who rarely condescended to play with us, because Shelley was adopted and I was not, because Shelley had Clue and Life, and I did not.

$\mathcal{T}$ H R E E

$\mathcal{M}$y father sold fruit from a truck, which was parked year-round in front of his small shop on Harvard Street in Brookline. Inside the shop were cheap straw baskets stacked to the ceiling and cases of the novelties that adorned them: jar grips, rabbit's-foot key chains, marshmallow chicks, wax lips, candy cigarettes, balls and jacks, bubble-gum cigars, decks of Old Maid and Authors, nickel-plated lighters, Chinese finger puzzles, paddle balls. To tease my mother and, on occasion, his mother-in-law, he'd answer a question about his line of work by saying, "Peddler."

"He owns a produce business," my mother would say, correcting any impression that we were poor.

"I specialize," he'd add.

"In gift baskets," said my mother. "He's famous for his arrangements."

He'd give the listener his card by this time, or at any point the listener evinced signs of sidling away. It said,

FRUIT BASKETS FOR ALL OCCASIONS, CUSTOM
"NOTHING SAYS CONGRATS OR OUR THOUGHTS ARE WITH
YOU . . . LIKE FRUIT."
OPEN 7 DAYS, EDDIE MARX, PROP.

My mother, doing homework for her perpetual college courses, didn't help with the business. If the red phone in the kitchen rang after hours and my father wasn't home, she let it ring. And who could have pictured her at the fruit truck, giving change from a dirty apron and tousling the hair of customers' kids? It wasn't just her tanned and finished look that made her girlfriends wonder how she had paired up with Eddie Marx, but that other thing—the college girl and the fruit peddler, the Jewish debutante and the blue-collar laborer, the tiny bathing beauty and the big *bulvan*.

She always told it the same way: "Eddie was in Boston the same time I was." B.U. would be mentioned, or Bay State Road, leading to the flat-tire episode that both of my parents liked to tell with their own twists, and that my maternal grandfather told best and most economically of all.

"You met him at B.U.?" the listener would ask.

"The last day of my sophomore year. I was packing the car, yelling at my father because he had driven right over a broken bottle."

"And Eddie?" they'd prompt.

"He said, 'Need a hand?' My father said, 'You mean it?' He opened the trunk, found what he needed, and thirty seconds later was on his knees."

And while my father was changing the tire, my grandfather was busy asking questions: What kind of business was his father in? What street in Chelsea? How many brothers and sisters did he have? What plans did Eddie have after graduation? Boston State? Not Boston University? Cost any less? Were his brothers big men too? Ever heard of Interlon? Well, know what interfacing is? Did his mother sew? Ever see her sew an extra layer of stiff cloth between the body of the garment and the facing?

It was inevitable that a conversation between my grandfather and a mechanically competent, friendly Jewish boy in which Interlon was mentioned would lead to a summer job offer.

Eddie said, "No, thanks. I help my dad in the summer. It's his big season."

"Fruit, did you say?"

"That's right," said Eddie.

"We go through a lot of fruit in our house," said Mr. Cohen.

Audrey, approaching with a huge Raggedy Ann doll, a tennis racquet, and a gooseneck lamp, heard "truck," and pictured exactly what Eddie's father's livelihood was: fruit sold from an open truck, a scale hanging from the back, and Eddie's father making change from a bus driver's coin holder. "This is everything," she said. "Let's go."

"I'd help," Eddie said to Audrey, showing his palms, "but I don't want to get your things dirty."

"You've helped enough already," said my grandfather, "and I just wish you'd let me buy you lunch as a thank-you."

Eddie looked down from his great height at Audrey. She smiled politely—the man had changed their goddamn tire, after all—but in sourpuss fashion. My grandfather asked her, "Where can you get a nice lunch around here? Where do the professors eat?"

"All my stuff is in the back," she said, hoping her father would understand that she couldn't have lunch near B.U. with this man—he looked old for a college student—especially with her sixty-year-old father along to pepper him with questions about the fruit business.

Eddie said, "Thanks, but I'll take a rain check."

My grandfather said, "You sure?"

"I had a late breakfast—"

"So did I," said Audrey, settling the question. Satisfied that he had made the proper overtures and had acted like a *mensch*, my grandfather performed one more ingratiating act. "You take my card, and if you're ever in Fitchburg-Leominster, anyplace close by, you come by the plant and I'll buy you lunch. Interlon—right on the main drag. Red brick with a big yellow brick smokestack."

"Thanks," Eddie said. He put the card in his wallet, which Audrey noted was embossed like a cowboy's and overstitched with gimp.

"Or need a summer job," Mr. Cohen added from the driver's seat.

From the safety of the passenger seat, Audrey waved to Eddie and granted him a brief, chilly smile. When her father steered the car into Kenmore Square, she spat out, "Big shot. He's going to show up one day and you'll be on the phone yelling at some supplier. Why offer something if you don't mean it?"

"I meant it," he said. And again, thinking it over: "I did mean it."

"And he'll be driving a fruit truck, with rotting fruit and flies," Audrey added, then laughed.

My grandfather smiled and checked the outside mirror. She wasn't the worst of the daughters, and she was the prettiest. This general absence of disappointment and these mild twinges of pride might mean that Audrey, the baby and only redhead, was his favorite.

𝓘t was almost precisely what my father did one day in late June—he showed up at Interlon and asked the receptionist for Mr. Cohen.

"And you're with . . . ?"

"Tell him Eddie Marx. From B.U. The flat-tire guy." The receptionist, who was wearing slacks of a print that looked to Eddie like Chinese wallpaper, said, "He's with an account right now."

My father sat down on a metal folding chair and waited until the human barking in the inner office stopped. The secretary didn't change expression or look up from the letterhead and two carbons she was typing. Mr. Cohen, dressed in gray trousers and a short-sleeved, white button-down shirt, came forward.

"You here for lunch?" he boomed in greeting.

Eddie said he had the truck, which meant he had the produce, which meant he couldn't leave it on a city street.

"How about my driveway?"

Eddie smiled, a grin that asked what "my driveway" meant exactly.

"My house! I'll call Florence."

Eddie raised his hands in protest. "Nobody likes an unexpected guest for lunch."

Isadore Cohen put his hand on Eddie's shoulder. "How old are you?"

"Twenty-five in September."

"I ask that because you don't act like a kid," said Isadore. "You act like you have half a brain."

Eddie laughed and said, "Tell that to my father."

"He gives you a hard time?" asked Isadore, pleased to be topping a guy's father as easily as this.

"He's got a short fuse, but he's harmless. I learned a long time ago to take it and not shout back."

"How many boys?" Isadore asked, a question he had asked before, and would ask again before lunch was over.

"Three," Eddie said. "Would have been four, but they lost one as a baby."

"I'm sorry," said my grandfather, and he was.

"The Marx brothers," Eddie said.

"Really? Are they related?" The secretary looked up for a few seconds, her hands poised above the keys.

"I meant us—we're the Marx brothers. My father says when he dies we can change the name on the trucks."

Isadore was dialing noisily, his index finger snapping the rotary dial faster than it was meant to go. "Florence! What's for lunch?" He nodded at Eddie—as if to say, Okay. It's gonna work. "You like salmon salad?" Eddie nodded back. "Florence! Can you make another sandwich? Or two? I've got a big strapping fellow here who looks like he can put away a coupla sandwiches for lunch." He banged the phone down happily.

"Follow me," he said.

Florence Cohen, trim and smartly dressed—early fifties, my father guessed—fed the interloper at the kitchen table after sizing up his Bermuda shorts and his big nylon shirttails. She was correct without being gracious. She offered Eddie seconds and thirds and, later, even some cookies for the road, but Eddie knew she wasn't pleased to have him.

"Is your daughter home for the summer?" he asked conversationally within minutes of arriving.

"She's home for the summer; she's just not home at the moment," Isadore explained. His wife's expression scolded him for giving away too much.

"Where is she?" Eddie asked.

"At Barbara's."

"My brother's daughter," he explained. "They have a built-in pool."

"Does she have any special summer plans?"

Florence didn't think this large, coarse-featured fruit peddler should be inquiring about Audrey's summer plans, either. "A few," she said.

Isadore was embarrassed by his wife's tone. He knew the deep freeze when he heard it, and thought Florence had turned into a snob despite having been a salesgirl in a dress shop when they met. "Florence's father grew up in Chelsea. And she grew up not too far from there. Maybe the two families knew each other," he tried, a warning.

Florence murmured, "I doubt that."

"Why not?" asked Isadore. He passed the plate of sliced cukes and tomatoes to Eddie, then helped himself to thirds. "A ragman and a fruit man might have had the same route," he said pointedly.

Florence returned her plate and her husband's, prematurely, to the sink. Eddie said nothing. His parents had their own version of this game (descendant of a horse thief versus descendant of a promiscuous tailor). Happily, the back-screen latch clicked and Audrey was home. Her red hair was pulled back into a careless ponytail—she'd never let a boy see her with her hair up—and her skin was tanned the color of a ripe Bosc pear. She was wearing scuffed white pumps and—to a boy with no sisters—almost nothing else: a two-piece plaid bathing suit with a bandeau top. Eddie jumped to his feet and said, "Hi, it's me—you probably don't remember—Eddie Marx."

Audrey took off her sunglasses and stared joylessly. "Is that your truck?" she asked.

He asked if it was blocking hers.

"I don't have a car," she said, and looked at her father disapprovingly. She reached over her mother's shoulder and took a cherry tomato. "Anything left to eat?"

Eddie eased himself back down into the kitchen chair. Audrey took a plate from a cupboard, opened the refrigerator, found a carton of cottage cheese, opened another cupboard, and found a can of cling peaches.

"Wait!" said Eddie.

Audrey looked up unhappily.

"I have fresh peaches on the truck."

Audrey, vaguely annoyed, asked, "Are they ripe?"

"They're ripe, they're juicy, they're delicious. I ate four driving out here"—inviting my grandmother to inspect his shirt for stains.

"Okay," Audrey said.

Eddie went quickly out the back door and returned with two peaches, a nectarine, and a pint of strawberries.

"I might be allergic to strawberries," said Audrey. "Sometimes I break out from them and sometimes I don't."

Eddie said, "Want to go out and choose something else?"

"This is fine." She looked at the fruit in his hands. It was quite perfect. "Unless you have a cantaloupe . . ."

"I do," said Eddie. "Let me see if I have one that's ready for eating."

"How do you know that?" my grandmother asked. Eddie signaled that they should follow him. He jogged to the truck, picked up a cantaloupe with one hand, and ordered them to sniff the melon.

Mother and daughter murmured their consensus: not much, a faint whiff of hard cantaloupe skin. Eddie chose another. "Now this." They sniffed. "It smells like ripe cantaloupe," said Audrey. He showed them one more trick: the green spot, the blossom end? It should give a little.

Audrey said sharply to her mother, "How have you been picking out cantaloupes all these years?"

"I thought you were supposed to shake them."

"Which is why *we* choose the fruit," Eddie said. He smiled at Audrey, his ally, and handed her his first-choice melon. She put her sunburned nose to it and, with a look that asked, "Here?" took a deep breath from its green spot.

"So," said Eddie, grinning the big grin that had earned him a reputation among the customers as the nicest of the Marx boys, "am I right?"

With the fruit lesson over and Audrey not a foot away, he allowed himself to take in the smell of her suntan oil, something like black olives. Her skin was shiny from it, and there was a line of sunburn at her waist and above her bandeau top, as if today's suit had exposed more skin than yesterday's.

Audrey didn't notice, or couldn't be bothered to interpret, the strain in his face. "Cut it up over the sink," she directed, my mother's first order to my father.

*A*s she explained to her cousin Barbara, when Eddie phoned, Audrey had agreed to go out with him because he was offering to take her to a movie Saturday night in Boston and she was dying to get out of Fitchburg. And there was something, frankly, about Eddie's jumbo presence, something like a bodyguard's or a football player's, that was normally off limits to a Jewish girl. Big hands and knuckles, big feet, wide calves below his Bermuda shorts, ruddy, even rubbery-looking face. She'd never dated a man who looked like Eddie, or who had one sunburned arm from driving the truck, or who viewed her as a prize beyond his grasp.

Audrey thought this might account for the strange goings-on in Boston, her kissing Eddie Marx in his brother's car when it was parked in Winthrop with a view of the beach.

"Are you going to go out with him again?" asked cousin Barbara, who in her life had kissed only Stevie Poppel, who had moved away. "I know I sometimes go for an older guy who I wouldn't have looked twice at if he was my age."

"Next Saturday."

Barbara had smiled. She admired Audrey, and was happy her parents had built the swimming pool, because Audrey might not otherwise have spent so much time with a younger cousin. "So don't worry whether you like him or not. Just go and see what happens," said Barbara.

*B*arbara was her maid of honor, because all three of her sisters had carried on so obnoxiously about her having to get married. Pregnant at nineteen by Eddie Marx. She hadn't even *told* her sisters; her mother had blabbed to Charlotte, the oldest, who'd spread the word until it reached Roberta, the next-to-youngest, who had actually laid eyes on Eddie, which made the astonishment bounce back up the sister corridor in record time.

"She doesn't love him!" Florence had screamed at her husband when he reported that Eddie had come by Interlon for a man-to-man talk and had left with money for a ring.

"How would you know?" was his mild retort.

"Because I know how she acts when she's in love," said her mother. "And it's not like this. Look at her."

"I'm nauseous," said Audrey, "and you know it."

Mrs. Cohen turned on her husband. "You brought this on. You had to invite him here for lunch. You had to find her a husband."

Red-faced, picturing a tiny grandson taking form, he said, "She doesn't have to keep our grandchild! His parents will raise him. Eddie told me this, about their offer." They had lost one of theirs, they said, and this might be the way God was replacing Solly. Audrey didn't have to be its mother! Audrey could go back to college, if that was more important, and study her singing and forget she'd ever met a *mensch* like Eddie Marx or had his baby.

Florence Cohen said it was not the parents' job to fix their children's mistakes, meaning, Don't expect me to start raising grandchildren like some woman off the boat.

So the Marxes drove to Fitchburg to have a somber engagement fish dinner with the Cohens. Mr. Marx, my other grandfather, was short, blue-eyed, and so utterly bald that whatever had taken the hair from his head had also taken his eyebrows and lashes. Mrs. Marx was big and heavy. Her dress was brown cotton, ironed and starched, buttoned down the front like a housedress, except for the big star burst of fake topaz above her left breast.

Eddie gave a short speech to the first joint session of future in-laws: He and Audrey had made a mistake. He was sorry, because he knew they had trusted him to date their daughter without any monkey business. But they loved each other, and now that they were going to have a baby, he didn't want anyone to think of their baby as a mistake.

Always, when my sister asked her how she felt to be pregnant at nineteen, my mother insisted it was welcome news once the shock wore off. It was the baby boom. People married and had babies young. Nineteen then was not like nineteen now. "And your father," she would say, slapping her hand to her cheek. "He was delirious. He was tickled pink. He couldn't wait."

The baby was Pammy, Pamela Arlene Marx, born seven and a half months after the garden wedding. She got my mother's small bones and my grandfather's former blond hair—an adorable combination, everyone agreed.

And I was proof, the planned second child, that they intended to stay married. I was named for my Grandpa Marx's baby sister, who had stayed behind in Europe. I had her exact name, once you took translation liberties with the Yiddish: Natalie Sarah Marx. It was a sacred honor I held over Pammy's head whenever I could: that I bore the name of our own personal Anne Frank, our forever-teenaged aunt, whose graduation photo from the gymnasium in Riga was presented to me at birth, our common initials engraved on the silver frame. To please my grandfather, everyone strained to see a resemblance between me and his beloved Nesha. I got her dark hair, her reputed height—she'd not been born when he left for America—and her head for science. She had corresponded faithfully ("like cluckvork"), the most beautiful letters in the most beautiful hand, to all her brothers and sisters in America. So regular, Papa Marx told me during a visit to the shrine on my bureau, that when they stopped coming in 1942, we knew.

FOUR

I can't remember what crusading impulse made us get dressed up and drive from our rental cabin to the Inn at Lake Devine, but I know my father and I were the ringleaders, and my mother was along to make sure we behaved. Pammy, at sixteen, said we were being several ridiculous things—hypocritical, low-class, uncool—and refused to change out of her bathing suit to go.

It was on that ride around the lake in 1963 that we invented our drop-in selves: Mr. and Mrs. Edward Martin and daughter Natalie, prospective guests. Mr. Martin owned a fruit—no, a grocery—store in Massachusetts. A superette. Mrs. Martin was a housewife.

A discreet white arrow, knee-high to the ground, marked the dirt road that led to the Inn. My mother announced that it smelled different on this side of the lake, and if you could bottle this air people would pay money for it. My father sniffed diagnostically out the window and said, "Wild blueberries." At the first crossroad, several slats nailed to a white pine announced the names of property-owning families: CARROLL, we read. FAHNSTOCK. DEL-BERTI. ALDRICH. McBRIDE, and the top one, lettered professionally, INN AT LAKE DEVINE.

"This way," I said, more nervous than I was admitting about my secret history of crank calls to Mrs. Ingrid Berry.

"Remember, we're just looking," my mother said. "We're considering it for a future vacation, so we want to see it in person."

Leafy branches scraped our truck as we lumbered along the narrow road, as if reminding us that these routes were meant for sleeker vehicles. Then the lake, steely blue, jagged shores. Our turnoff ended in a paved parking lot filled with late-model cars. The lawn before us looked darkly bluish-green and golf-course perfect. Adirondack chairs shone with what looked to be a just-dry coat of high-gloss green. We parked in the space farthest from the Inn so no one would see MARX FRUIT painted on the doors.

My father and I jumped out of either side of the truck's cab, and my mother inched her way toward the passenger door. She had worn a sleeveless sheath of pale yellow linen, with a tear-shaped cutout centered at her collarbone. Her clutch pocketbook and pumps were of woven straw. My father was wearing navy-blue chinos and a white short-sleeved shirt, and I was wearing shorts and a matching sleeveless blouse of red-and-white-checked seersucker: the nice, neat Martin family, arriving to inspect the possible site of next year's summer vacation.

As we convened at the passenger side, another car drove up. It was a station wagon driven by a teenage boy, with two teenage girls as passengers, all in bathing suits. They didn't greet us, although they assessed us as they walked by with the air of returning regulars who had driven a father's car to town for suntan lotion and Noxzema.

My father started off on the white-pebbled path to the Inn, but my mother and I held back. We didn't want any too-self-assured teenagers to hear us wonder aloud if we had the right entrance or the right clerk. He turned back and said, "You coming?" My mother held up one finger and said, "Give me a minute. I have to check something."

I knew my father didn't know what the delay was. He had no guile. He couldn't figure out what my mother had to check. I walked over to him and said, "Wait a sec. We don't want to catch up to those kids."

He used the intermission to face the lake, inhale appreciatively, and massage country air into the hair follicles of his big forearms. My mother and I waited until the teenagers disappeared into the buildings before we set out on the white-pebbled walk, my father last in our procession. We walked up the wide stairs of the big white house, crossed the veranda, its floorboards glossy green and its ceiling sky-blue, and entered through the front door. Inside, the wallpaper depicted mural-size scenes of riverboats on the Mississippi at Natchez. There was a room-size braided rug in the reception area, a large dining room straight ahead with round tables set for dinner, an unlit stone fireplace, and not a soul in sight.

"Hal-lo!" my father sang out.

Still no sign of life. There was a blackboard on an easel outside the dining room. In blue, pink, and green chalk, someone had artfully lettered

> FRUIT CUP OR HEARTS OF PALM
>
> LAMB CHOPS OR RAINBOW TROUT
>
> SUNDAE OR BAKED APPLE

My father followed me over to the sign and said, "Sounds good. Lots of fruit. And I like how they give you a choice."

From nowhere, a woman with graying blond hair pulled back into a bulky and imperfect french twist glided over to us and said, "May I help you?" She was wearing a wraparound skirt in a Pennsylvania Dutch print, and the short-sleeved white blouse I had seen in a hundred Ship 'n Shore ads.

My mother said, "We've just stopped by to see the Inn, because we're thinking of a future stay here."

With the briefest of insincere smiles and no other sign of cordiality, the woman asked, "And you are . . . ?"

"Audrey Martin. And this is Mr. Martin, and our daughter, Natalie."

"Ingrid Berry," she said coolly, as if it were a brand name of high quality and customer loyalty.

"Are you the manager?" Eddie asked.

"Yes," she said. "My husband and I are the owners."

I stared at the woman I had made it my business to harass by telephone and mail, a federal offense for sure. She looked perfectly nice, I thought, with her high color and her Canada mint–pink lipstick.

"You've got a beautiful piece of property here," said my father. "You must have the best shoreline on the lake."

"We think so," said Mrs. Berry, staring a bit too serenely back.

"Are you open all year?" my mother asked.

"Just Memorial Day to Labor Day."

"Not too long," said my father cheerfully.

"We fill up a year in advance," said Mrs. Berry. "It's not uncommon for our guests to reserve their rooms for the next summer as they're leaving."

"You all booked for this year?" asked my father.

"I'm afraid we are," said Mrs. Berry.

"Wow," he said.

"Maybe you could check your guest register," said my mother.

"Shoehorn us in," my father added.

Mrs. Berry glided around to the other side of the dark wood reception desk. She opened a black-cloth ledger and pretended to inspect handwritten entries every few pages. "Well!" she said after a dry silence.

"Did you find something?" my mother asked.

"I have . . . let me check one other thing . . ." She opened a wooden filing box and moved deliberately, front to back, through the index cards until she found the object of her search. "Okay. It looks as though we have the last weekend in September open. A family suite, meaning two connecting rooms."

"You're not closed after Labor Day?" asked my mother.

"We're open weekends year-round," said Mrs. Berry. "A two-night minimum."

"We were kind of hoping for a summer visit," said my father. "The girls and I love the water. Our other daughter, Pammy, didn't come with us." He added, as if that sounded irregular, "She has the sniffles."

My mother said, "Why don't we think it over. The girls go back to school the Wednesday after Labor Day, so it's not what we were hoping—"

"It's a cancellation," said Mrs. Berry. "I can't promise it will be available when you call back."

My mother waited a few seconds—probably only I noticed her gathering her will—and said smoothly, "I guess it's a risk we'll have to take."

"Where do you live?" asked Mrs. Berry.

"Newton," said my father, one detail we hadn't thought to fine-tune.

I saw something in her gray-blue eyes, a flicker of triumph, as if we had moved our queen foolishly, setting her up for checkmate. "Newton, MassaJewsetts?" said Mrs. Berry softly, sarcastically, the offending syllable almost lost in her 180-degree pivot to the file box. She stayed that way, her back to us, pretending to be doing some critical paperwork.

"Okay, then. We'll be in touch," said my father.

Mrs. Berry murmured something affirmative, and we left.

I was the only one who was sure. I insisted for most of the ride around the lake—until my mother forbade me to say another word on the subject—that I had heard "Jew" as plain as day cross the lips of Ingrid Hitler Berry.

"Nobody would say that," my father argued.

"But I heard her."

"Natalie," said my mother. "Someone might think that, but

would never say it to our face. You thought you heard it because you know she's prejudiced. You were listening for it."

"Or maybe she had some kind of Scandinavian accent," said my father. "Maybe that's what you heard—'Massayoosetts.' "

I yelled that Mrs. Berry had no accent whatsoever—none. And why was he sticking up for her?

My mother said, "Don't yell at your father."

"She didn't know we were Jewish," I continued. "She thought we were the Martins who lived in Newton and didn't like Jews either. She expected us to say something like, 'Ha, ha, you said it: "Newton, MassaJewsetts" is right!' "

"She didn't say anything of the kind," my mother insisted. "You imagined you heard 'MassaJewsetts.' " And later, as if to herself: "It's ridiculous. No one would say that kind of thing out loud to strangers. Especially the manager of a resort. Not in this day and age. I don't want to hear another word."

ℱ I V E

I had stopped dwelling on Mrs. Berry and designing campaigns against her, but suddenly she was back. At overnight camp in New Hampshire the next summer, a bunkmate mentioned that when camp was over, she and her parents and brothers were having their real vacation, a week at a hotel on Lake Devine. Suddenly, Robin Fife in her Bermuda shorts and white camp T-shirt, though a mildly annoying and not very bright bunkmate, represented the ideal Gentile guest. I asked the name of their destination, and she answered, a little off the mark, "The Lake Devine Hotel."

I asked what it was like.

"Kind of boring, but my parents like it."

"What kind of people go there?" I asked.

"Boring people," said Robin. "Old people. People who don't even use the dock half the time."

I asked what people did at a lake if they didn't use the dock.

"Sit in big chairs and look out at the water through binoculars. Stuff like that. They're old."

It sounded more peaceful to me than anti-Semitic. Old Jewish people liked to sit in lawn chairs and stare out at the water, too.

For the remaining three weeks of camp, I employed all the tricks acquired at the knee of my sister, queen of brainwashers and cajolers. I began my campaign by saying, "I wrote to my parents and asked them if they could make reservations for the same week you and your parents would be at the Inn."

Robin began to sit with me at meals, copy my candy-bar choices at the camp store, squeeze next to me around the campfire. I gave her progress reports every few mail calls: "My mother's checking with the Inn" or "They're waiting to hear from Mrs. Berry."

Weren't older sisters and brothers a pain? I confided. My sister bossed me around, never let me play with her and her friends or talk in front of them. She had her driver's license and wouldn't take me places just for fun, ever, unless my parents made her.

"Me too," said Robin. "Only it's worse, because my parents don't make Chip take me anywhere. They don't trust his driving."

"At least you don't have to share a room with him while you're on vacation," I grumbled.

"That's true," Robin agreed.

"I have to share a *room* with Pammy." I shook my head, my eyes closed, as if the prospect of her slovenliness and general discourtesy were too much to bear.

Robin pondered this, as I had intended: rooms, room assignments, roommates. I could see her silently counting beds in her single. Finally, she said, "If you're there at the same time I am, maybe we could share a room and your sister could stay alone."

I said, "My mother wouldn't like it. She'd think I was imposing."

"Why would you be imposing? My parents are paying for the room anyway."

"True," I said. I promised to write to my mother immediately and to propose such an arrangement, despite her known aversion to imposing.

"Tell her I'm afraid to sleep alone," said Robin. "Which is kind of true. If I have to go to the bathroom in the middle of the night, I go next door to my parents' room so one of them can walk me down the hall. And sometimes I can't fall asleep because I'm nervous, so I make one of them sleep in my other twin bed."

It was all the ammunition I needed: I'd position myself as a companion. A baby-sitter. I'd be so nice, so well mannered, so appreciative, and I'd perform several custodial duties that would free Mr. and Mrs. Fife from the burden of Robin. I'd be Heidi helping Clara in Düsseldorf: She'd get out of the wheelchair and I'd get to experience a holiday on the other side of the tracks.

It wasn't that difficult to fake the rest: Soon I reported that there were no rooms at the Inn for us—my parents had made their inquiries far too late. Robin was bitterly disappointed. I reviewed the might-have-beens of our week-long partnership, the croquet and the sessions with Dippity-Do now evaporated. She thought it was her idea when she hit on the solution: "What if you came with us? I already told my parents that I was going to have a friend there." She wrote immediately to her parents, and I wrote to mine, too, as soon as the Fifes formally invited me. I wrote, "Robin Fife, the girl from Farmington, Connecticut, has invited me to join her family on vacation in Vermont. She has two brothers who don't play with her, so her parents want her to bring a friend. Can I go? Please?"

They didn't think to ask right away the name of the Fifes' lodging, because I was careful to focus on mission—Robin's need for company and her bad sleeping habits—rather than setting. Our mothers spoke, and it wasn't until the end of the exceedingly cordial conversation that Mrs. Fife pronounced the name of their destination.

My mother could hardly withdraw her permission then. What could she say?—"Uh-oh. They don't like Jews there. Did Robin tell you we're of the Jewish faith?" I was sure the reason she didn't renege, besides the bad etiquette of it, was the crusading impulse running through the Marxes. We all wanted to cross the threshold as guests and not visitors, and maybe I, in my early-teen disguise, was best suited to be a spy in the house of Devine. It was our duty to show that we—with the blood of Moses, Queen Esther, Leonard Bernstein, and Sid Caesar coursing through our veins—were the equal of any clientele. And if the Berrys still didn't think so, wasn't it our duty to set them straight?

I'd like to say that my mother and I prepared for my week away with no eye toward outward appearances, no thought to what constituted high-quality Protestant summer clothes. We pressed and packed for days: Bermuda shorts and Villager shirts; a sleeveless shirtwaist dress of a muted plaid with a braided rope belt; a new Catalina bathing suit in blue jersey; a terry-cloth cover-up piped in pinpoint blue gingham; tops, shorts, and something then in fashion called a skort. New Keds and new Peds. A bathrobe of yellow seersucker, and two new pairs of baby dolls. A white cable-knit cardigan for cool evenings and a Radcliffe sweatshirt for cool days.

The Fifes picked me up at our house in Newton on the Saturday morning of our departure. My parents invited them in for coffee and fruit, but they demurred gaily and said, "Next time! We don't want to lose a minute."

My father looked into the car and said, "No boys? I thought you had a couple of boys!" Pammy, who had sauntered out in her most fetching cutoffs and in bare feet, froze, then retreated at my father's bald question.

Mr. Fife explained that Jeff and Donald Junior were driving up separately. My mother said, "I hope that your taking Natalie didn't change your plans to that extent."

"Not at all," they said, graciously and adamantly. "We need two cars up there, with the suitcases and the boys' long legs. This is grand." The Fifes swiveled around to smile at me and Robin, and said, "Are we ready?"

My parents kissed me through my half-open window, and my mother mouthed, "Be good. Help out."

"We'll give you a call toward the middle of the week," said my father.

"Don't worry," said the Fifes. "She's going to have a wonderful week. We'll take good care of her."

My mother said weakly, "It's just . . . she just got home from camp."

"I know," said Mrs. Fife. "I know exactly how you feel."

My father put his arm around my mother's shoulders and walked her back to the curb. They waved and smiled bravely. At least in my memory, I winked.

$\mathcal{W}$e sang in the car. Robin had taught her parents her favorite camp songs, and the Fifes were a family who could harmonize. I learned that Mr. Fife taught music and directed both the a cappella choir and glee club of a private school in West Hartford. After we exhausted our repertoire of camp songs, they asked if I knew any Gilbert and Sullivan. I said *I* didn't, but please. For the next ninety minutes, except for a sherbet and bathroom stop at Howard Johnson's, they sang the entire score of *H.M.S. Pinafore.* I smiled and nodded as if this were how my family occupied itself, too, on a long car trip. They awarded themselves an encore, "Edelweiss," from their best Broadway outing ever, *The Sound of Music.* I began to worry about the week ahead—about the medleys, the rounds, the three-part harmonies, the low speed at which Mr. Fife drove and his reluctance to pass another living soul. They stopped to take photographs from scenic turnouts as if they'd never passed them before and would never return. Mr. Fife pulled into the breakdown lane when he spotted a car with its hood up. He jogged over to interview the unhappy driver, and jogged back to us, satisfied. "Radiator overheated," he said, "but he's carrying water. He's just going to let it cool down a bit." After a few minutes of driving in uncharacteristic silence, Mr. Fife expressed disappointment in himself: *He* didn't carry water, but from this day forth certainly would, especially on long trips, especially at these elevations.

As soon as we turned onto the dirt road that led to the Inn, everyone but me started counting down from sixty in another happy chorus. Mrs. Fife turned around to explain: They had figured out the previous summer that the drive from the main road to the parking lot took exactly one minute! I joined in at thirty-five, less enthusiastically, but smiling like a good guest. We would do it after every outing, every errand, over the next week. And hitting "One!" as we crossed the first inch of asphalt never failed to delight my host family.

Before I went, my parents and I had discussed whether or not I should announce myself as the daughter of the couple who had stopped by the previous summer to admire the property. We decided against full disclosure. We had posed as the Martins, and I was arriving as Natalie Marx. We'd look like liars. Besides, my mother assured me, adults like Mrs. Berry don't notice children. If you look familiar, she'll think she saw you once in a department store.

Mrs. Berry, with her gray-blond hair shortened to a Jackie Kennedy bouffant, greeted the Fifes the way paying guests would hope to be received on their fourteenth visit—warmly and on a first-name basis. And because I was there under the Fife banner, Mrs. Berry shook my hand and welcomed me with a short, cloying speech about how lucky I was to be there with the Inn's absolute favorite family. . . . What was my name?

"Natalie Marx."

"Marx," she repeated.

"Like Groucho."

Mrs. Berry laughed politely. The Fifes chuckled wholeheartedly. "I love his show," said Mrs. Berry. "He can be so . . . irreverent."

"Did you get a television?" asked Robin.

Mrs. Berry wagged her finger in the manner of a school principal who had no rapport with children. "With all there is to do here, young lady, would you want to stay in your room and watch television?" Ugh, I thought; she's horrible on all counts. She looked to the Fifes for ratification; they continued to smile proudly and vacantly.

"The boys beat you to it," Mrs. Berry announced to the adults.

Mr. and Mrs. Fife exchanged more looks of pride and disbelief. "When did they get here?" Mr. Fife asked.

Mrs. Berry said, "Close to an hour ago, before check-in time. They changed into their suits and flew down to the water."

"They must have *flown* up the interstate," chuckled Mr. Fife, the slowest male driver Connecticut had ever licensed.

"Let's get into our suits, too," said Robin.

I said, Great, I couldn't wait to jump in.

"Girls, girls," said her father with mock sternness. "Luggage! We're old enough to carry our own bags. Robin?" He led us back down the white-pebbled path to the car, where he ceremoniously handed Robin an undersize piece of luggage and me a canvas beach tote. There was something deliberately good-fatherish and annoying about the way he did it: two hands on each bag, estimating its heft with a thoughtful frown before passing it on. I could see what was ahead: a week of Mr. Fife's scientific teaching and fathering methods, ratcheted up a few notches for me.

I soon figured out that the brothers, Jeff and Donald Junior/ Chip, were the reason Mr. and Mrs. Fife took such pains to be Perfect Public Parents. Their sons were a walking cockfight. They were horrible together and dullards apart, partners in a kind of boy play I hadn't seen in my all-girl life on Irving Circle. In the name of horseplay, they strangled each other in wrestling holds, and couldn't walk within swinging distance of each other without grabbing and twisting whatever limb swung free. They found this fun, giving it or taking it. In the lake they'd race, thrashing and grunting, with the loser then attempting to drown the winner. Separately, each could be civilized; but together, they were a two-man litter of puppies, nipping and yelping and rolling around on each other's food.

When I brought up the subject one night—How can you stand them? Why do they have to crack every knuckle separately? Why don't your parents do something?—Robin said her parents yelled at Jeff and Chip at home, and made them shake hands and go off to their separate rooms and cool down. But here, her parents needed a vacation. They dumped the two boys in one room, figuring they'd kill each other or get it out of their systems.

I said, "They can't get it out of their systems. It's hormones."

"It is?"

"It's teenage-boy hormones. Why do you think they're always wrestling and rolling around on top of each other?"

Robin, wide-eyed, shook her head.

I told her it was like girls getting our periods: Boys got hormones. I asked her again: Why didn't her parents *say* something? It looked to me that her brothers didn't get yelled at or punished, no matter how much they horsed around and got the lifeguard angry.

"They're showing off for the people on the dock and for you," she stated calmly.

"For me?" I asked.

"That's what Mrs. Berry said."

I asked her when Mrs. Berry had offered this opinion.

"When you were swimming out to the raft and I stayed on the dock. She said to me, 'I guess your brothers are showing off for your little friend.' They were doing cannonballs from the raft trying to hit you."

"And what did you say?"

"I didn't say anything. I was shivering. And she was just walking down the dock to tell Nelson something." Nelson Berry, the oldest of the three Berry children, was the exasperated lifeguard caught between wanting to banish the Fife boys from the waterfront and needing to maintain good guest relations. Robin and I liked him.

I said, "Mrs. Berry doesn't like me because I'm Jewish."

"How does she know you're Jewish?"

"She just knows."

"What's 'Jewish' again?" Robin asked.

"Jewish means you go to temple instead of church."

"Oh," said Robin.

"You know lots of Jewish people."

"I do?"

"Janet in our bunk was Jewish. And Melody."

"The counselor Melody?"

"Yup. And you know famous Jewish people," I said: Sammy Davis, Jr. Lorne Green. Marilyn Monroe's husband. Ed Sullivan's wife.

"I think my senator was Jewish," she said.

I couldn't resist the opportunity, Robin being as much of a blank slate as she was. I said, "We're God's chosen people, so Mrs. Berry has no right not to like Jews. Especially now. The law says you have to like everybody equally if you own a hotel."

She asked me if I thought Nelson went to church or to temple. I explained patiently that religion ran in families; there was no way Nelson Berry went to temple.

"Good," said Robin. "I mean, I'm glad he's the same thing I am."

I asked her if she had seen *The Diary of Anne Frank*, with Millie Perkins, the model, because that explained what happened when things got out of hand.

She said she'd heard of Millie Perkins, but not Anne Frank.

I shut off the lamp between our two beds. After a minute, I whispered, "Robin?"

"What?" she asked groggily.

I said, "Don't say anything to your parents about Mrs. Berry not liking me because I'm Jewish. People hate it when you think that, and she'd say it wasn't true."

"Okay," said Robin.

· · ·

*T*he next day, at breakfast, Mr. Fife asked me if I wanted to take a little ride with him to the grocery store. He was going to buy a newspaper and would like the company. He also needed—wink— help choosing the penny candy. I waited for him to sweep Robin into the invitation, but she didn't look up from her cereal, the same Sugar Pops every day. I said, "Okay. Sure. If you want me to."

He waited until we had turned onto the paved road, then said, "Natalie, I hope you know that we think very, very highly of the Jewish people."

I was stunned by the subject matter and by Robin's overnight betrayal.

He said, "We live in a state that sent a Jewish man to the U.S. Senate."

"I know. Robin told me."

He said, "I work with several very smart and dedicated teachers of the Jewish faith."

I said, "You do?"

"And you know I love music. I don't have to tell you that. Do you know how many of the world's greatest composers and lyricists are Jewish?"

"Lots?"

"George and Ira Gershwin, Richard Rodgers, Irving Berlin, Sammy Cahn . . . I could go on and on."

It was so Mr. Fife-ish, but so earnest and well meaning that my eyes prickled with tears. I pictured the emergency conference he and Mrs. Fife must have had before breakfast—how would they handle Natalie's religious crisis?

I managed to say, my throat a knot, "I know you're nice to everyone."

"And I wouldn't tolerate anything else. Not in my family. Not in my classroom, not in my church, my choir, not anywhere."

"I know," I said.

"I play golf at a club that has several Jewish members. And Mrs. Fife and I have voted for Senator Ribicoff every time he's run for office. He would *not* get elected in Connecticut if only Jewish people voted for him, would he?"

I said that must be right. What I didn't know how to say was, Haven't you noticed that you've been vacationing at a Christians-only hotel for the past fourteen years?

"Do you promise me you won't worry about this anymore?" he coaxed.

I said I wouldn't worry about it anymore.

"If you ever hear a word that insults you or your religion, then you'll come to me. Promise? Even if it's a month from now? A year?"

It was just the gassy gust of wind I needed to dry my eyes and restore my skepticism. "Okay," I said. "Thanks." Yeah right, Mr. Fife, my lifelong friend. Father of the stupidest girl at Camp Minnehaha.

"So do we feel better?"

I said I felt much better.

"Maybe a little homesick?"

"Maybe that was it," I said.

"We're your parents this week. And Robin is your sister. And Jeff and Chip are your brothers as long as we're at Lake Devine."

"Thanks," I said, for the twentieth time.

"Can I say one more thing?" He flashed me the coy grin of a leading man about to break into song.

"Sure," I said.

He smiled, waited a beat, then said proudly, "*Shalom hah-vay-reem.*"

Oh, God—Hebrew. *Hello, friends.* I asked how he knew that.

"It's a round! I had a counselor at music camp when I was about your age who was from Palestine." Then Mr. Fife sang in his most cantorial baritone: "*Shalom, chaverim, shalom, chaverim, shalom, shalom . . .*"

"You come in . . . now!" he instructed, chopping the air between us.

And so we sang, round and round in a minor key, all the way to the store and back—"*Shalom, chaverim, shalom, chaverim, shalom, shalom*"—until the final sixty seconds, when we turned onto the dirt road and had to switch to counting.

$\mathcal{S}$ I X

could only speculate from Mr. Berry's outward display of good humor that he was, at his core, more Christian than his wife. The term was supplied by Robin, who, quoting some Sunday School lesson, said that *Christian* meant kind, fair, good . . . *exactly* like Jesus and his disciples—nice like her parents, like Nelson, like Mo, our junior counselor, and Mrs. Abodeely, the camp nutritionist, and, and . . .

"Me?"

She thought this over, frowning, her first bump into the guardrail between temple and church.

"If it means 'nice' or 'fair,' " I argued, "then you must be able to say it about anyone." I didn't really care to win the point I was making. I found that needling her in the brains department relieved the tedium of talking to her—she who couldn't take, make, or get a joke of any kind. Not that it was satisfying, with no audience to play to. By midweek, I was even missing my sister, the queen of disdain, the master of the withering smile.

I said to Robin one chilly morning on the dock, plucking a ruse out of thin air, "You know, in Tuesday Weld's family, all the kids are named for days of the week."

"Really? They are?"

"There's Domingo, which is Spanish for Sunday—her brother—and a sister named Wednesday."

"Really?" Robin said again.

"They call her Wendy for short."

I heard a laugh behind me.

"Good one, Natalie," said Nelson Berry. He walked right between us, his bare feet grazing our towel. At the edge of the dock, he hesitated for a few seconds, took his whistle off, and handed it to me for safekeeping. Feet together, he dove head-first, no tricks, into the shirred surface of the lake. He came up for air halfway to the raft, then switched to the backstroke, eyes conscientiously watching us, the minor guests.

Robin said, "It's good that he can just jump in and doesn't have to get used to the water first. I'd freeze."

I, who had tried for my junior lifesaving certification at camp but had failed all parts of the test involving the rescue and towing of deadweight counselors, said, "That's what a lifeguard does, runs and dives. You're even supposed to do a kind of belly flop so your head stays above the water and you don't take your eyes off the person who's drowning."

Neither one of us took our eyes off Nelson and his straight-edged, rhythmic backstroke.

Robin said, "I never saw him have to jump off and save anyone's life."

"Not in all the time you've been coming here?"

Nelson executed a snap of a racing turn against the barrels of the raft and was doing a slow crawl back, face out of the water and eyes meticulously forward.

"I think everyone who goes out to the raft knows how to swim really good, and everyone who doesn't stays inside the buoys," said Robin.

I stood up, the red cord of his whistle wrapped twice around my fist for safekeeping against wind and water and Robin Fife. Nelson Berry, age sixteen, with the Red Cross badge sewn to his navy-blue trunks, knew my name and had used it in an unmistakably sympathetic manner. I slipped the whistle's cord around my neck. Any second now it would be around his.

$\mathcal{N}$elson, everyone said, took after their father, who seemed happiest playing handyman, crisscrossing the lawn with a wrench or a trowel in his hand. Where Mrs. Berry was superficially gracious but internally cranky or worse, her bashful husband blossomed into a low level of jolliness, especially around kids. He called me Nat almost immediately, in what sounded like election to his exclusive club of favorite guests.

He seemed to like me, even appreciate me. He flagged me down the first time I passed him kneeling in a flower bed and asked if I was having a good time on my vacation.

I said I was. It was very nice here.

"The lake's not too cold for you?"

I said, "Well, sometimes, but I get used to it."

"Our little one's not bothering you?"

I said, well, that was okay.

He sighed. "She can be a pest, no matter how many times we tell her not to bother the guests."

I said I lived on a street in Newton, Massachusetts, with all girls. Every single family on my street had girls, so I was used to dealing with pests . . . in Newton. Newton, Mass.

"Is that right?" he asked happily. "I had an aunt and uncle in Newton and I used to love to visit them. They lived near a lake. Right in the middle of the town, it seemed like."

"Crystal Lake?"

"That was it. Their house backed right up to it." He chuckled. "Big stone house. They were the rich relations."

By midweek, he was my favorite company. I'd abandon Robin on the croquet court to stand by him and wait for his questions.

"What does your dad do?" he asked early in the week.

"He owns a fruit store."

Mr. Berry looked up and grinned. "Does he farm?"

I said no, he was strictly on the retail end.

"In Newton?" he asked.

I said, "Brookline, Mass. It started in Chelsea as my grandfather's truck."

He'd point to the burlap sack of bulbs or the potted seedlings, and I'd hand him one at a time. "You ever help him out there, Nat?" he asked amiably.

I said, "I sometimes help him with his fruit baskets."

"Oh yeah?"

I explained about this sideline: the special orders, the novelties.

"That sounds real nice," he said.

I listened carefully. There were no signs that Mrs. Berry had poisoned Mr. Berry. Sometimes, as she hurried past us to the dock or to a plumbing emergency, she'd say primly, "Hello, Natalie."

I'd return a wan hello. She wouldn't stop, but might glance back, at which time I'd take care to have resumed conversation with the far superior Mr. Berry. After we'd had a few daily chats, he said, "You miss your folks a bit?"

I said, "Not really."

"I think my boys would miss us if they were away. And Gretel? We'd have to ship her home."

I told him, "Mr. Fife said I was supposed to think of him and Mrs. Fife as my folks while I'm here."

"Easier said than done, right? Only your parents are your parents, no matter how nice your hosts are. That's what I'd say. Family is family."

I handed him another cutting, and said after a pause, "They're really nice, but they're not like my parents."

With two hands, he flattened the soil around a new seedling. "I'm usually around—you know me, puttering in some flower bed or other."

I said, "I know."

"Always around," he said, "and usually hoping for a little company."

I nodded but couldn't speak. I knew he was looking at me when he said, "Good company and good conversation."

I loved Mr. Berry at that moment, a wave of gratitude that left me mute.

"Any time, Nat," he repeated.

Robin had neglected to tell me that Gretel Berry was an annoyance factor to all girls vacationing at her parents' inn. She was only eight or nine that summer, and was like a yappy dog who wanted to play fetch with every passerby. "Want to see my room?" she asked the daughters of every guest, regardless of their age.

Mr. Berry had apologized for her, and it was for his sake that I said yes. The small two-story house was down a path, about fifty yards into the woods. As I followed the annoying Gretel, she chatted in a run-on fashion that didn't require answers. The back door was wide open, revealing one knotty-pine room bisected by a squat wood stove. I asked Gretel if they lived here year-round and she said they did. It wasn't the house of a very formidable enemy. The kitchen had open shelves with no cupboard doors and a narrow two-burner stove, which, if the box of wooden matches were an indicator, needed its pilot light ignited with each use. I could see stacks of milky green dishes and sturdy glassware, the same dime-store variety that came with the cabins we had rented over the years. The living room was shabby gold and brown. An orange cotton bedspread with pom-pom fringe covered the couch. Good, I thought; Ingrid Berry has dreadful taste.

Gretel said, "C'mon upstairs."

At the top, the knotty pine of the stairwell had given way to a dull lettuce-green woodwork. We passed what had to be, thrillingly, the boys' room: bunk beds and plaid wallpaper extending to the eaves and ceiling. The parents' room had a high double bed covered with a yellowed chenille bedspread and decorated with a lone throw pillow of green polished cotton. Gretel's tiny room at the end of the hall had ballerina wallpaper. Her headboard was tufted with pink oilcloth, and a flat gold button sat in the middle of each tuft. There was a doll bed with a flannel doll blanket in a pastel plaid. A baby doll in what I would soon learn was a christening gown was under the covers, the blanket tucked under her rubber armpits. "Her name's Annette," said Gretel.

I asked her if Annette was named after Annette the Mouseketeer, because I used to have a boy doll I called Cubby.

"No, she's not," said Gretel, an obvious lie, since there was only one Annette in the universe.

I said, "What did you want to show me?"

"Oh." She looked around and lunged for the closest object of possible interest: Annette's miniature baby bottle, which was attached with a pink rubber band to the doll's stiff wrist. "She drinks and then she wets down there," said Gretel.

I told her I knew. I used to have a Betsy Wetsy.

"What happened to her?"

I said she rotted. I used to shove food into the little hole between her lips, and it didn't come out the other end. Of course, I was only three or four then. She started to stink and my mother threw her out.

She asked if I wanted to play dolls. I said I hadn't brought any dolls with me, and, besides, when you're fourteen, you're not that interested anymore. She said, deaf to my answer, that I could use hers. She had a Ginny with four bought outfits and about ten more that her Aunt Ann had made, including a kilt with a gold safety pin and a knitted sweater with a G on the front for Gretel.

"Or Ginny."

"She said it was Gretel."

I asked if she was supposed to be playing in the house by herself when there were no adults here.

"They let me."

"No one's watching you?"

She said, "I'm in fourth grade and I get all A's."

I told her I'd better go find Robin, who was waiting for me to, um, play tennis.

"I play tennis," said Gretel.

"It has to be an even number of players. Two is even. Three is odd."

"We could take turns."

I said, well, she could watch.

She said, N-O. Did I know her parents owned this hotel?

I said, "The tennis courts aren't at your parents' hotel. They belong to the town, and this is a free country."

Gretel said, "I knew Robin before you did."

I said, "You're a baby—Baby Gretel. I'm not playing with any baby." When she screwed up her face, I made a big show of leaving, exactly the way my sister did when I pouted after an insult. The message in my feigned exit was: You're proving my point, aren't you? You're a crybaby. I'm going to play with girls who are older, who don't pick fights with the very people they want to make friends with.

Still, she was a pathetic little thing. And I had been the same pathetic little thing on Irving Circle when I stood on our front porch trying to snare my sister's friends' attention. From the narrow stairwell, I called back, "If you want to come and watch us play, you can. Maybe Mr. Fife will play with you."

She took her time. I made an audio display of pounding my feet on the steps to the bottom, then yelling, "You coming or not?"

Soundlessly, Mrs. Berry had approached on the path of dried pine needles and was opening the screen door. As accusingly as if she had interrupted a burglary, she said, "May I help you?"

I yelped at the sound of her, then said, "I told Gretel she can play tennis with me and Robin. I'm waiting to see if she's coming."

"Oh?" She glanced around the room, in a quick survey of valuables.

I said, hoping to sound indulgent and charitable, "She wanted to show me her room and Annette."

"Where's Robin?" she asked.

"In our room. Changing."

"Gretel!" she sang out, her eyes fixed on mine. "Are you playing tennis with Natalie?"

"I don't know how to," the brat yelled back.

"Well," Mrs. Berry said smugly to me, "I guess you're free to play tennis with someone your own age."

It was painful to see how pleased she looked, to see that an adult and mother could take satisfaction in humiliating me.

I said, "Gretel wanted me to play dolls with her, so I was just trying to be nice." I walked past her and out the screen door. I stopped on the small brick rectangle that served as the back stoop and said, "I didn't think someone nine years old should be alone all day."

*M*rs. Berry reported me to Mrs. Fife. I had teased Gretel and I'd been fresh.

I said, "Mrs. Berry hates me."

"She said you were in the little house without an invitation."

"Gretel invited me to see her room. She invites everybody. I'm the only one who ever said yes."

She said, "There's an unwritten rule that hotel guests don't go in the owners' residence."

"Doesn't Gretel know that rule?"

"She's only six," said Mrs. Fife.

I said, "She's nine. She's going into fourth grade."

Mrs. Fife said, "Natalie, I know Mrs. Berry doesn't hate you. She's just looking out for her little girl, the same way your mother does and the same way I do for Robin. Gretel's her baby."

I repeated, "She's nine. And I was being nice to her because I felt sorry for her."

Mrs. Fife advised that in the two days we had left, I should be especially polite to Mrs. Berry. After all, we were guests at her hotel, and I might want to come back someday.

I said, "There's a lot of kids here who I wouldn't want at my hotel. All *I* did was let Gretel show me her dolls. I didn't touch anything and I didn't make a racket—"

She raised a finger to her lips. "Natalie, nobody likes a tattletale."

I considered the short time remaining, the claustrophobic ride home, and my parents waiting for the Fifes' report about what a pleasure I had been. So I didn't say, "Nobody can stand being around your sons, but I don't hear Mrs. Berry complaining about them."

Because in three days I'd be home with people who appreciated and loved me, and I'd never have to endure another vacation with strangers, I told her she was right.

$\mathcal{S}$ E V E N

$\mathcal{I}$t was generally assumed, because I didn't talk about the painful parts, that I'd had a lovely week at Lake Devine. My parents darted into the street to greet me as if the Fifes' Chevy needed flagging down, then invited my hosts to stay for dinner, for tea, for coffee. The Fifes said, "We'd love to—great little girl you've got there—but at this rate the boys will beat us home." My father produced our thank-you gift: a basket of fruit with a pineapple, a box of stationery, and a roll of pastel mint patties straining against pink cellophane. Trying to speed up their retreat, I thanked the Fifes repeatedly. Finally, parents and daughter piled into the front seat, but not before Mr. Fife grasped my hand and shoulder in a meaningful shake: I had, he assured me, enriched everyone's week.

My father repeated an earlier offer. "I wish you'd let me cover—"

"I wouldn't hear of it," boomed Mr. Fife. "Natalie was our guest."

"Then Robin has to come stay with us."

My parents waved good-bye, both sorrowfully and enthusiastically, as if the Fife station wagon were carrying their last child off to college.

Dinner was ready—my mother's sweet-and-sour meatballs, which I had requested as my welcome-home meal from camp the month before. My parents wanted to hear about the hotel, the clientele, the activities, the food, and what they called "the climate."

I said my favorite meal had been roast beef au jus with popovers on the first Sunday.

"Who cooked?" my father wanted to know.

I told him a woman, the cook, Mrs. Knickerbocker, Mrs. K. And my favorite part was that she came out of the kitchen after dessert and people would applaud. *Every night*, even when it wasn't so great. She took a bow. If she didn't appear at her usual moment, people would clap until she did. It was a hotel tradition. She'd been there for a long time, as long as the Fifes had been going there.

"You applauded even when it wasn't good?" asked my mother. "Isn't that a little insincere?"

I repeated that it was a *tradition* at this hotel. Perhaps at all hotels with dining rooms. I was an expert on such things now.

"What else did you have besides roast beef?" my father asked.

I said, squinting into space to recall my seven nights, "Chicken croquettes, baked stuffed sole with Mornay sauce, Yankee pot roast, Irish lamb stew, New England boiled dinner, turkey pot pie, meatloaf surprise."

My mother made a face: *ordinary.*

"Fresh vegetables or canned?" my father asked.

I said both. And good bread.

"What kind of bread?" he asked.

"Rolls."

"Rolls every night?" my mother asked. "Those soft white ones?"

"Good, though. Homemade . . ." I moved the subject out-of-doors; my mother held no strong opinions on nature. "Remember the raft?" I began. "We swam out there and sunbathed all afternoon."

"Did she do the desserts, too?" my mother asked.

I said I thought so. Here, look at my tan.

I knew I was close to blurting out something that would put

Mrs. Berry on the anecdotal hot seat: the pork at Lake Devine. It appeared more and more frequently during my stay, until it seemed that every dish left the kitchen scrambled with ham or garnished with bacon.

So I asked, incapable of leaving it unsaid, "Do most restaurants put ham in everything?"

"You like ham," my dad said.

I told them it wasn't a problem, just a question.

"Ham at every meal?" my mother asked.

I said no: sausages, bacon, ham steaks, B.L.T.s, pork roasts, the pale *goyishe* frankfurters of sporting events, meatloaf crisscrossed with limp strips of bacon, deviled-ham sandwiches on a picnic lunch.

"That's how the *goyim* cook," said my mother.

"I hope you didn't complain," said my father.

I said no, I had not complained. I had thought of mentioning it to Mr. Fife, but I didn't know what people outside Irving Circle put on their table, and I didn't want Mrs. K. to think that Jews were difficult.

"I think you used good judgment, Nat," said my dad. "I'm sure it wasn't any different from what they usually served."

I said, Maybe. But ham on salad?

"That's a chef's salad," said my father.

"Bacon on turkey sandwiches?"

"You've had club sandwiches," said my mother, "and you loved them."

I said they must be right. Once I had gotten the idea in my head that Mrs. Berry was testing me, I must have tasted ham everywhere. But it couldn't have been the case, because other people would have noticed, people who didn't like pork for their own reasons. Yes, I was mistaken, I could see that now. Grown women don't pick on little girls. Mrs. Berry had better things to do than send a message to me personally with every meal.

. . .

*R*obin wrote me letters in the off season that sounded like someone had forced her to. Her pale personality faded even more on the page: "Dear Natalie. How are you? I am fine. How is school? What are you doing this weekend? Maryellen is coming over for a sleepover. I have Mr. Souza for math." As if I knew who Maryellen was, or Mr. Souza, or as if I cared to discuss ninth grade with someone in eighth. I did write back, dashing off one side of a page of notebook paper, "School is fine. Judy and Donna and I saw *Lord of the Flies* on Saturday. I have Mrs. Polga for English. I'm in study hall now. My cousins from Swampscott are coming here for Thanksgiving."

It was all the effort it took to keep the correspondence alive. I was surprised that Robin still liked me after my summer's mental cruelty, though I suspected that, when compared to her brothers, I was the best friend she'd ever had. With her in another state, I selectively remembered the tolerable parts of Robin—how she rarely got mad at anyone for anything, and would defer to my preferences in sports and games. She liked to read, although I found most of her books woefully babyish. When I read aloud to her from *The Fountainhead*, she promised she'd find a copy in Farmington.

My family received New Year's greetings from Robin's family on Rosh Hashanah. Three months later, a big Hanukkah card arrived on the dot of the first day, signed individually by every Fife, including Jeff and Chip. My parents asked why I thought the Fifes were so keen to acknowledge Jewish holidays, and I said, "They have a lot of Jewish friends."

"How do you know that?"

"Mr. Fife told me all his Jewish stuff."

"What Jewish stuff?" asked my mother.

I said, "You know—like he teaches with fine Jewish teachers. Plays golf with Jewish golfers. Reelected a Jewish senator."

My mother made a face.

My father said to her, "That's okay. He was trying to make Natalie feel more comfortable. He wanted us to know they like Jews."

I said, "They meant well sending us cards."

"That's right," said my father proudly. "Nat's right."

My mother stood the Fifes' Hallmark menorah up on the kitchen table without a word. I knew she thought my father was too uncritical ("Name one person you don't like," she would challenge him from time to time) and that I was too much my father's girl to have noticed the earnestness of the Fifes' every act.

"Maybe I'll make them up something," said my father.

I said, "You already did, remember? With stationery and mints?"

"You don't have to send them anything," my mother said. "I'll put them on our Christmas list."

*T*here was a quarterly newsletter in the off season, *The News of Lake Devine*, which I had signed up for in the clearest possible handwriting before I left. The first one I received was the holiday issue, which had a black-and-white photo of the staff, Nelson included, surrounding Mr. and Mrs. Berry, who were sitting in matching wing chairs.

I spent at least fifteen minutes poring over a Christmas tree formed by the typed names of the Inn's guests. It was labeled "The 1964 Season." Long names made up the diagonals of the tree, while shorter names formed the horizontal cuts of the branches. I found "Fife," at the very bottom, the base of the stump, and, on further study, "Stewart" and "Rice," fellow sunbathers. I didn't expect to find "Marx" as part of the framework, but I felt a stab of hope when I saw that the pile of presents under the tree had guest children's names crisscrossing each package in lieu of ribbons. I found *Chip, Jeff, Robin* bisecting one side of a box but, after a futile examination, no *Natalie*.

I read "Chef's Secrets," which revealed that Mrs. K. basted her turkey with Crisco every thirty minutes for the entire length of the roasting; that she put her piecrust dough in the freezer for ten to fifteen minutes before rolling it out between two sheets of waxed paper; that she saved the wrappers from sticks of margarine to grease her baking pans.

"**Next issue,**" the last line promised in bold type: "**Mrs. K's raisin-and-vinegar pie.**"

"Buildings & Grounds" announced that Mr. B., in consultation with the pro at the public golf course, was going to install a putting green around the flag pole. Also, new gutters, a color TV in the public room, and an aluminum canoe by the summer of '66.

"What's New with You," reported two births, one thirty-fifth wedding anniversary, one successful cataract operation, one engagement spawned at the Inn, one change of address, one Eagle Scout induction, one midyear college graduation, one early admission to Clark. "We'd love to hear from each and every one of you," the Berrys added.

"Mushroom Musings" carried Mr. Berry's byline. "The woods around the Inn have given me a new hobby," he wrote, "something I have more time for now that our guests have departed and our children are back in school. I set out with my field guide, a knife, and sometimes with Mrs. B., who carries a basket in the crook of her elbow à la Little Red Riding Hood. A recent foray into the state forest (off Routes 7 and 125) turned up a 20-lb. Hen-of-the-Woods in perfect prime condition on the stump of an ancient oak. (It is pale gray with a ruffled, feathered appearance, and is considered a delicacy in Italy, where it's known as 'Griffo,' and in France, where it is called, not surprisingly, 'Poulet de Bois.') We also came upon several gorgeous fruitings of red caps, which we promptly sautéed in butter and ate on toast for lunch. (Remember, never pick every mushroom in an area.) Let me know if you liked the column, or the 'boss editor' may yank it! Karl B."

Within a week, I sent a note to Mr. Berry, reporting that I had enjoyed "Mushroom Musings" and hoped to see more FUNgus columns in the newsletter. He didn't write me separately, but quoted my pun with attribution in the next issue ("Mushrooms belong to a group of organisms called 'fungi,' " he explained), and credited me with an interest in horticulture beyond my years.

In order to make that false statement true, I took two books out of the library with chapters on mushrooms. Neither triggered any sincere interest in the subject, but they dovetailed nicely with a science assignment—any topic in the physical world, three to four typewritten pages. I wrote on *Amanita*, the most famous poisonous mushrooms, and made a cover out of construction paper, showing a carefully rendered human skeleton (5 points extra credit I wasn't even fishing for) eating a chalky white specimen. I found an *Amanita* in the woods off Jolson, or at least something that matched the illustration in the book, and brought it in for the oral presentation, peat clinging to its poison cup. The girls wouldn't touch it; the boys passed it around and faked bites to its cap. Everyone loved the description of death by toxic mushroom—the illness, the apparent recovery, then the violent relapse and ultimate organ failure. Mr. Noonan gave me an A+. My foray into mycology was my excuse for writing a second letter to my summer ally: "My science paper this marking period was on North American *Amanita*. I found out they're everywhere, like loaded guns lying in the woods. Hope you don't sauté any of *them* in butter for lunch!"

Immediately, Mr. Berry sent me a book from his own library on toxigenic fungi, with a note on Lake Devine white stationery, with its unchanged green pointillist etching, saying that he was glad I was aware of the dangers; here were some other killers for me to study; no hurry; keep the book until I came up for my next visit.

The night his letter arrived, my parents asked at dinner—a dinner at which I had picked the canned gray button mushrooms out of my mother's pot roast—what it was that was making me and Mr. Berry such fast friends.

"Mushrooms," I said.

"You hate mushrooms," my sister noted.

I explained that this was the science of fungi, not the *eating* of mushrooms. Mr. Berry and I shared a passion for mycology.

"Since when?" said Pammy.

"She did a paper on it," said my father.

I said, "Mr. Berry writes a mushroom column."

My mother postulated that I was quite taken with the hotel owner, her voice and eyebrows signaling to Pammy that little Natalie had her first crush.

I said, "Mr. Berry was very nice to me."

"They usually are," my mother said, "to your face."

My father rebuked her. "You don't send someone a book and say, 'Bring it with you when you come back' if you're just being polite." It was meant to shush her and elicit some backpedaling where she'd admit that Natalie was right about Mr. Berry: He was a fine man and the world was, after all, a benevolent and open-minded place.

"*Are* you going back?" Pammy asked, as if parents didn't exist, as if I were in charge of my own vacations.

I said yes, someday.

"I think you're nuts," she mumbled.

My father stabbed the unwanted mushrooms on my plate with his ever-roving fork and popped the yield into his mouth. It was a display of table manners, I thought, that was unsuitable for public dining. I said, "Can't you eat off your own plate, or at least ask me before you eat off mine?"

"Yeah, Dad," said Pammy.

He laughed good-naturedly, as if we couldn't possibly be finding fault with an honored custom. "Oh, of course, Miss Marx," he said, mushroom flecks dotting his gums. "I beg your pardon."

"They're right," my mother said. "It's a disgusting habit. One day you're going to do it to some stranger in a restaurant—reach over and stick your fork in his french fries."

Rising to walk his plate to the sink, he asked happily, his spotted napkin billowing from the neck of his sweater vest, "What kind of a lout do you take me for?"

On a Friday afternoon the following April, I came home to find the house spotless, my room tidy well beyond what my mother usually accomplished in one of her bursts of irritation. My eyelet bureau scarves had been starched and pressed, and my stuffed animals were lined up like prizes at a shooting gallery. Inspecting the refrigerator, I spotted a white frosted oblong I knew to be her chocolate icebox cake. I asked what was going on. She said airily, "Nothing. I was in a cleaning mood."

"Is someone coming tonight?"

She looked at the stove clock and said—cleverly, she thought—"Tonight? No."

"What did you make for dinner?"

"Spaghetti and meatballs."

Normal food, except that on Friday nights we had chicken, an echo of my parents' childhood Shabbat dinners.

"How was school?" she asked.

"Fine."

"Did you get back your algebra quiz?"

I said not yet. Mr. Hogan was out, so we had had a substitute, who didn't do any math with us.

A car turned onto Irving Circle and drove slowly, as if the driver were reading house numbers. I went to the picture window in the living room: An olive-and-ochre Chevy with blue license plates came to a full stop in front of our house. Robin Fife bounced out of the passenger side, a blue-and-green kilt visible below her short Tyrolean jacket.

I whipped away from the window and flattened myself against the wall like a parolee on the lam.

"What's the matter with you?" my mother asked, untying her half-apron from behind her waist.

"It's Robin," I hissed.

My mother said, "I know. She's spending the weekend."

"No she's not—"

But we were out of time: Robin and her mother were on the front porch. I could hear Robin asking, "What's her sister's name again?"

"Rachel?" Mrs. Fife offered.

Without uttering a sound, my mother ordered me to get the hell over by her side and wipe the scowl off my face. She opened the front door with a gracious sweep and a welcoming smile. Robin cried, "Surprise!" and threw herself against me. I said blandly, "Hi, Robin." And to her mother, as she crossed our threshold, "Thanks for arranging this, Mrs. Fife."

My mother served coffee in her bone china cups, and chocolate-covered cherries on a two-tiered candy dish, even though Mrs. Fife had declined with a flutter of her hand. They agreed to call each other Audrey and Sissy and to do this again soon with Eddie and Donald. After a half-hour, Mrs. Fife said she'd be on her way: Her college roommate lived in Lincoln, and they were planning a *wicked* weekend without the hubbies—shopping, a matinee at the Schubert, and dinner out.

"A musical?" I asked.

"Yes!" said Mrs. Fife, amazed as always by such extraordinary intuition. "*West Side Story*, though not the Broadway cast."

"Can I see your room?" asked Robin.

"I'm leaving in a minute, so give me a kiss if you're running upstairs."

There was no upstairs. We lived in a ranch house, but neither my mother nor I corrected her.

I asked—for no reason beyond what my family had begun to call my one-track mind—"Are you going back to the Inn this year?"

Mrs. Fife murmured, "We're not sure yet."

I knew that couldn't be true: The newsletter announced on every page that guests returning for the summer of '65 must notify the Berrys, as was their standard policy, on January first.

"Are you?" Robin asked.

My mother said, "It's awfully hard for my husband to get away in the summer."

"Of course," said Mrs. Fife gaily. "Your husband is in the produce business. He must wait all year long for summer so he can sell native fruit."

"You don't think you'll be there this summer?" Robin persisted.

"Robin," said her mother. "You know how far in advance they fill the rooms, don't you?"

"I bet if you called the Berrys up, or wrote them a letter . . ."

My mother's eyes showed that she understood quite clearly what Bunk Eleven had been like, how long seven additional nights of double occupancy at the Inn had felt, and why she'd be making this weekend up to me.

I pointed out to Robin that Mrs. Berry didn't like to bend any rules, especially where I was concerned. Remember?

Sissy Fife translated with an indulgent smile, "Ingrid Berry can be something of an iron hand in a velvet glove."

Her own gloves went on, signaling the end of that unpleasantness. Kisses and handshakes all around, and she was gone.

Robin didn't grasp that we had exhausted the topic of the Inn at Lake Devine. "I had much more fun last summer with Natalie in my room," she told my mother, "and this year they're getting a color TV."

I said, "I can't go there this summer, Robin. Okay? Your father has the summer off, but not everybody's father is a teacher. It's my father's busiest season, and we all help him out."

"You do?" said Robin. "You work?"

"That's right," I said. "I wipe the fuzz off peaches when a customer wants nectarines."

Before Robin could express amazement over that piece of science, my mother silenced me. "It's very nice of you to want Natalie along, but it's probably not going to happen in the foreseeable future," she said, holding out the dish of dark chocolate cherries to Robin, who hesitated.

I bit into one and showed her how it worked: See, a whole cherry inside, runny but delicious. I said, "You've had cherry pie, right? And you liked that."

She took a dainty bite, then another, chewing unhappily, as if she'd been instructed to clean her plate while at the Marx house, no matter how exotic the offering.

"Have another," I said after her pained last swallow. "The pits won't hurt you."

My mother said, "Maybe Robin doesn't want to spoil her appetite, *Natalie*. Why don't you show her your room now."

And to me, in Yiddish, "Enough."

PART

Two

$\mathcal{E}$ I G H T

$\mathcal{I}$ had no nostalgia for Camp Minnehaha, no active curiosity about my fellow Hiawathans, until a mimeographed invitation arrived for our tenth bunk reunion. Suddenly I found the idea irresistible, mythical, the before and after with a flourish: Julia Child bringing the finished product out of the oven—*voilà*—seconds after the raw demo went in. I couldn't not go; couldn't not see what kind of adults had sprung from the cheerful and the cranky, the swift and the slow, the pretty and the homely we had been at fourteen.

$\mathcal{E}$very December without fail, the Fifes had sent a card and we had reciprocated—Hanukkah greetings from them with their Lung Association stamps, and Christmas/New Year's tidings from us—with hopes expressed annually for visits and good health. I had let my friendship with Robin fade to nothing, recognizing that if it weren't for the artificial bonds formed through my Gentile ambitions, we never would have shared a room or exchanged a word.

The reunion invitation came to Irving Circle, with PLEASE FORWARD stamped on the envelope. In my case, it was hardly necessary. I visited Newton faithfully from eight trolley stops away, often spending the night, usually speaking to both parents daily.

After four years in the country at UMass, two friends and I had rented rooms in an MIT fraternity that had lost its charter and had become something like a boardinghouse. In another century, it had been a narrow, elegant bowfront house on Commonwealth Avenue with a magnolia tree on either side of the stoop. I prepared meals gratis for my housemates, turning their weekly grocery dollars into crocks of soups and giant casseroles. I got better and more adventurous with cheap ingredients: gigantic packages of chicken backs and necks; beef from shinbones; lamb shanks; day-old bread, bruised fruit, turbot fillets flash-frozen in Iceland. By midyear, as my housemates were taking national boards and writing theses, I announced to my friends—and admitted to myself—that I had found my calling.

I paid my cooking-school tuition from my wages as an assistant to the artist who designed Star Market's circular. BUY ONE, GET ONE FREE, under a six-pack of ginger ale; 10¢/LB., below a cabbage; GOOD THRU 11/9/73, in the corner of a coupon, were my contributions. I had the right idea—that I belonged around large quantities of food—and for a while it seemed a drafting table in a supermarket's corporate office was a step in the right direction.

Within weeks, I found myself lingering at the deli counter where I picked up my lunch. There was nothing creative going on there, but I envied the short-order cook his quirky sandwich-making, knife-wielding mannerisms. He caught me watching, and teased me into confessing my restaurant dreams. It's a profession, he said, not a trade. This was his day job. Nights he worked at the Café Budapest, where the mayor ate, he told me; where Red Auerbach and John Havlicek ate, and actresses from the Wilbur. And picture this, kiddo, as long as you're considering rewarding careers: Their pastry chef? A college graduate who trained in Paris? She could bring tears to people's eyes with her desserts.

"Chips?" he asked as he bagged my turkey sandwich. He leaned closer and confided, "Restaurants are going to be the double features of tomorrow. By that I mean people will consider a beautiful meal and a bottle of wine all they need for an evening's entertainment." He winked.

"I'll remember that," I said.

It took thirty weeks of training at the unaccredited Ecole les Trois Etoiles in Newton Centre, working alongside housewives who wanted to master the art of pâté brisé and take the occasional catering job with their husbands' firms. With my executive-chef dreams, I was something of a novelty and a teacher's pet. I completed ten weeks, signed up for ten more, took ten more again. The head of the school, M. Tardieu, was an imperious Alsatian, who would grab my rolling pin or my cleaver and finish what I had not so skillfully begun. Because he knew I was looking for a career instead of a hobby, and because he had five daughters of his own, he turned his exasperation into resolve. He called me his "valedictorian" in one reference letter—I'd stuck around long enough to be the best knife handler and saucier—and that word above his unreadable signature was enough to get me my first job.

Pammy had disappointed my parents by marrying Danny O'Connor, of Jolson Terrace, one of the boys we'd chased off our street a dozen years before. He'd gone to Immaculate Conception through eighth, then switched to Newton South, where he and Pammy had gone steady for their entire junior and senior years. My parents were privately heartbroken, even though they'd never forbidden us to date boys outside the fold. Danny was no genius, just a polite young man with a head for agribusiness. At sixteen he had made deals with neighbors for whole seasons' worth of mowing, raking, and shoveling. After high school, Pammy had gone to UMass, and Danny, though planning to make landscaping his life's work, had gone to Framingham State. He dropped out with no regrets when his June birthday came in at 366 in the Selective Service lottery.

My parents had not raised us to be observant Jews, with our High Holidays–only attendance at the Reform temple, and our fuzzy observation of a Hanukkah-Christmas hybrid. Still, Pammy surprised my parents one April night, not calling first from Amherst, but arriving home at suppertime with an announcement. She and Danny, who was at that very moment two streets away breaking the same news to his parents, were *engaged*. Not "thinking of getting married" but formally engaged, with an .85-carat perfect diamond held by five prongs that Danny had had on layaway since his sophomore year. He could have chosen something bigger for the same price, Pammy told us proudly, her fingernails freshly lacquered in hospital-white, but Danny had chosen the better gem over the grander one.

She saved for last what would become the central embarrassment of the match—that she had agreed to be married in a Catholic church by a priest. Otherwise, she explained, their marriage wouldn't be recognized by Rome or by God, which not only mattered a great deal to Danny's parents, grandparents, and one great-grandmother, but had everything to do with where he spent eternity.

That made sense, didn't it? Pammy demanded. Danny's parents were religious and we were not. She was just going to sign a piece of paper that said she'd raise her children Catholic—no big deal. Danny could take them to church. She'd still be Jewish.

The big deal was that all the Jews we'd heard of who married outside our religion picked people who were lukewarm about their own. Affianced young men and women from other denominations converted. There were Hebrew lessons, circumcisions, ritual baths. My parents saw it all around them—the hotel weddings, the justices of the peace, the judges, the Unitarian ministers uniting Jews and halfhearted Christians in ceremonies that didn't mention God. Even if the outsider stopped short of full conversion, he or she embraced Judaism, joining discussion groups at the temple, presiding at seders, topping bagels with lox.

Not Pammy and Danny. They were married in a Gothic cathedral of a Catholic church on Beacon Street, on a Saturday, by a pre–Vatican II holdout of a priest, with most of the not-very-religious Jewish relatives boycotting both ceremony and reception. Those who did come didn't mix. Danny's relatives, to a person, took communion. At the reception, college friends and cousins initiated a big loud hora, elevating the new Mr. and Mrs. Daniel O'Connor, Jr., in chairs while the O'Connor kin clapped and cheered the way only *goyim* and Hasidim do in the face of such extremes of religion and folk dancing.

My grandparents refused to go. The Cohens, we lied, were now living year-round in West Palm Beach. The Marxes—well, you understand: Saturday is the Jewish people's Sabbath.

The no-shows failed to send presents. My mother, ignoring the one-year grace period allowed by Emily Post for wedding gifts, called the laggards and gave them a piece of her mind: Danny O'Connor was a good boy. Pamela could have done a lot worse. His love for her was written all over his freckled face, and always had been. Maybe he wasn't a doctor, a lawyer, a dentist, but he had a serious and quiet way about him, and his draft number was the highest in the land. He wasn't afraid of work—he'd been putting money in the bank from the moment he could push a lawn mower.

Give us some credit. Do you think we would have gone along with this for all these years if Danny O'Connor was—what?—some Irish hooligan? The wedding you missed to make some point that was none of your damn business had been a beautiful affair, and Pamela the most gorgeous bride.

But *this*, no present—not a candy dish, not an egg cup, not a, a, a Whitman's Sampler—was too hard to hold her tongue over. How did they think it looked to the O'Connors, whose relatives attended regardless, and put on a smile even if they weren't thrilled that Danny was marrying outside his faith?

And don't send one now. We don't want it. It's too late. Pammy doesn't know I'm calling; Pammy doesn't need your present. But someone had to tell you—you broke her heart.

My mother would slip the receiver into its cradle and cross off another name. Having just finished pinning medals to the chest of her new son-in-law for the benefit of Aunt Lee or Uncle Myron or a distant cousin's widow, she'd growl to me, the unattached daughter in the next room, "Don't *you* do this to me, ever."

The Green Ridge Turkey Farm and Restaurant on the Daniel Webster Highway in Nashua, New Hampshire, was the original site of the reunion, but after I'd mailed my check, Donna Paquette called to say it had been changed to her house in West Roxbury. A scarce seven women did not justify the renting of a function room, so Donna had offered her finished basement on the Orange Line. I should bring a sleeping bag, a side dish, and any snapshots I had from 1964. Directions by car, bus, and T to follow.

I asked who would be there, and she rattled off names as if ten years had not passed since the last roll call—Robin, among them.

"Great!" I heard myself saying. I was increasingly curious. The lines handwritten at the bottom of the Fife holiday cards had mentioned Miss Porter's and, later, Connecticut College, which led me to believe that Robin had outgrown her childhood simplemindedness. A reunion would give me a perfect view of a new, educated, possibly even bright Robin. She'd carry on equally with all of her old bunkmates; she'd have many of us to sing with, to squeeze her sleeping bag between, to smother with her grateful attentions. Or maybe none of that. Maybe she'd changed in the ten years I hadn't been looking and was neither silly nor excitable nor still humming to fill in every gap.

"Graduated with honors from UMass (Amherst) in '72 with a B.S. in biology. I am living in Boston and training to be an executive chef" is all that I sent Tookie Boutselis, a third-grade teacher and our bunk historian. On her own initiative, and on her school's mimeograph machine, she produced a pictureless yearbook, which she mailed to us a week before the party as a consolation prize. The party had been indefinitely postponed due to a lack of interest in the scaled-down basement sleepover. ("Thanks just the same to Donna and her family and to those of you who offered potluck contributions.")

From Tookie's double-sided ditto sheet I learned that Callie Kochanek, the bunk beauty, was already divorced from someone named J.B. Her full-page report was both intimate and sketchy in a way that made me feel I had missed several installments: "If anyone had ever told me that I could have loved anyone as much as I had loved J.B., I would have said it was impossible. The year in Georgia was tough. J.B. shipped out in February, and for the next six months I cried, wrote letters to him, and watched soap operas. Maybe I should have moved back in with my parents while J.B. was 'in-country,' but I had made friends with the other wives who were in the same boat. Finally, I went to work. I met Dean my first day at First Co-operative, and the rest, as they say, is history."

Callie claimed the most column inches, and I had the fewest. In between were the two-paragraph autobiographies from the remaining bunkmates: a nurse on an oncology floor (Joanne), a secretary at Hanscom Field (Carol), a saltwater taffy concessionaire (Linda), a graduate student in speech pathology (Donna), and an assistant manager at Pappagallo on Newbury Street (Robin).

I found the last item startling, not so much occupationally as geographically, for it meant that ten blocks down Comm Ave and two blocks over to Newbury, stood, at that very moment, the real-life, adult Robin Fife. I called my mother immediately and said, "Guess where Robin Fife works."

"Robin *Fife?*"

"Yes, Robin. From camp. The *Fifes.*"

"Where?"

"Like, ten minutes away. At Pappagallo."

"What happened to college?"

I said presumably she had just graduated.

She reminded me that the Fifes had sent me a graduation card the year before, and it looked as if we had failed to reciprocate.

"I wouldn't worry about it."

"You should walk over and say hello. Maybe you and she can go to the reunion together."

I told her that event had been canceled.

"I wondered about that," she said. "Who'd want to go to a pajama party at your age?"

Clearly not enough of us, I answered. I was heading downtown now for a few errands, then on to school.

"I want a report," she said.

I answered sharply that I was busy day and night for the next few days and couldn't promise any such thing. Who knew if I'd even have time to drop by the shoe store.

"You were always funny about her," my mother noted, a sigh of a sentence that faded to good-bye.

Twenty minutes later I was at Pappagallo, staring at a window full of the flattest flats, adorned with the floppiest botanically ac-curate leather blossoms ever stitched by man or machine. Little gloves of shoes in hot-pink, kelly-green, lemon-yellow for feet that would never know the hazards of falling food or dripping butter. I walked inside in a big-footed pique. Who wore these stupid ballet slippers, their slivers of leather functioning as both sole and heel? I hadn't thought to change from my wrinkled coral overalls and faded chartreuse T-shirt into something more Newbury Streetish. And worse than anything in sight—my white-and-brown saddle shoes with soles like thick bologna.

I headed for the one display of brown and brick loafers. A sales-woman, not Robin, was handing an aqua shoe and a shoehorn to a middle-age customer in a chino safari outfit—to my mind suggest-ing that Pappagallo didn't expect its employees to cradle a stranger's sweaty feet.

From behind me I heard footsteps, then the beginning of a sales-woman's offer of help, then softly, as if the speaker were testing a hunch—"Natalie?"

I turned, then faked a look of awestruck rapture. *"Rob-in?"*

She didn't hurl herself at me the way she would have ten years before but, in the same incredulous and charitable way she had whispered my name, stepped forward and hugged me for a long time.

I was stunned by my own response, a sudden wash of affection at the sight of her, now a tanned woman with yellow Alice in Wonderland–beribboned hair, and miniature door knockers for earrings. "I can't believe it," we said together, then repeated from arm's length. "I can't believe it's you."

I asked how she had recognized me, and she laughed.

I laughed, too, quite sure she meant only that I'd been this tall and this unadorned at camp. I said I wouldn't have recognized her. Well maybe, after close examination, I could see her younger self in there. She looked like Chip now, the taller, leaner brother. She was dressed in a navy chino miniskirt, a starched man-tailored shirt with fine green stripes, a gold bangle, the kind that opened and closed mechanically for a tight fit around thin wrists. Even in the flattest shoes in the universe, she was taller than my five-feet-eight.

And I, who used to have the height and the upper hand, who had enjoyed a joke in her company as long as it was at her expense, cried, "I'm such a mess! If I had known I was going to see anyone, I'd have changed."

"Don't be ridiculous," she said. "You look wonderful."

"I'm on my way to school—"

"Where do you go?" she asked, looking pleased enough to put a card of congratulations in the afternoon mail.

"You won't believe it," I began, "but I'm studying to be a chef."

She pronounced it—me—wonderful. A chef!

I said, "I was a biology major—"

"And cooking is a kind of science, right?"

She was, no question, what my mother would describe as darling. I explained my ten-year plan . . . to learn every station—did she know that term?—to work my way up, and to specialize in regional American cuisine, which was starting to be recognized by food writers and even by Europeans, and to one day own my own restaurant: Natalie's.

Robin was too distracted by her own delight to congratulate me. She called to her fellow saleswoman, a dark-haired, blue-eyed colleen of a pretty preppie, "Betsy—this is Natalie! We went to summer camp together." Betsy smiled, as did her customer, who was now holding a swatch of fuchsia fabric to a cobalt-blue shoe.

"I love those together," Robin first assured the customer.

"*Seeee*," said Betsy.

Robin backtracked: Betsy! This was *Natalie*, from camp ten years ago. "I was the youngest girl in the bunk," she explained, "and Natalie was like my big sister." Suddenly something glinted at my elbow. The hand that had pushed me into the spotlight wore a diamond ring, round and plain and set in yellow gold like Pammy's perfect stone. I said nothing, as if an engagement ring were far too bourgeois an object for me to spot or acknowledge. Robin continued to describe our overlapping histories, the first footnote being, to my surprise, that her brothers had made fools of themselves over me one summer.

Kneeling among a dozen boxes, Betsy asked, "Did you tell Natalie your good news?"

"What's that?" I asked.

Robin had the grace to look slightly pained. "I'm engaged," she said.

"Show her," commanded Betsy.

Robin held out her left hand, the long fingers relaxed as if she were reluctant to show off. I didn't take the proffered hand, in the manner of the admiring guests at Pammy's shower, but said, "Wow. Cool."

Robin asked softly, in the silence where I should have been embellishing my compliment and peppering her with questions, "Do you remember the Inn at Lake Devine?"

I said, "Of course I do."

"We still go there, believe it or not."

I knew then that she was not changing the subject but moving toward the heart of it. "You met your fiancé there?"

Robin said yes . . . perhaps I remembered the owners?

In the face of such delicacy—her not filling in the crucial blank—I knew what the other name on the invitation had to be.

". . . their older son? Nelson?" she continued.

For the first time that afternoon, I said an honest and generous thing: "Oh God, I had such a crush on Nelson!"

Robin's face reddened. "I know," she said. "We all did. Everyone who ever went there did."

"Even people who *never* went there did," chimed in Betsy.

I asked when it had happened, meaning, *How in the world?*

"The summer between my sophomore and junior years—not the engagement, that was this past Christmas—but the beginning."

"The understanding," amended Betsy.

"After that, we wrote and saw each other over the winter. I was in New London and he was teaching in Rhode Island. Not so far away."

"She, of course, had been in love with him since day one," added Betsy.

"The funny part was, I'd been hanging around with Kris, his brother. Not *seeing* him or anything, because they had a rule about the boys dating guests, but just palling around with him, miniature golf and tennis. One day Nelson started tagging along and making Kris sit in the backseat."

Betsy told her customer she'd check for an 8 wide in navy, and excused herself, her chin anchoring a stack of black-and-turquoise boxes. Lowering my voice, I asked Robin, "Are you going to get into trouble shmoozing at work?"

She said no, she was in charge today. Their manager had Wednesdays off, and Betsy was a pal. She touched her watch with two fingertips. "I could even run out for a quick cup of coffee if you had the time."

I said I didn't. School began in thirty-five minutes—restaurant hours; we served light meals—which I could make if I got a River-side car outbound in the next few minutes. I said I would be back, though, now that I knew where to find her.

"Promise? My day off is Monday," she said. "And, here—take my home number." She hurried to write hers on a blank Pappagallo receipt and to record mine. Another hug, then a wail: "I didn't even ask about your parents or Pammy!"

I said they were fine. And hers?

"They'll be delirious about this," she said. "When I was in high school they used to say, 'Why can't you make friends with girls like Natalie?' They put me in private school my junior year so I'd get more serious."

I grinned and said it looked like she turned out fine without me.

"Still," she said, "I'd love it if we could keep in touch."

I said, "I used to write to Nelson's dad, you know. Is he still mushrooming?"

"Probably. I'll ask Nelson."

I said, "Please remember me to him, and to Mr. Berry, too."

Robin's whole face seemed to be consumed by a fresh inspiration. She asked in a rush of syllables and an intake of breath, "What are you doing next December twenty-first? It's a Saturday."

"December twenty-first? Why?"

"Our wedding! Will you come?"

I remembered how easily I had conned my way into the family vacation, and how readily the Fifes had added me to their roster. I said, "It's very sweet of you, but it isn't necessary."

"My parents would love it," she said. "They still talk about that summer, the week you came with us to the lake."

I said, "So do I."

"You'll be the surprise guest. I mean, I can't wait to tell Nelson, but I won't get anyone else's hopes up until you know for sure."

I said I would. At least, I'd try. I'd go home and put it on my calendar. December twenty-first, the winter solstice.

She turned to the customer, who was again fingering her fuchsia swatch. "That's just like Natalie. She knows things off the top of her head." She turned back and said, "Wait until everyone hears who walked into Pappagallo today . . . Oh God, did you want to try anything on?"

I said no, really. Just looking.

She shook her head in self-reproach. "All this time, and I never asked."

I said I had to go, had to catch the T, but . . . soon.

"I hope you mean it," said Robin, "and I hope you meant what you said about putting the twenty-first on your calendar. Invitations go out November eighth."

I said I'd do my best—though I hoped to be a full-fledged souschef by then, and chefs worked every weekend. As I reached the end of the walk, she called after me, "Please try, Natalie. It's going to be a winter-white wedding up at the lake."

I stopped. "At the Inn?"

"Of course at the Inn. It's going to be small, so they'll have a bed for everyone, a wedding weekend." She cupped a hand to the corner of her mouth and said, "Ingrid's treat. Do you believe it?"

She glowed with the pride of a fiancée and a future Berry. "Did you ever see *White Christmas*? It's like that, so beautiful. You have to see it in winter, Nat; you won't even recognize it. When was the last time you were there?"

"With you," I said.

"Is that *true*?" she asked. "Ten years?"

I said it would be ten years in August. We were fourteen and thirteen, remember? Nelson was sixteen. And Gretel was, like, nine?

"Gretel's at Middlebury. She's going to be a bridesmaid . . . I had to."

But, she assured me, it would be great just the same. Kris, Chip, and Jeff as ushers, and, oh, the Inn in winter—ice-skating on the lake, lights strung in the trees, a fire in the big stone fireplace. They got engaged there last Christmas Eve, on snowshoes. It was so beautiful, they decided to be married there.

She took my hand and buffed it lightly, maternally with her knuckles. Imagine: all of us grown-up, her brothers civilized, Mrs. K. retired, the road paved, the cabins heated, the Adirondack chairs painted red.

So peaceful, like a painting, like the movie, like a song. She didn't know if I remembered anything from the old days, but I would love—*love*—every minute at Lake Devine, every snowflake, every mushroom, every Berry.

$\mathcal{N}$ I N E

$\mathcal{B}$y the time the invitation arrived in November, I was working at the elegant Ten Tables, salad-prepping in a tight space for a man who liked me a little too much. His name was Monsieur P., known in Boston cooking circles for his butterless reductions from essences of this and that. I was thrilled to get the entry-level job, thrilled to wear the white jacket and to answer, "Ten Tables," when people asked where my training had led. Monsieur P. was both chef and owner, never married, probably only forty as I look back, with a pied-à-terre above the kitchen. I learned quickly of his unwavering preference for female helpmates, and too late that he always liked the newest hire best.

He had a way of squeezing past us, never murmuring, "Pardon," but placing both hands on shoulders or waists to move us out of his way. Occasionally he'd land a kiss on the back of a head or neck, accompanied by a murmured endearment. An expert at the phony embrace, he'd circle me with his arms and lift me off the ground for no reason except to celebrate the punctual arrival of the cheese purveyor or the successful unmolding of a charlotte russe. At first I thought, How warm, how enthusiastic, how well we get along. He's French; the French act this way. They use their hands. His are not the caresses of a Casanova but the normal gestures of a European male.

I never stated that I preferred he keep his hands to himself. He was my teacher, my boss, my ticket to full-fledged chefdom. And, in a kitchen full of aspiring sous-chefs, Monsieur P. implied that I was the chosen, that I alone had ze touch.

I'd been working only four months when Robin's wedding invitation arrived. Monsieur P. said, Sorry, but you have not yet earned the right to a day off.

I said I knew that, but what could I do? An old friend was getting married and I had more or less promised to go.

"Natalie, this is a very large favor you are asking of me—the weekend before Christmas."

I said I'd make it up however I could.

He said, "We'll decide."

"When?" I asked. "I have to let them know."

"Monday evening. You come for dinner."

Mondays and Tuesdays we were closed, so the kitchen and dining room were dark when I arrived. I called out his name and heard a spirited, "Yes, chérie, I'm above. Would you bring the champagne from the Frigidaire?"

Decades of maternal warning signals flashed, but I ignored them. I wasn't crossing any line. I'd been upstairs several times—had retrieved Band-Aids and salve from his bathroom for our burns; had snipped herbs from pots on Monsieur's sill.

I was not pleased, therefore, to find Monsieur P., like a caricature of a Frenchman with seduction on the menu, in a brown silk dressing robe, vigorously scaling spaetzle batter through a colander into boiling water. Edith Piaf warbled from the speakers. I said, "Am I early? Do you want me to take over so you can finish getting dressed?"

He asked if his informal attire made me uncomfortable.

I said, "Actually, yes."

"Well, then," said Monsieur P., "I wouldn't want my esteemed guest to be uncomfortable." He walked the three steps into his bedroom, failing to close the door between us. The robe came off, but no clothes materialized. He seemed determined to chat with me and pretend he was the least self-conscious man ever born. "Natalie?" he began. "How do you like your work at Ten Tables? I mean, does it please you, the restaurant?"

"Very much," I said, eyes on the sauté pan, the salt cellar, the highly compelling knobs on the stove.

"Do you think I'm a good teacher?"

"Yes I do."

"I agree," he said. "I think I'm an excellent teacher." By then he was leaning against the doorjamb as if lost in conversation, holding some undergarment in front of his private parts, but not too squarely.

I said, "Would you mind closing the door? Or should I wait downstairs while you dress?"

"No, no, no. Not at all. *Pardon*. When you live alone, you learn bad manners. But, no, stay. I thought tonight it would be nice if you did the honors."

I asked, "What honors?"

"The veal! You make it."

I looked at the platter of pink meat and asked if it had been pounded.

"Everything's ready. I didn't want you to pound veal or peel apples on your free night."

At last he was dressed—a pair of tan slacks and a baby-blue V-neck sweater over nothing but dark chest hair.

"Should I begin?" I asked.

"*Oui*. First the champagne."

I sautéed the shallots, the *escalopes* of veal in another pan, the slivered mushrooms; executed a one-handed squeeze of lemon, a big pinch of kosher salt and several grinds of pepper, more butter, a flourish of chopped parsley. With a wink, he added a big splash of champagne, on his way to putting the finishing touches on the small table—cloth napkins that weren't from the linen service, two wineglasses apiece, a Wedgwood ashtray, a small silver candelabra.

When I said from the stove, "*Fini,*" he said, "*Bon!*" He pulled out my chair, pushed me back in with his whole body, sniffed the air above my hair and said I smelled good. Bread appeared, and the spaetzle; a green vegetable that I don't recall. The lights were dimmed. Some French male crooner replaced Piaf. When Monsieur P. sat down, our knees bumped. My napkin slipped off my lap, to be patted back into place by my host.

I brought up the very reason for this dinner. Had he remembered? Saturday December twenty-first and Sunday the twenty-second?

"Ah, *oui,*" said Monsieur P. "A wedding of an old friend." He refilled his flute and added a gulp to my full glass.

"Is somebody going with you?" he asked.

I said no.

He leaned closer. "Why is it that I don't hear talk of any man?"

I said, "It's hard to have a social life when you work nights and weekends."

He broke off a bite of bread and chewed it slowly. "I agree. It's most difficult in our work. . . . Did I ever tell you," he confided, lifting his glass to view me through it, "I find Jewish women very beautiful?"

I swallowed my mouthful of veal, then laughed.

He blinked like a stunned owl and asked what I had found so amusing.

I said, "*All* Jewish women? You find *all* Jewish women beautiful? Because there's a pretty wide range."

"Ahhphff," he said, lips vibrating, as if to say, "I couldn't agree more."

"In my family alone we have a redhead, a blonde—"

He shook his head, his eyes closed in profound contradiction. "Not blondes, not redheads . . . I meant *your* kind of looks, exotic, sultry, brilliant dark hair."

I said, "Thank you," but tersely. I'd heard this before from boys at UMass, usually graduates of Catholic high schools, who believed that Jewish girls were easy once the flattery hit its mark.

He reached over and tugged at the upper sleeve of my jersey. "You dress like a trash collector, of course, which is a shame."

I pointed out that he and I dressed exactly alike at work. I was hardly going to wear a party dress—

"But tonight a dress would have been nice. I've never seen you in a dress. I've never seen your legs."

I wondered: Normally flirtatious, or uncalled for? Time to decide.

The veal, he announced, was acceptable, sixty seconds too long on the fire, but tasty.

"Would you send it back?" I asked.

"If I thought it would bring the chef to my table," oozed Monsieur.

I stood and said, "Why don't I clear the plates for the salad."

He lit a cigarette and squinted through his own smoke, watching me scrape the dishes at the sink. After a long silence, he said, smiling, "Come here, *chérie*."

Ever the good employee, I walked back to the table.

"Here." He patted his lap.

I ignored the invitation and reached for the bread basket.

"Leave it." He drew me onto his lap. "I have some extraordinary Camembert."

I sat there silently, my back rigid. After a few playful bounces I said, "That's enough."

"Why? This isn't nice?" He gathered my hair into a high ponytail and let it fall. He smoothed it, divided it, used it as a paintbrush against my cheek. The next words, whispered moistly at close range, were, "I was hoping you might let Jacques make love to you this evening. An early Christmas present to one another."

I said, "We Jewesses don't celebrate Christmas."

"You would enjoy it very much," he murmured. "I am a very good teacher, you know."

I said, "I'm sure you are, but no thanks."

He rubbed out his cigarette in the ashtray and took my face in both of his hands. I sat there while he administered little licks of kisses all over my face as if to say, "Here is the famous seduction technique that in my country substitutes for love."

When his tongue hit my teeth, I pulled away, thinking several distressing things at once: I don't want to hurt his feelings. I don't want to lose my job or move back home. I want to go to Lake Devine.

"Is it that you're afraid of getting pregnant?"

I said, "What?"

"Because there are ways to prevent that."

I stood, finally, and said, "You think I don't want to sleep with you because I might get pregnant?"

He smiled as if the seduction were progressing exactly as he had hoped. "*Non?*"

"You think it's fair to ask me to have sex with you?"

He shrugged.

"Did you ever hear of the casting couch?"

He said eagerly, "I don't know about that."

"It's where a Hollywood director says to an actress, 'If you want a part in my film, you'll have to sleep with me.' "

No censure registered in the square Gallic face; in fact, it lit up with admiration.

"It's the same thing," I said.

"It's not the same thing. Those directors have no feelings for those girls. And if those girls do whatever the bastard is asking, they'd be wrong, wouldn't they? They'd be very stupid and naïve."

It was undeniable, finally: Benign little porky Monsieur, who hugged and nuzzled every woman on his payroll, was not benign at all. I persevered, thinking the point would be won as soon as I framed it correctly. "I meant, would you want to have sex with me if I didn't want to have sex with you?"

"*Chérie*—it's the woman's job to say no, so how do I know what you want?"

I said, "I have to get home. My parents are expecting me."

"What about salad? And dessert?"

I said, "It's late. And I'm not feeling well."

"I thought you'd spend the night! I was so looking forward to your . . . company."

I said again, "My parents are expecting me."

"You don't have to stay the night. You'll stay for another hour, and then I'll call a taxi."

I said—for the record; for anyone who might wonder if I had imagined the proposed horse trade—"It's my choice, then: no sex, no days off?"

He thought I was asking if anything short of intercourse would do the trick. He smiled an oily smile and said, "It would be very nice, I assure you."

"Not for me," I said.

He looked perplexed. Could I stay thirty minutes? Fifteen? He'd made a *tarte tatin*.

I wondered if there was a place to go—an office at City Hall, a bureau in the State House—to report such an embarrassing personal thing. I said, "I can't. I'd be crazy. And I can't work for someone who—"

"Natalie," he cried. "I need you at Ten Tables."

"You've got more hands than you need," I said, fastening the snaps of my parka.

"I won't mention this to anyone. You'll have a nice day off tomorrow and I'll see you Wednesday."

I said, "I'm afraid you won't."

"Natalie. Don't be childish. I always ask. If the girl says no, what's the harm?"

I raised my voice. "Do you think it's right to ask for sex in exchange for two vacation days? Do you think it's ethical?"

His eyes narrowed. "Ah! Your ethics; your famous ethics." He harrumphed as if everything inexplicable I'd said now made perfect sense. "I forgot while you were sitting on my lap that you come from a race of social workers and agitators. All I was thinking was how much I'd like to fuck you."

The word seared my ears, his intention exactly. He poured an angry splash of wine into his glass and gulped it down.

He waved me out—*out!*—his hand thrashing the air.

Shocked by the hate in his voice, by the loss in one quick hour of a job, a reference, a champion, I said only from a great distance, "Well, good-bye then."

He heckled me in French, sputtering, his arms folded tightly across his chest.

I shrugged: *No comprendo.*

"You hurt my feelings very badly," wailed Monsieur.

$\mathcal{T}$ E N

$\mathcal{I}$ traveled north by bus, holding a gift-wrapped wok and its companion Joyce Chen cookbook on my lap. It was Friday, the day before the wedding, and raining in Boston. The drizzle turned to light snow as we neared New Hampshire, to larger flakes as we crossed into White River Junction. I looked for Fife-Berry wedding guests among my fellow passengers, but had no visual test. The only other person who disembarked in Gilbert, a young man in a pea coat carrying a laundry bag, hitched a ride so fast and so playfully that I knew the driver had to be a buddy. I called the Inn, and found the stranger at the other end helpful, even warm, in a way that made me think I had been right to come.

$\mathcal{K}$ris Berry, the dark-eyed, dark-haired younger brother, who resembled his father, came to pick me up at the bus station. I had no summer recollection of this Berry; there hadn't been anyone tall and angular, and certainly no one wearing cross-country skiwear, right down to the knickers and square-toed shoes.

He had volunteered, he told me, to make the transportation runs while everyone else was decorating the dining room with—literally—boughs of holly. He preferred to be outdoors and active.

Very nice to meet me, or meet me again. He knew I had been a guest of the Inn before.

I asked if everyone had arrived. He said not every guest was coming a day ahead; that was only for close friends and out-of-towners. Robin wouldn't be arriving until morning—hair or dress or nails or some such thing. I asked if I was too early, and he said, "Hell, no; rooms are ready. Vespers at four in Middlebury, then dinner back at the Inn. A special deal—roast beef and Yorkshire pudding."

I said, "I understand Mrs. Knickerbocker left."

He grinned. "You remember the name of the cook from all those years ago?"

"I remember that curtain call she took every night."

"Every *meal*, is more like it," said Kris.

"And wasn't the dishwasher Roland?"

"I can't remember anything," he said, adding, "I'm not the natural-born innkeeper they had hoped for." He said Mrs. K. had quit about two years ago—lured to the Trapp Family Lodge, the last anyone heard.

"That seems right," I said.

"Standing O's for the Wiener schnitzel."

"Does she like it?" I asked.

"We don't talk about the big betrayal under our roof. High treason, according to my mother."

I thanked him for the warning. "I might have gone on and on, talking about my fond memories of Mrs. K.'s roast beef au jus," I said, immediately regretting my own last syllable. In the company of Ingrid Berry's son, I had to name the one entrée in the world that sounded Semitic.

"Right, the roast beef and popovers," he said. "That was probably her best meal." He smiled a fond, distant smile. "And some desserts weren't bad, compared to everything else on the menu."

Good sign, I thought—derision toward Ingrid and family business.

The tires crunched on snow as the van turned onto the access road. I said, "You know, every time I drove this road with the Fifes, we had to count down from sixty to one."

"Why?"

"They liked to."

"How perfect," said Kris. "How exceedingly . . . cheerful."

I wondered how he knew he could say this in front of me. I said, "It was awfully nice of them to invite me."

"Oh, they're the nicest," said Kris, and laughed. "Nobody's nicer than our soon-to-be-related Donald and Sissy and Miss Robin."

A Yiddish word came to mind, the collective noun my mother applied ironically to the O'Connors. I had the urge to pronounce it, to unfurl the banner that advertised my team. I wavered for a few seconds, then said, "The *mekhutonim*."

He repeated the strange syllables.

"It means 'in-laws, the extended family,' in Yiddish."

Kris asked me if I was Jewish.

I said I was: Natalie Marx. M-A-R-X.

"Cool," said Kris. "Any relation to Karl?"

I said, Maybe; who knows?

"I, of course, am an offspring of the famous Karl-with-a-K *Berry*," he added.

"Famous mushroomer," I said.

"You know about that?"

I said I had corresponded with him a few times over his column in the newsletter.

"I think I knew that," Kris said vaguely, then grinned. "I knew some little brown-noser was writing to him about her science projects." He began moving his lips without making any sounds until he murmured, "*Oy gvald.*"

I asked where he had picked that up.

"My college roommate."

"Was he Jewish?"

"He wasn't, but he was from Brooklyn, so he pretended to be."

He said he knew a few more words, but they weren't for mixed company. "What's the in-law word again?"

"*Meck-oo-tun-im.*"

"Too bad the Fifes aren't Jewish. Then I could really impress them: 'What time will the *mekhutonim* be arriving, Mrs. Fife?' 'How are your *mekhutonim* enjoying the amenities of the Inn?' "

"Excellent," I said.

"*Shmuck*, I know," mused Kris. "And *tush*, of course."

I said, "Who doesn't?"

"What does *shlep* mean again?"

I said, "Drag. Go somewhere unwillingly: *shlepping* to the bus station to pick up wedding guests."

"Not at all," he said.

Suddenly we were at the lake. A new circular driveway took us right up to the steps of the main building, where shaggy pine, red-ribboned wreaths hung on every window and electric candles flickered on every sill. Kris said, "My mother goes a little crazy with the Christmas decorations. . . . Hope you don't find it a bit too much."

I said most of the world decorated for Christmas, and I looked forward to it. I liked blue lights best, or white when they outlined a house and all its shrubbery. No, I said, it wasn't too much at all: It was beautiful.

*P*eople looked up from their eggnog and their sprinkle cookies to view the arrival of the new guest. Ingrid glided over with a smile meant for someone else, easy and gracious. I plucked off my right mitten and extended my hand. "Ingrid. Natalie Marx."

"Karl!" she called sharply, in a voice that might have been summoning security. That impression passed in seconds, because the next thing Ingrid did was hug me. Mr. Berry hurried to our side with a glass for me and blushed as I kissed him on one cheek. I asked if he remembered me, the Natalie who wrote him those show-off letters about mushrooms?

"You're so tall," he said.

"She was always tall—"

"And lovely," said her husband—which made Ingrid stare at me, evaluating the compliment, and then check her son's face for signs of confirmation.

I said, "The place looks every bit as charming as I remember it."

"Does it?" asked Ingrid.

"More contemporary, of course, but just as comfortable." My hostess waited, unblinking, so I continued. "Love the circular driveway"—then a quick survey of the room—"and isn't this new furniture?"

"New slipcovers," said Ingrid.

"And you've paved the access road," I gushed.

"How's the driving?" Mr. Berry asked Kris.

"Fine. No worse than this morning."

"Have you seen the bridegroom yet?" his father asked me cheerfully.

I had, from the corner of my eye. It was most assuredly Nelson on his knees in front of the stone fireplace, feeding what looked like wedding trash—silver-belled wrapping paper and flattened gift boxes—into the flames. I watched him stand, replace the screen, survey the room. Spot me. We both smiled.

He was, once and still, adorable, much the same as the teenage Nelson on the dock, which meant not only a diver's stride in my direction but the mixture of wholesomeness and sex appeal that few boys of my acquaintance had ever possessed. He kissed me lightly, releasing an acute pang that had no business surviving for a decade. "Robin's talked about nothing else since you RSVP'd," he said.

I murmured, "*Nothing* else? You poor guy."

"It's true! She called me from the store that day you turned up and had me paged, which she never does."

"And you knew who she was talking about?"

"Immediately."

I took a sip of eggnog, which had a fleck of carton wax floating on its surface. "You have a good memory for stray guests," I said.

Nelson raised his punch glass and said, "I'm glad you could come."

I smiled, the wistful kind of smile that dismisses an untenable subject. I asked if any of the Fifes were here yet.

Nelson raised his voice, "Are there any Fifes here yet?"—a cue for the broadly smiling, portly, and mostly bald man standing a few feet away to open his arms.

"Mr. Fife?" I asked, pretending to be astonished.

He alternately hugged me and inspected me like a long-lost favorite graduate who had returned to student-teach. Throughout the extended greeting, I marveled at the depth of his unearned affection for me—the friend of Robin who'd spent one week a decade ago feeling persecuted while under his supervision. I joked between hugs, "Boy, I'd like to see you with someone you spent *two* weeks' vacation with."

"Why, Natty," said Mr. Fife. "We may not have seen you as much as we might have liked, but we've always felt very close to you, and your parents, too."

It gave me the second pang since my arrival—Mr. Fife's asking so little in the way of friendship, and my feeling even less in return. I wanted to say, "But we're not close. We hardly know each other. Spending a week together a decade ago does not exactly make you Uncle Donald."

I said instead, "Congratulations. You must feel as if Robin's marrying into the family of your oldest friends in the world."

"You're right about that," chortled Mr. Fife. "We were already one big happy family."

Kris called my name from the punch bowl. He held out a refill in one hand and coughed into his other fist with a guttural explosion that only I would hear as "*mekhutonim.*" I laughed.

Mr. Fife volunteered that Mrs. Fife was upstairs attending to some mother-of-the-bride business, and Robin was driving up first thing in the A.M. with the boys, who, believe it or not, had become doting big brothers.

Ingrid interrupted with, "Maybe Natalie would like to change before she officially joins the party." I was wearing jeans and a purple parka. I said, "I *would* like to change, thank you," picturing the clash of my short orange part-angora sweaterdress among the embroidered jumpers of Santa red.

"We're getting up a group to go to vespers for anyone who's interested," she added.

I didn't know what vespers were and didn't ask. Mr. Fife confided that it was a late afternoon/early evening service, more singing than scriptures today.

"Show Natalie to her room," Ingrid ordered any male Berry within hearing range.

When Kris and I both reached for the suitcase handle, he offered dryly, "Um, I believe this is my job, miss."

"We should leave no later than three-forty," said Ingrid.

Kris said to me, "There's no hurry. I mean, it's optional. Some of us aren't going."

I said, "I'm game. I like Christmas music." I stopped at the first landing and surveyed the room below. Almost nothing had changed, except that the wallpaper was no longer murals of Natchez but fronds that looked like juniper or weeping willow. Ingrid was gesturing and organizing the transportation: I would join the boys and Mr. Berry in the van. She would lead the Fifes, and we'd caravan.

"Gretel's a soloist," said Mr. Berry proudly.

"You remember our Gretel, don't you?" asked his wife.

$\mathcal{M}$r. Berry, next to me in the backseat, said, "Maybe Natalie doesn't want to talk about it, boys." He meant the circumstances of my job reversal, a short conversational journey from his question "So, what do you do, Natalie?"

I said I didn't mind. In fact, I was pleased. In the few weeks since I'd erased Ten Tables from my résumé, I had discovered that people found this chapter in my employment history something close to enthralling. I chose my verbs carefully in front of Mr. B.: Monsieur P. demanded that I have . . . that I go to . . . that I have relations with him in exchange for the granting of this weekend off.

"*This* weekend?" Mr. Berry repeated.

I nodded.

"You quit in order to come here?"

"What choice did she have, Dad?" said Nelson.

"Boy," said Kris, "this better be one great weekend," drawing a swat from his brother.

"I asked six weeks in advance, as soon as the invitation came."

"Could you have said no to the sex and kept the job if you had backed down on the time off?" asked Kris.

I said, "How could I stay after that?"

"How could you even ask her?" said his father.

"Did he try to talk you into staying after you called his bluff?" Nelson asked.

I said, "No. He was angry."

"He didn't call you up and apologize after he cooled down?" asked Kris.

I said, "No, although I had secretly been expecting he would."

"It may still happen," said Kris.

Mr. Berry, patting my arm, said, "Of course you couldn't stay after that, working for such a man. You had no choice."

Kris said, lowering his voice to a stage whisper, "Dad, you didn't make any sexual demands on Mrs. Knickerbocker, did you?"

Only Mr. Berry, staring forlornly, failed to laugh. I said, in the voice I had used to coax my stunned father back from a similar state, "It's okay. I got out of there in time. I'll find another job."

*I*f ever a Jew wished that Christmas were a secular holiday, it was me at vespers on the eve of Robin's wedding. The choir, dressed as Edwardian carolers, entered from the back of the chapel, singing softly, their individual voices distinct as they passed me, then back to a blended whole. I saw white-gloved bell ringers in black evening gowns and tails. I fell in love with an entire brass ensemble of handsome men. Most beautiful and moving in a repertoire of beautiful and moving carols was "Silent Night," in German and English, by candlelight.

I knew from the way the Berrys came to life along the pew that it was Gretel singing the solo in the choir loft. I studied everything about her, noticing, besides the resemblance to her mother, something irritating and superior about her. She enunciated the words too carefully, and looked too beatific for a member of a red-blooded college glee club. Her blond hair was ringleted, and her lips were cotton-candy pink; her white blouse was at once coyer and frillier than anyone else's. Gretel's clear soprano climbed higher up the scale than any voice before hers, distilling the whole program into one piercing note of Christmas ecstasy.

Like all the Berrys, I had tears in my eyes as the lights went back on. No one knew me, so no one knew how much of an outsider I really was. A love-in of some sort started with handshakes in the front pew and worked its way back to us. Strangers grasped the hands of those around them, saying—or so I heard—"Pleased to meet you . . . pleased to meet you." How civilized and welcoming, I thought, until I realized that everyone else was murmuring a holier "Peace be with you."

Later, I would compare the evening to the funeral of someone I hardly knew: disrespectful and a little presumptuous of me to be there at all, but terribly moving just the same.

E L E V E N

From my austere single room under the eaves, I heard the news indirectly. A far-off phone rang; not words but footsteps thundering, then crying and, unmistakably, the sounds of grief. For a quarter of an hour I surveyed the possibilities, wanting to know, gauging the etiquette of the situation. When footsteps approached my room I froze, suddenly sure that the disturbance was devastating news from Newton, for me. The footsteps passed. I put on my bathrobe and ventured into the chilly hall holding my toothbrush and toothpaste. The sounds from below were louder but no more decipherable. After brushing my teeth, I walked down the two flights of stairs to the main floor, where I found Kris and his father on a sofa, white-faced.

I said, "What's wrong?"

Kris closed his eyes and shook his head as if the answer were unbearable. Mr. Berry said something softly, words I couldn't put together. My hearing didn't work, or refused to. I said, "No," and dropped into the nearest chair. They slid forward from the couch to prop me up. What they had tried to say so very carefully had to be repeated and amplified until I grasped it: an accident.

"Who?" I whispered.

"Robin," Kris told me, in a cry of brotherly grief that made the next question unnecessary.

Chip and Jeff were hurt but would survive. The details came from outside—newspapers and television. Robin, in the backseat with her wedding dress, had received the blunt force of a skidding car that had hit black ice and swerved into their lane. The other driver, an elderly woman, killed. No one could bear to ask questions or speak at all, including me, except to offer to go home and leave the Fifes and the Berrys to their pain.

Mostly, I stayed out of the way by cooking. Breakfast on trays, handed to Kris for delivery. Comfort foods for lunch and dinner—plain custards and clear soups that were sent without fanfare and returned untouched.

I kept asking him, then Mr. Berry and Ingrid, whose kitchen I had effectively taken over, "Am I imposing? Should I leave? I'll understand."

Someone always said, "You've been so helpful. Please stay."

I did stay, despite the chill of the poorly heated rooms and my fear that trays of food and cups of tea didn't adequately express my own sorrow.

A few wedding guests who couldn't be reached in time—it had been Gretel's job, with her trained voice and her poise, to go down the list—arrived Saturday morning in wedding finery. The families asked if I could turn the horrified guests away, or register those who couldn't face a return trip. I did. I assigned rooms in the same far-off corner as mine, and made sandwiches. In the morning, they slipped away.

Mr. and Mrs. Fife, under sedation by the Berrys' family doctor, left their room only to talk to the undertaker and the minister. Someone said that if Robin had wanted to be married at Lake Devine, then surely she would want to be buried there. The Berrys must have spoken privately with the minister, because plans for the grave site changed. The Fifes were helped to see that there was no cemetery per se on the property, and since Nelson and Robin had not yet been formally . . . well, united in matrimony, it might be more comforting for all concerned if Robin were buried closer to home. The funeral was a different matter entirely, the minister said. How utterly fitting that it be in Gilbert.

Mr. Berry drove Mr. Fife to Mary Hitchcock Hospital in Hanover the first day and drank tea in the cafeteria while he and his sons talked and cried. Jeff was recovering from surgery for a ruptured spleen and several broken ribs. Chip, with less trauma of the physical kind, came back with them, bruised, stitched, silent.

When the few woeful guests checked out, it was just the immediate families and I who had to get through the five days until the funeral. I woke up when it was still dark, made coffee and French toast dipped in eggnog, and kept it warm as the mourners drifted in and out of the kitchen in bathrobes and a state of near befuddlement. My parents called, asking if I wasn't intruding on the families' privacy and worrying that I was running up an enormous bill. I said, "I can't be sure, and I don't want to ask, but I'm sort of managing the place. I don't think they'll charge me."

By Monday, according to my standards, supplies were running out. I approached Mr. Berry and offered to restock the pantry.

"Could you?" he said. Then vaguely, as if it were difficult to address anything material from before the accident, "Can you drive a manual transmission?"

I said I couldn't, so sorry. But was there a market that delivered?

"Nelson will drive you," he said rotely.

I said, "Do you mean Kris?"

"I meant Nelson," said his father. "He needs to get out."

I asked about a grocery list. "Use your discretion," he said. "Nelson can sign for anything."

I could barely engage Mr. Berry in the face of his helplessness, so I was relieved and surprised by Nelson's near-normal demeanor when he appeared, jangling keys. Kris, swigging juice at the refrigerator, quipped, "Natalie, you know where we keep the herd, right?

Two gallons is probably enough—good strong yanks. The half-and-half comes from the black-and-white cows." When Nelson laughed, I did too. Having not seen mourning at close range, I had assumed that in the raw days following a tragedy there were no breaks in the pain, no moments when an older brother might laugh at the goofy joke of a younger brother, or that anyone would dare provoke laughter at all.

On our ride to the supermarket, I told him how terribly sorry I was, and sad; how inadequate words of condolence must sound. Nelson said matter-of-factly, No, words of condolence helped, although he hadn't heard from many friends.

I said, "It's too soon. They probably think you don't want to talk."

"I don't," he said. "At least not every minute."

"People don't know what to say. That's why they send flowers to the funeral and leave casseroles on the front porch. It's their way of doing something and taking care of you."

"Did someone leave a casserole?"

I said no, but it hadn't been that long. And leaving a casserole at a hotel . . . well, people assume there's a working kitchen.

"Speaking of that," said Nelson, "has anyone thanked you for all your help? Because I don't know what we would have done." His voice caught, and I could see his hands tighten on the steering wheel. He forced a grim smile. "Well, I do know what we'd do: We'd be eating my mother's cooking."

I said, "She's taking care of everything else. Much harder stuff."

He said it had to be a sacrifice at this time of year, my being in a joyless house at Christmas instead of with my own family.

I said no, it was no sacrifice at all.

He turned on the radio, fiddled with dials, and snapped it off.

I said, "I stayed because I thought it would be good to have someone around who can . . . well, function. Don't get me wrong, not that you can't function, but someone who wasn't . . . so close. Someone who can help."

"But, still, this can't be easy for you."

I said, "When I'm working, I feel as if I'm helping. When I'm in my room, I feel strange about being here."

"And lonely," said Nelson, "with all of us disappearing into our own rooms." After a pause, he said, his voice hoarse, "I'm dreading the funeral."

I wanted to do better, but confessed only, "So am I."

"The minister said it would help."

I said I'd heard that.

"Even if it doesn't, at least I'll have it behind me."

I asked him if he believed in life everlasting and all that.

"Do you?"

I lied. "Sure."

He said, "I wish I did."

I told him I didn't either but had wanted to say the right thing. I said, "I think religion was invented to deal with death. It's when it helps the most." I checked his face in profile and saw tears rolling down his cheeks, which were scratched as if he had shaved blindly. When I didn't look away he said, "I'm all right."

As our fellow shoppers expressed their condolences, I listened to what people said so I could memorize graceful and helpful phrases. Women were better at it, or at least said more. Men had to mention the black ice. Everyone asked what they could do. One woman, after testifying that her heart was breaking for him and his family, confided that a lifetime ago her fiancé had broken off their engagement just before the wedding, and in some ways—

Nelson said tersely, pushing the cart forward, "I appreciate your sympathy."

From the privacy of the next aisle, we made horrified faces: the absolute gall of that woman to compare . . . to bring up her own . . .

Quietly I said, "I'm sorry I dragged you here."

Nelson acknowledged the sad nod of another shopper, then said, "I had to get out sooner or later."

I went back to my list: eggs, milk, butter, bread, chicken, grape-fruit, vegetables, real syrup. He glanced at it and said, "Looks so practical."

I asked him what he'd do differently.

"Shrimp cocktail, ice cream sandwiches, Rocky Road, Mallo-mars, pizza, hearts of palm."

"By all means," I said.

"Seriously, you should get whatever strikes a chef's fancy." He smiled sadly. "Or anything poor Nelson wants."

I asked what his family liked for dinner.

He stopped to ponder the hot fudge, butterscotch, and sprinkles section. "Probably the same thing your family likes for dinner."

I didn't think so, but I said okay. At the meat counter, I selected two loins of pork, four chickens, three pounds of bacon, two pounds of hamburger for lasagna. And there was Christmas to con-sider. I rang the bell at the meat counter, and a man in a blood-stained apron waved from behind the glass divider. When he came out, I asked him if there were any fresh turkeys to be had. He said Christmas orders were in already, sorry.

I whispered across the tubs of chicken livers, "I'm shopping for the Berry family. From the Inn?"

He winced and said he'd heard about the accident. What an awful tragedy.

I asked again, "Do you think you could find a fresh turkey some-where for their Christmas dinner?"

He said, "They always have a ham on Christmas. I have a couple of beauties," and motioned that I should follow him. I told Nelson I'd be right back; why didn't he fill up the cart with everything he'd ever wanted. The butcher called to me from cold storage. "I have one I was saving for myself—it's not from my usual provisioner but a smokehouse down by Manchester. It's a beauty. No chemicals. Just under twenty pounds."

I asked if he was sure, because I didn't think the Berrys would know the difference.

"I insist. It's the least I can do."

I said, "I know they'll be very grateful."

He reappeared cradling an enormous haunch, which he slid onto a metal slab. After wrapping it in yards of butcher paper, he pushed a few buttons. The machine discharged a price sticker, which he slapped onto the bundle. He winked at me and said, "Almost twenty bucks; she won't be *that* grateful."

He hauled it to our cart in the cereal aisle, where I explained to Nelson that this was the butcher's private family Christmas ham, which he selflessly insisted on us having—well, on us *acquiring*, instead of a frozen turkey.

"That's very kind, Stan," said Nelson, and, with more difficulty, "Christmas is Kris's birthday."

The butcher wiped his big hand on his apron, then squeezed Nelson's shoulder, assuring him that ninety-nine cents a pound covered his costs and no more. Softly, he asked me, "You gonna put that pink glaze on it from a jar?"

I said, unsure of his leanings, "No."

He smiled and said, "Atta girl."

That evening, for the first time since the accident, everyone came down to dinner. The big stone fireplace was ablaze, and I had arranged hurricane candles and pinecones into a low-key centerpiece. Mrs. Fife, the last to arrive, murmured almost inaudibly that she couldn't possibly eat a bit of this lovely food . . . so sorry, after all the hard work Natalie had done. Her skin was gray and her eyes were so dull that I didn't think she understood anything being said. Mr. Fife cut her food. She sat with her hands in her lap, clutching a Christmas handkerchief. Every few minutes her husband would pick up her fork and try to feed her a morsel, but she would shake her head. He'd whisper something to her, and she would open her mouth obediently and chew without expression. I said, from my seat next to him, "Is there anything I could make her that she really loves?"

He shook his head and patted my hand with a pained, grateful smile. "It wouldn't matter," he whispered.

I had cooked what my grandmothers would have produced on a cold, woeful winter's night—*gedempte fleysh* and *lokshn-kugel*—or, as I billed it for the Fifes and Berrys, pot roast and noodle pudding. For dessert I made trifle, guiltily, disguising a layer of wedding cake that had been stored unfrosted and labeled in the walk-in freezer.

With everyone at one table, it was clear to me that the Berrys had bitten off more than they now wanted to chew. The Fifes were suffering the loss of their dearest, only daughter, while the Berrys, next door in their white house, were going through something several degrees less profound. Conversation was hopeless with the funeral and a ragged Christmas still ahead. Every topic except the food on the table brought tears to someone's eyes. The weather and the forecasts raised the specter of bad roads; the subject of home reminded everyone of what had to yet be endured before leaving and what heartbreaking memories would ambush the Fifes in Farmington. Between courses, Kris prompted me to tell my Ten Tables/Monsieur P. story, which, after it was sanitized, had no point except my joblessness.

To Gretel's credit, she found the most self-centered and therefore neutral subjects to chat about: her term paper on whether *The Magic Flute* the movie did justice to the opera; her friend Suzanne's new black Lab puppy; what did Mr. Fife think Middlebury should sing in the New England Barbershop and Sweet Adelines Invitational?

It was also apparent to me that Gretel was making a play for poor, bruised, dazed Chip. She maneuvered next to him at meals with the technique of a musical-chairs champion; she kept his milk glass refilled, reminding him of the healing properties of vitamin D. I wondered if I was the only one who noticed, until I saw Kris watching a particularly fawning waitress act, and we exchanged split-second smiles.

Away from the table, Gretel was unfriendly. I tried to enlist her for kitchen chores, thinking she'd welcome the occupational therapy. Kris and Nelson appeared regularly to chop and peel, but Gretel, I soon realized, regarded me as hired help. "Go put your feet up, Natalie," the boys would order after dinner. "We'll stack the dishwasher." I knew they viewed the kitchen as a free zone where they could be less lugubrious for an hour between sad conversations. They wouldn't let me wash dishes, but they wouldn't let me leave, either; they liked me to sit at the long, chipped enamel kitchen table and recount temperamental-chef stories in a bad French accent.

Ingrid would march in and out to supervise. When I stood up, one of the boys would tell me to sit down. Kris would ask Ingrid, "Do you think your daughter could lower herself to pick up a dish towel?" to which their mother would reply that Gretel was helping in other ways, tilting her head toward the stairs: the packing up of wedding gifts; the Fifes.

Nelson broke the silence, after his mother had left, with, "Quite the little nursemaid, my sister."

"Hoping for the night shift, I think," added Kris.

I asked how old Gretel was.

"Old enough to be setting her cap for Donald Junior."

"And how quaintly you put it," said Nelson.

"She's nineteen," said Kris.

"And how old is Junior?" I asked.

"My age," said Nelson.

"Not too old," I said.

"Haven't you noticed?" Kris asked. "Our sister's middle-aged. Personally, I think she's a little old for the Chipper."

I hesitated, worried that a line had been crossed in front of the bereaved Nelson, but he smiled wanly.

"Don't get me wrong," said Kris. "I love my sister." He pounded his own chest with a fist and coughed.

"Of course you do," I said.

"You're so nice," said Nelson. "You must not have any sisters or brothers."

"Or she's on her best behavior," said Kris.

I said I certainly did have a sister, who had tormented me for the first fifteen years of my life, then had gone off to college and found she couldn't keep it up long-distance.

"What's her name?" Kris asked, spooning trifle into his mouth from someone's untouched bowl.

I said, "Mrs. Daniel J. O'Connor."

"Interesting," said Kris. "Was that a big deal?"

I said, "Some days."

"Just one sister? No brothers?"

"No brothers."

I think it was Nelson who asked quite solemnly, "And what about male friends?"

"Well, I guess I have you guys," I replied.

With that, I remember thinking that the next logical remark should have been a wisecrack, at least from Kris. Something like, "You need a pal, Nat? Or a brother? No problem. I'm your man." But there was only an uncharacteristic silence. I watched each brother turn back to the pot he was drying, the plate he was scraping. A notion and a complication formed in my mind—that I was being wooed.

Was such a thing possible, I wondered, in the midst of a tragedy?

I knew Robin had wanted me there. Out of nowhere, she had materialized on Newbury Street; had convinced me, a virtual stranger, to come to her wedding, to do whatever was necessary to get to the Inn.

I had arrived with good intentions and, to be fair, just a little curiosity. Then disaster. I tried to help the best way I knew. In this very kitchen I had made trifle from her wedding cake and stir-fry in her virgin wok. And now, from the grave—actually, from the stately Victorian funeral parlor in Gilbert Center—the angel Robin in her Priscilla of Boston wedding dress seemed to be pitching me her bouquet.

$\mathcal{T}$ W E L V E

$\mathcal{E}$arly on Christmas Eve, after four nights in a room that was too small and too drafty for someone whose role was evolving, I moved down the hall to an unlocked double with a cushioned window seat. Relocation was easy: I hung my orange sweaterdress and my brown velvet suit—the wedding, and now funeral, outfit—in the closet, and washed my inadequate supply of underwear in the chipped pedestal sink. I noticed that my new bed was rumpled but didn't give that detail much thought. Chambermaids were seasonal at the Inn; probably one of the waylaid wedding guests, wanting to be no trouble at all, had straightened the bedclothes a bit haphazardly before departing.

Within hours I learned that this pretty room with its lake view and its yellow chintz headboard was unlocked and disheveled for a reason, which revealed itself at midnight in the moonlit silhouettes of lanky Chip and bouffanted Gretel embracing at the foot of my squatter's bed. I watched as silently as they had tiptoed over my threshold, then snapped on my reading lamp and pronounced calmly—relishing Gretel's imminent mortification—"Excuse me? Kids?"

Gretel managed to muffle her scream and clamp Chip even tighter. He swore softly and broke free. "It's not what it looks like,"

Gretel sputtered. The loneliness and insomnia, she explained in her patronizing fashion, had driven them to a kind of waking sleep-walking. She had slipped away to the Inn, where there were longer hallways for pacing than in the Berry quarters, and they'd chanced upon each other outside this very door.

I wanted to say, Yeah, I caught a glimpse of that loneliness and insomnia practically poking through his pajama bottoms. Instead I said, "I understand. It's a terrible time."

"Yes," said Gretel, bridelike in a white peignoir set. "Exactly. The nights particularly."

Chip remained mute. He turned his attention to the knob at the end of the drapery cord as if he were not a party to the discussions and not trysting with his *mekhutonim*. I propped myself up prettily with a second pillow and said—not out of charity, but to let them know the room was mine to give away—"Look, we're all adults. Why don't I go back to my old room and let you two have this one?"

Gretel, of course, couldn't allow me the last word. "Will you be moving back to this room tomorrow?"

"Gee, Gretel," I said. "Do you suppose that in a virtually empty hotel I could spend my last night in a deluxe room, and you and Chip could find another place to talk?"

"Oh," she said. "Probably."

I made a fairly elaborate show of packing my belongings, sur-veying the bathroom, and collecting my damp underpants from the towel bar. I murmured to Gretel as I left, my two dresses held high on their hangers as a curtain between me and Chip, "You're using something, I hope."

She stammered that if she understood my comment, then they certainly didn't need "something" for talking and consoling each other, no matter how it looked to me.

"Fine," I said.

She signaled to Chip that we girls needed a word alone: Two minutes? There, the bathroom would be fine.

"Tonight is Christmas Eve, the saddest, most horrible Christmas Eve in either of our lives," Gretel began as soon as the bathroom door closed, "which I know is not your holiday, but to us—"

I said, "You don't have to make up excuses for being with him, as if I wouldn't understand."

She looked perplexed. What didn't I understand—Christian tradition or popularity?

I tried again. "Do you think I've never felt the way you feel? Or is it that I need you to explain the meaning of Christmas?"

Her condescending smile faded. "I only meant that I hope you understand what's at stake here, because if we ever got caught by our parents—"

I said angrily, "You know, maybe they'd be upset for a good reason. Do you think this is a good idea?"

Gretel sagged. "We're desperate," she whispered.

"So you scouted out this room and set up a midnight rendezvous?"

"We spend time together here during the day," Gretel said. "So far, no one's come looking for us."

I didn't let her off the hook immediately. "How old are you?" I demanded.

"Twenty."

"And you think you can pull this off without getting anyone upset?"

"No one will know!" she cried.

I shrugged as if to say, I certainly hope you're right, little girl.

"You'll be very, very quiet going back to your room?" she coaxed.

I said, "I think your timing couldn't be worse, but if you're worried I'm going to squeal, then don't."

"You won't tell my brothers, either?"

"Why can't you tell them? They don't seem like the kind of big brothers who would beat up the man who seduced their baby sister."

"The man who *loves* their baby sister," she corrected, smiling to signal, woman to woman, that this was no garden-variety seduction: If things went her way, she could wake up engaged.

In the light, I could see the full effect of her getup: white chiffon, with satin ribbons crisscrossing her bosom for a Grecian-goddess effect. What kind of advance planning, I wondered, put such a trousseau item in the drawer of a college sophomore?

"Chip is so miserable," she confided, "and I think this will make him happy. I mean, as happy as he can be, considering Robin. And even though it looks as if we're rushing into this, if you think about it, we've known each other our whole lives." She offered me a chummy smile and a half-hug. "Thank goodness it was only you."

We heard a knock, then a pathetic "Gretel?" from the bathroom.

"You'd better let him out," I said.

I dreamed that Robin and Nelson's wedding went on in the cathedral where my sister was married. Behind the altar, a cellar-like passageway led to my father's store, where the immediate families plus me reconvened for a sit-down meal. There was no joy or laughter. Something we couldn't name was wrong.

I had learned that no matter how much warmth had been generated in the kitchen the night before, the emotional temperature reset itself to bleak by morning. I was up before anyone else, flipping banana-walnut pancakes and frying bacon in honor of Kris's birthday. As always, he appeared first; he needed a shave and was wearing wrinkled summer clothes, as if he'd exhausted his clean laundry and dug these out. I told him to find a table and close his eyes.

I shut off the dining room lights and set his pancakes down with a flourish. One pink birthday candle flickered in a star-shaped pat of butter, which was centered in a wreath of green and red gumdrops.

"How'd you know?" he asked.

"Nelson mentioned it to Stan."

"Who's Stan?"

"The butcher at Foodland."

Kris cut a neat triangle from the stack. I said, "Aren't you going to blow out the candle?"

He chewed the large bite and said, "Delicious. And, no, I look better in candlelight."

"But the butter's melting."

He pushed the candle a centimeter deeper.

"No wish?" I said.

He shook his head almost imperceptibly.

I said softly, "May I?"

He blinked, waiting.

"May today be as . . . decent as it can be," I said. "And may future birthdays not remind you of Christmas nineteen seventy-four."

His knife and fork didn't move.

"Kris?"

He mumbled an apology and rushed out of the room. I dropped into the adjacent chair and reflexively burst into tears—for Robin, for Kris, for me on my fifth day as mourner without portfolio, for a Christmas that was sadder than I could have imagined, even in a gloomy off-season hotel. After a minute or two, I heard footsteps behind me.

"Do you believe?" Kris asked, trying to be jocular, his eyes red-rimmed and his voice unsteady, "that in this century parents would name their Christmas baby after Kris Kringle?"

I sat up straighter and said—in the same spirit of ignoring what had just happened—"It could be worse. Kris is a nice name."

"The choices, as they saw it, were Nicholas, Noel, or Kris." He sat down and replaced his napkin on his knees. "The first was rejected as sounding too Italian. 'Noel,' while unmistakably Christmasy, was eliminated for being the name of a famous homosexual—"

"They told you that?"

"Not in so many words. They said the only other Noel they'd heard of was Noël Coward, and they wouldn't want people to think I was named after him. So it came down to Kris." He closed his eyes for a long few moments, then blew out what remained of the candle. He opened his eyes and said, "Sorry."

"For what?"

"You were holding up better than everyone else put together— and now look what I did."

I said, "It wasn't you. Any little thing would have set me off. It was overdue. We both were."

Kris exhaled and rubbed his face.

I said, "And then there's me—named after a dead teenage aunt." We forced bleary smiles.

He picked up his fork and knife. "You're joining me, aren't you?"

I didn't think I could get pancakes past the lump in my throat, but I said yes. Did he think I'd let him eat alone on this of all days? I took a few steps toward the kitchen, but stopped to say, "Anyone would be depressed when his birthday falls the day before his brother's fiancée's funeral. You don't have to try to be cheerful just because I stuck a candle in your breakfast."

He said, "I wish I were that unselfish. I wish I could say it was all for Robin. But it's not. What got to me was—" he stopped, then gestured: the plate; the effort; me. "I wasn't expecting a thing from anybody."

I touched his shoulder. He hunched it upward until my hand was pressed to his unshaved cheek. It seemed a brave act, and one that deserved addressing.

*J*eff arrived after lunch, on furlough from Mary Hitchcock Hospital. We'd been told he was consumed by the belief that if he had driven faster or slower by three seconds—hadn't stopped for that yellow light at the Jack in the Box, or hadn't passed that horse trailer on Route 84—the deadly, swerving Chrysler would have missed his sister.

Accompanying him was his girlfriend, Bonnie Valluzzi, who had not been romantically entrenched enough to be invited to the wedding, but had rushed to Jeff's bedside the minute she'd learned of the accident and spent two nights sleeping in the nurses' lounge. Reportedly, she had been inspired to switch her major to nursing as soon as she could transfer to a four-year college, to forgive the wedding snub, to retract the breakup it had provoked.

I was silently celebrating the absence of parents at the table and my rightful role as carver and server. The Fifes had stayed in their room, believing that Jeff needed a few hours with the young people, and the senior Berrys had driven to Brattleboro to visit Karl's father in a nursing home. We drank beer from the gaudy Germanic stein collection and sang "Happy Birthday" to Kris, with Gretel harmonizing. Even Chip and Jeff joined in, smiling from time to time. Gretel, like a mole for the older generation, proposed we say grace, but Nelson killed the idea. "Grace? That's just what I feel like saying these days—thanks, God."

Kris stood and said, "Well, then, I'm going to make a speech." After a deep breath and an exaggerated exhale he said, "Today, friends and relatives, is my twenty-third birthday. As we all know, I've had better." He raised his stein, looked directly at me, and said, "But, still, I'm grateful for who *is* here."

Nelson said, on the downswing of everyone's hoisting, "Quite the toastmaster, Kristofer. Hope you were going to do better than that as my best man." Instantly, Kris reached across to squeeze Nelson's shoulder. "Buddy," he said softly. "I promise. Someday."

We ate the ham, a Grand Marnier sweet potato soufflé, a wreath of steamed broccoli with cherry-tomato ornaments, shoe-string onion rings in a milk batter from *Alice's Restaurant Cookbook*, and a three-layer chocolate birthday cake. As I stood over the ham, massaging the Inn's best knife against its carving stone, I apologized for what might be seen as an inappropriately festive meal. My words, I knew, were unnecessary because I had discovered in my five days of consolation cooking that life went on: Gretel seduced Chip; Bonnie Valluzzi switched her Christmas plans and her

major; Nelson received guys from high school, who arrived looking terrified, as if their parents had forced the sympathy call, then
left having played boisterous hockey on the lake.

"It's Christmas," said Gretel in her headmistress fashion, "and it's
Kris's birthday. You did a lovely job with the food and the presen-
tation." She turned to address the newcomers, Jeff and Bonnie.
"Natalie's a professional chef."

Bonnie said brightly, "Here?"

I said, No, I was just helping out.

"Where do you work?" she asked.

I said I'd quit my job the month before and would be looking for
another post as soon as I returned to Boston.

"My dad has a restaurant in New Haven," said Bonnie. "Valluzzi's."

"It's pizza," said Jeff.

"I could give you his number. He knows a lot of restaurant owners and could make some calls."

"Thanks," I said, "but I'm going to exhaust the Boston possibilities first."

"My dad has an inn in Vermont," said Kris quietly.

I didn't answer him directly, but smiled as if it were a stray,
rhetorical compliment. Of course I had thought about the hole in
their lineup, the unmentioned job of head chef in high season, and
had decided it would be a terrible mistake. I couldn't relax around
Ingrid, and the food that pleased her would never please me. With
these ingredients, these recipes, I had stopped auditioning for the
role, stopped thinking about cuisine with roots along the Rhine.
Tonight I was the executive chef instead of the visiting hand in the
kitchen, and within the limitations of a huge smokehouse ham, I
had cooked the way I'd been taught.

After dessert and coffee, the members of the party excused
themselves in twos. Bonnie said she'd take Jeff upstairs, along with
plates of this unusual and original food for his parents, and water

for everyone's pills. Gretel said she'd get Chip settled and would return in about forty-five minutes to help with the cleanup.

" 'Get settled'?" Kris repeated. "What does that mean, exactly?"

Chip, for once, answered first, avoiding my knowing stare. "I need my leg elevated, and I can't do it without help."

"And it's really, really hard for him to fall asleep, Kristofer," Gretel said, in a tone that pronounced her brother the least sensitive man in New England. "I read aloud to him and it lulls him to sleep."

"You never do that for me," her oldest brother said.

"I'll do it," cooed Kris, with a few comic strokes to Nelson's brow.

"Poor Gretel," I said. "Having to explain herself to a panel of brothers."

Apparently, it took more than one midnight mediation session to turn Gretel into my ally. She took Chip's good elbow and guided him between the vast number of empty tables, away from her inquisitors.

"Good night," we called in a chorus, gaining only a toss of Gretel's stiff hair and a raised hand from Chip.

"You don't suppose . . ." Nelson began, as soon as they were out of earshot.

"I'd bet on it," said Kris. "Tonight's the night. Or else she'll have to work it out long-distance."

I said, "Unless she's already worked it out."

With that I turned my attention to collecting silverware, knowing I had their full attention.

"Natalie?" I heard.

I looked up, projecting as much counterfeit innocence as I could in one expression.

"Do you know something we don't know?" asked Nelson.

I said, "Guys. Please. Let's change the subject. Anyone want thirds on cake?"

"We're waiting for your answer," said Nelson.

"We have our ways," said Kris. "You think we can't interrogate you till you drop?"

Had I promised the brat anything that I wasn't dying to betray? I reached for and scraped a few plates. Finally I said, "Would you guys beat him up or anything?"

"*Us?*" they said. "*Chip?*"

"And you don't have a lot invested in your sister's . . . how shall I say this—honor?"

"She's answered it," said Nelson. "Let's not give her the satisfaction of eating out of her hand."

"Good," I said. "I'm glad you feel that way."

Nelson and Kris wheedled further: How did I know? When did it happen? Where were they?

I said, Okay, but they wouldn't tell their parents, would they?

They protested that they never told their parents anything.

I waited a few beats longer, then said only, "Okay."

"Okay what?" said Kris.

"They sneaked into my room last night."

"*Your* room?"

"Well, my new room. I moved my stuff into a double, and woke up around midnight to see two figures at the foot of my bed. Locked in an embrace."

"Dressed?" asked Kris.

"Do we want to know?" Nelson asked, wincing.

"Dressed to kill. At least Gretel was, in this getup—the goddess Aphrodite, in this white chiffon number—"

Nelson's expression changed. I saw something in his face that was unrelated to a big brother's chagrin over a sister's sexual escapades.

"Just a nightgown," I backtracked. "Nothing scandalous."

"What did it look like?" he asked.

I proceeded carefully. "White? Like a tunic. Crisscrossed"—I traced the path quickly, clinically, on my own body—"with white satin ribbons."

Nelson looked at Kris.

Kris said, "What?"

"That doesn't ring a bell?"

"I don't know what the hell you're talking about. I was hoping Natalie would get to the good stuff."

Nelson murmured, "Of course you weren't there."

"Where?" Kris and I asked together.

"That nightgown," he said. "It was Robin's. I mean, it was Gretel's gift to Robin at her shower. Robin loved it."

I said, No, there must be some mistake—

"Gretel was packing up and returning the presents so I wouldn't have to . . . so Sissy wouldn't have to."

I said, "Nelson, I had no idea—"

"Don't be ridiculous. You didn't know . . ."

I said, "Except it's one more thing for you to be upset about."

He stood up, and pushed in his chair as if to a precise, reserved spot. "Would you folks mind if I turned in?"

We rushed to say, No, God no. Of course not.

"Natalie, as always, a magnificent dinner." He reached for my hand, kissed it sadly, distractedly, then walked away, his fists in his jeans pockets.

Kris directed me to a perch on the counter, outside the work zone, and coaxed me to pick up Gretel's adventure from the unfortunate junction of the repossessed gown.

Whispering in case there were principals or parents eavesdropping, I said, "So I wake up and I hear this sound"—I smacked my lips on the back of my hand to approximate smooching—"and I don't say anything for a few seconds, then I pipe up, from the depths of my pillow, 'Kids? Excuse me?' "

"No!" said Kris, laughing. "Did Gretel jump out of her skin?"

I shushed him. "Practically. She grabbed Chip. Meanwhile, I've turned on the light, so they know it's me, which is when Gretel starts negotiating with me. Or interpreting for me—how they couldn't sleep and had been pacing and happened to run into each other outside my room."

"Chip wasn't undressed or anything. I mean it wasn't totally embarrassing, was it?"

"Pajamas." I fixed my eyes on his for comic effect and said gravely, "Thin cotton hospital pajamas."

He groaned. "And you weren't, like, embarrassed? I mean, you were decent and everything?"

I said, "I was most decent. No question."

"I only asked because my family . . . several times a day, it seems—me included—does something that is totally . . . embarrassing."

"No you don't," I said.

"I'm just picturing the whole situation, and I know Gretel, and I would put money on the fact that she made you feel as if you were the one who was trespassing."

I smiled and said, "Maybe. But I handled it."

"Who stayed? You or them?"

"Them."

He smiled. "But you had the last word?"

"Damn right," I said.

He picked up a dish towel and dried his hands. "Still, pretty brazen, huh? Leading him off to bed tonight for all the world to see. Knowing you know the whole story."

"I'm just a temporary cook," I said. "The young mistress of the house doesn't have to kowtow to the help."

He came over to where I was sitting on the linoleum counter above the cabinets. Solemnly, as if speaking for the entire ungrateful management, he said, "I want to thank you for dinner . . . not just for dinner. For breakfast today, too. Especially for breakfast."

He took a step closer, so there was no room left between the toes of his sneakers and the cupboard door. Without meaning to—or at least without planning the next step—I hooked my legs around his playfully. Which led to his arms around my neck, and my arms around his waist.

"You're welcome," I said.

We would have kissed. We were a second from it, an inch, which is where things froze on Christmas night 1974. We might as well have been kissing for the effect we created, the alarm we tripped.

The well-oiled door swung inward, delivering Kris's mother for her nightly inspection. We jumped apart, but not as cleanly as we would have if our arms and legs hadn't been entwined.

Ingrid stared for a few unforgiving seconds, then hissed, "Remember tomorrow," and turned on her heels.

I jumped off the counter and sputtered, "Do you think we *forgot?*" at the same time Kris called, "Ma!"

The door swung hard, vibrating. If she heard us, she didn't look back.

$\mathcal{T}$ H I R T E E N

$\mathcal{M}$y parents came to the Inn an hour ahead of the service, so when Mrs. Fife couldn't go to the funeral, couldn't even be propped up, it was my mother who stayed behind with her.

Mr. Fife said, No, he couldn't endorse such a plan; it was his duty to stay if Sissy couldn't go. My mother insisted. She assured us that she'd locate what she needed—the tea bags, the scotch, the cold compresses—closing the door on our procession with a firm and competent click.

Mr. Fife, his sons, and Nelson got into the undertaker's limousine; the remaining Berrys took the van, while I drove with my father, somberly dressed in his black overcoat and the gray felt homburg that he wore only for rides to churches and to synagogues. He kept shaking his head and repeating, "That poor Sissy. That poor woman. These poor people."

I said, "It's been hanging over everyone's head for so long, they never thought this day would come."

It set my father off, as if he had been mulling over this ill-gotten delay. "Why in God's name did they wait so long?" he demanded.

"I told you—Jeff was in the hospital. They wanted him to be able to go. Then there was Christmas."

"The Jews have it right," my father said. "We bury our dead before the next sundown." He muttered, "Waiting and waiting in a strange place, away from home. It's ridiculous! It's cruel! And for what? To put a sick boy at his sister's grave? Jesus, I couldn't believe it when you told me they were waiting this long."

I said, "It seemed right when the decision was made, to have the funeral up here, where Robin wanted to be married."

"*Meshugas!*" my father said. He patted my hand, and I knew he was saying, I'm riled up, honey, but I didn't mean that you had anything to do with this lousy decision.

I said, "I think it's been torture for the Berrys."

"Well, isn't that too bad."

Surprised, I said, "No one complained. I just meant that it's a huge responsibility."

"They're innkeepers! They're professional hosts. Tragedies happen. You make your living inviting strangers into your home, you can't always expect it's going to be easy."

"First you say the funeral should have happened days ago, and in the next sentence you're saying, 'Too bad for the Berrys. They have to accept whatever happens under their roof.'"

"All of a sudden you admire them? You think I'm wrong to hold a grudge?"

We were at the YIELD sign that marked the end of the shore road and the beginning of the route to Gilbert Center. Two cars ahead of us, the limo driver, as if mindful of recent tragedies, was driving with studied slowness.

I said, "That was a different time."

"And you think people change?"

I said, "Whatever Ingrid Berry thinks of me, she hasn't passed it down to her children." To her sons, at least, I thought.

"They'd be fools if they didn't appreciate you, with all the help you've been. They got a free cook and bottle washer, and a very nice, soothing, helpful girl, who the Fifes happen to love, so it's all very convenient. Just because you dislike someone doesn't mean you won't take advantage of her. And now, your mother."

"Mom? I thought you said that was fine."

"It's fine because there was no one else, apparently. But what kind of system is this? Your mother's practically a stranger! Where are Sissy's sisters? Her best friends?" He shook his head with deep disapproval. "The Berrys are takers, Nat. That's all I'm saying."

I said, "Dad. They invited me here as a special friend of Robin's—before anything went wrong. I couldn't leave them in the lurch."

"Who?" he asked. "Who couldn't you leave in the lurch?"

"Everyone: Mr. Fife, Sissy, Nelson, his brother."

At just that juncture, Kris, from the backseat of the van, turned around to check on us. I waved discreetly, and he waved back.

"Which one's that?" my father asked.

"Kris," I said. "Kristofer."

My father said nothing. His badly aligned tires thumped the country road. "Are you packed?" he asked me finally.

I said, "I hardly brought anything."

He said quietly, "Natty, we'll go back there to get your mother and to pay our respects after the service. Then I want you to come home with us."

*C*ars with Rhode Island and Connecticut license plates lined Union Street outside the church. Undaunted, my father pulled his truck into a driveway between a luncheonette and a card store several blocks south.

I hissed that he couldn't block someone's driveway, but he was already out of the cab, opening the restaurant's front door and announcing loud enough for me to hear from the sidewalk, "I'm up for the funeral. Can I park in your alley for maybe a half-hour? I'm up from Massachusetts. Marx Fruit. I'll leave my keys."

It was the way he conducted himself, asking only what he would have readily agreed to if it were his town, his driveway, and a brother truck in need of a favor. Of course the counterman agreed.

"You and Pamela," he clucked as we walked back up Union.

"You're so afraid you're going to offend someone. You know why? 'Cause you never had to finagle anything. Never had to fight your way to the front of the line." He smiled. "You and your sister. You go into a bakery, and if some shmuck cuts in front of you, you say, 'Excuse me, sir, but you're not supposed to cut in front of people who were here first.' You don't get that from me, and you sure don't get it from your grandfathers."

I said, "You think you can bend every rule. You think you can ask the chef to cook you up some liver and onions even if they're not on the menu—"

"You're never gonna let me forget that—"

"I wouldn't accommodate you. I'd refuse. Because I know you: You have to try. That's the fun of it. I'd refuse because if the waitress went back and said, 'Sorry, sir, no deal,' you would've ordered the meat-loaf plate and have been perfectly happy."

"You!" he said proudly, squeezing my shoulders, missing my point entirely. "As if you'd work in a joint that had a meat-loaf plate."

An usher directed us to a guest book on a pedestal, where a dozen schoolboys in crested blue blazers—Mr. Fife's boys' choir, I would soon learn—were carefully inscribing their names. After signing "The Edward Marx family," I caught up with my eternally unselfconscious father, now barreling toward the front of the church as if snagging good seats at the North Shore Music Tent. It put us where no one else, apparently, wanted to be—directly behind the families, and therefore only yards from Robin. The sight of a small nosegay on her immense, gleaming cherry coffin instantly made my eyes sting and my throat ache. I knew, and the assembly would soon learn, that the violets, sweetheart roses, and stephanotis were to have been her understated bridal bouquet.

Before anyone said an official word, Mr. Fife's boys' choir rose to sing. I was astonished to see Donald himself stand, touch the cheeks of the saddest, well-scrubbed faces, and conduct them in the singing of "You'll Never Walk Alone." With the first note I could see his spine straighten, his shoulders lift, his elbows square; when his face turned, I could see his eyebrows flexed and his lips moving, and I knew that these verses and this refrain were four minutes of relief. When the song ended, the dozen boys dropped to the ground, cross-legged, instantly motionless, like ball boys at a tennis tournament. Donald returned to his seat, his body sagging again.

The minister from Gilbert was joined by a robed man he introduced as Robin's beloved and lifelong clergyman from home, the Reverend Hatch, who was square of jaw and wild of eyebrow. He turned toward the coffin and began, as if a lifetime of ministerial composure were required to keep his voice from breaking, "Dear Robin . . ."

But then, facing the congregation, he said what men of God say about senseless, accidental deaths of persons who have never spoken an unkind word or entertained an uncharitable thought in their twenty-three years on earth: that the Lord had His plan and His reasons, as much as we didn't understand them. As much as we might question Him. As much as we might turn away from Him at a time like this. The Reverend Hatch read the Twenty-third Psalm as if it would help, as if we had needed him to travel from Connecticut for this contribution, as if these weren't the most rote, all-purpose public school stanzas in the entire Bible.

It wasn't enough for me. I wanted someone to state the obvious: that this was not bearable. That Robin had been horribly cheated. That old ladies shouldn't drive. That shmucks and criminals still walked the earth, while Robin lay here bruised and dead. I wasn't going to start it, but I hoped if it had been me, there would be keening and wailing reminiscent of mothers at the graves of sons killed in the Six-Day War.

Gretel sang a hymn beautifully between eulogies, the first by the Reverend Hatch (young Robin), followed by the host minister (bride and adult).

It ended with the saddest sight of all, the pallbearers carrying her away, Nelson and friends on one side and what must have been doting uncles on the other.

Donald Fife and his sons followed, but barely.

I held my father back so that we didn't merge into the recessional directly behind the Berrys, but minutes later, after the coffin had left the church.

I said, Yes, I *would* go home with him as soon as we picked Mom up at the Inn; that I had paid my respects already and had more or less said my good-byes.

$\mathcal{F}$ O U R T E E N

$\mathcal{I}$ returned home from Robin's funeral grateful for my parents' rescue and believing that my family life, measured in love, democracy, and the intimacy of a modest ranch, was far superior to anything I'd seen up north. I slept rent-free in my old room, cleaned a little, cooked, and shopped—but only when I felt like it. Across the street, paralleling my own career trajectory, Shelley Loftus was clipping ads for job fairs and go-getter seminars that we might attend together.

My parents suggested I work for one of them while I job-hunted—either do the things in a real estate office that didn't require a license or uncrate Florida citrus at sunup. I chose the desk job at Audrey Marx Properties, under the wing of Pamela Marx O'Connor, Associate.

I developed an itch on my hands and wrists that neither of the dermatologists I consulted could relieve with hydrocortisone cream or environmental adjustments. The longer I lived at home and played receptionist for Audrey Marx Properties, the worse it got. A third doctor asked questions that verged on the psychiatric: My age? Marital status? Medications? Occupation? Had I always lived at home? How was that working out? Any new stresses concurrent with the onset of symptoms?

I answered each question briefly but honestly: I was twenty-four years old and single, with no prescriptions to my name. I was an unemployed chef, looking for work in a recession, in a certain caliber of restaurant. Living at home was trying, not that I could put my finger on why, but I was beginning to feel myself shrinking.

Recent stresses? Those would include working for my frighteningly similar mother and sister in a field I had only contempt for, waiting for my phone to ring on any number of counts, and the death in a car crash of a friend en route to her wedding.

My last answer startled the doctor, who reached over and squeezed one of my itchy hands. "How awful for you," she said.

I wanted to tell this sympathetic and relatively young dermatologist the whole story, but sensed I had already exceeded the space allotted on my medical history. I hesitated, then asked if this was the kind of thing she had time for.

"I'll make time."

"Briefly, then: I was up at this inn, where the wedding was supposed to be. Then we got the awful news. I found myself in the middle of everything, taking care of people I hardly knew. My parents had to come up and drag me home."

"Against your will?"

I said, Not really. The funeral was over. I had no clothes and no concrete reason to stay. No spoken invitation.

"But you have unfinished business there?"

I said, "I guess I do."

"When was this?"

"Christmas."

"Have you been in touch with these people?"

I said no.

"Are these people men?"

I said yes. None of whom I had heard from.

"Have you called them?"

I said I hadn't.

She said I should. Waiting was stressful. Stress caused all sorts of systemic misfires. "I'm writing you a prescription for some lotion, but it's not going to do anything more for you than the steroid cream you've been using." She tore a page from her prescription pad and handed it to me. "I have parents, too," she said. "In Newton. Maybe you need a place of your own."

In late February, Hilda Simone, a plump little game bird of a woman in a short, shiny black suit, walked into Audrey Marx Properties and asked me if this office handled commercial space. I swiveled around in my chair to consult Pammy, who glided to the reception desk, hand outstretched, eyes round with pleasure and fixed on Mrs. Simone. "Of course we do, Natalie," she chided.

Hilda Simone then said, "You see, my husband and I are looking for a site for our restaurant."

Pamela had the instincts to hold back until she had interviewed Mrs. Simone and effectively counted her money. "Tell me more," she said.

Just then my mother walked in with a couple she introduced as the Schenkmans, Dr. and Dr., relocating from Manhattan to work at Mass Eye and Ear, referred by such-and-such, also at the Infirmary. Would either of them like coffee, tea, Cup-a-Soup? Natalie, would you mind?

Pammy said, almost shrilly, "You know what, Audrey? Mrs. Simone wanted to talk to us about space for a *new restaurant*. Maybe I could get the doctors coffee and talk to them, since you're so much better with commercial space, and Natalie could act as consultant."

I said blandly, "I can get the coffee."

My mother reconfigured the message for the doctors: "You know what? Because Mrs. O'Connor is our residential specialist, I'm going to ask her if she'd speak with you." She then announced gaily to the office at large, "Natalie gets our coffee because she's the food and beverage specialist de la maison."

I asked, "Who wants what?"

Nothing for me, they all said. My mother pointed to the empty chair next to her new client. "Sit down. You've met Mrs. Simone?"

I said, "More or less."

"Natalie is helping us out temporarily while she secures work in her own field."

Mrs. Simone did not take the bait. My mother tried again: "She's a very talented chef."

Mrs. Simone perked up slightly. "Where?"

"I'm between jobs," I said.

"She worked at Ten Tables," my mother supplied. "I thought she'd be the perfect person to consult about properties. Considering her expertise."

"Are you a broker, too?" Mrs. Simone asked me.

I said no. I wasn't licensed. Or inclined, I wanted to say.

I saw nothing auspicious in Hilda Simone. I sensed the soul of a franchise owner or a server of bottled dressing.

"What kind of restaurant?" my mother asked.

Mrs. Simone said, "Not . . . inexpensive."

"French?" my mother chirped.

"In certain ways."

"Such as?" I asked.

"Well, French bread. Butter not margarine. Desserts from scratch. Wine."

I said, "I see."

Mrs. Simone said, "I've always thought it would be fun to own a restaurant and to greet people at the door. So we've been eating at a lot of different places and taking notes. My husband has his ideas and I have mine."

"It's a huge job," I said, "and the hours are brutal."

"You're looking for what kind of square footage?" asked my mother.

"We thought enough for twenty tables. No more than that."

I asked, "Are you or your husband a chef?"

"He's a lawyer," she said. "I would be the manager."

My mother said, "Do you *need* a chef?"

I said, "Mom, they need a space first."

My mother opened her big loose-leaf notebook. "May I ask about renovations? Is there a budget for that?"

Mrs. Simone said they fully expected to renovate even if the space had been previously used as a restaurant.

"Newton, right?"

"We're starting with Newton."

"Natalie's cooking school was in Newton," my mother said.

"Les Trois Etoiles," I supplied.

My mother confided to me, "I'm thinking Piccadilly Square." She flipped to a tab in her book, which fell open to the precise listing. "It's too perfect," she said. "I can't believe it."

Mrs. Simone asked what had been there before.

"A pastry shop," Pammy offered from across the room, "which was a gold mine, but the owner had some problem with his feet or his legs and had to close."

"Phlebitis," said my mother.

"It was darling," said Pammy. "I used to love their Mexican wedding cookies."

"Good foot traffic," my mother said, "with a nice courtyard."

"It's two minutes from here by car," Pammy offered.

The Schenkmans couldn't have known why an entire office was doting on an unprepossessing woman in a short shiny suit. Mrs. Dr. Schenkman said, "Should we come back at a better time?"

Pammy snapped to attention. I could see her lean across her desk, presumably to explain to the ophthalmologists that they had been caught in the middle of a campaign to get her unemployed sister back to work; *please* excuse the inattention.

My mother led Mrs. Simone away, signaling God-knows-what to me with her eyebrows and her warden's bracelet of master keys. "Any last-minute thoughts on location, Nat? Something you'd think of that I wouldn't?"

I shrugged. "Parking?"

My mother beamed. "See. A chef *would* think of that."

"There's two big public lots, each a block away, and a T station across the street," said my sister.

An hour later my mother called, triumphant, from a phone booth. No sale or lease yet, but these people were serious. I should go home immediately. The Simones were coming to dinner, and I was cooking.

The first thing I did was talk them out of Chez Hilda as a name for their establishment. And next thing I knew, I was auditioning for the post of head chef as if I really wanted it. Earlier, between the hours of four and seven P.M., I had staged a small rebellion, shopping for ingredients that had no chic. It would serve my mother right: She clearly didn't understand that restaurants were not created equal, and I was not so pathetic a candidate that I needed her crude employment services. So I bought chuck and cheap Burgundy and the lettuce and cellophane-wrapped tomatoes of a prosaic salad. I made a stew, which my mother billed as Beef Bourguignon à la Natalie, and mashed potatoes—all of which unwittingly hit the nail on its head.

Mrs. Simone may have been dreaming of haute cuisine and pale pink linens, but Mr. Simone loved diner food. "You understand what I'm trying to do," he said, a solemn oath, looking up from his first bite of my Grape-Nut custard pudding.

"Have some more," my mother said.

"These old standbys? I just made what I thought you'd like."

"We're in the market for a chef," he announced.

"I can't believe it," said my mother. "Eddie, did you hear that? Natalie! Show him the letter from your cooking teacher."

Mr. Simone, eyes closed, licked the front and back of his spoon. Finally he asked what else I could do, dessert-wise, in this genre.

"What genre?" I asked.

"Home cooking, but top-notch."

My mother rose and said pointedly to my father, "Let's do the dishes and let the professionals talk." She commanded Mrs. Simone to sit and to have another helping.

"Desserts," Mr. Simone prompted.

I thought of my childhood and the UMass dining commons. "Fig squares. Brownies à la mode. Chocolate icebox cookie cake."

"With real whipped cream between the cookies?"

"Of course. And Boston cream pie."

He said happily, "Who makes that anymore?"

By that point, I was enjoying my own acting ability. "Apple pie, cherry pie, chocolate cream pie." I thought of the revolving pie display at the now defunct luncheonette near my father's store. "Lemon meringue pie, strawberry-rhubarb pie, grasshopper pie, blueberry pie . . . lattice tops on the fruit pies—"

"Oh my," he breathed.

I remembered the custard family. "And there's rice, coconut, Grape-Nuts, of course, and bread puddings—"

"With raisins?"

I gave him a sly look that said Raisin is my middle name.

He was not a restaurateur. Anyone with Betty Crocker on her shelf could have passed this test. I said both grandly and modestly, "This is supposed to be pleasure, not business. We've put you on the spot."

He said, "You know, hon, I'm a pretty good judge of character. She strikes me as the kind of person we're looking for." He asked if I had a résumé.

I told him what was on it: UMass, B.S. in biology, cum laude. Les Trois Etoiles under Chef Pierre Tardieu; Star Market; Ten Tables.

My father piped up from the kitchen sink, "Ask *me*. Natty worked for me more summers than I can count. And she was always my best worker."

Mrs. Simone said, "We were going to put an ad in the *Globe*."

From the kitchen pass-through, my mother said, "It's very common to sell a house through word-of-mouth without an ad, before it ever goes on the market. Those deals are easiest on everyone concerned."

I asked Mr. Simone, "Do you like soups?"

He looked at me with a soulmate's gaze of joy and astonishment, so I continued, now addressing his wife. "There's so many modern twists on the old standbys: a chicken soup with fresh herbs, an onion soup with shallots and without the baked-on cheese, a black bean, a white gazpacho, a Mexican vegetable, a cabbage, a cream of carrot, a shrimp gumbo, a cock-a-leekie—"

"Holy cow!" cried Mr. Simone. "You do all those?"

"Of course. And dozens more."

"It gets better and better," chuckled Mr. Simone.

His wife murmured, "I do like the fact that she worked at Ten Tables."

I said, "I have to be honest. If you call my boss there, he may say less than flattering things, but it's because he made sexual advances and I rebuffed him. It's why I quit."

Attorney Simone liked even that—a sidebar confession. "Thanks for telling me, Natalie."

My mother materialized with my résumé, my To-whom-it-may-concern reference letter, and a framed photo of my third and final graduating class at Les Trois Etoiles. Mrs. Simone skimmed the papers, and passed them to her husband. With a wink, he folded my vitae once, twice, then stuffed it into an inside breast pocket.

"What do you think about a salad bar?" asked Mrs. Simone.

"Love 'em," my mother snapped.

"What do you think, Natalie? People love a salad bar," Hilda said.

I said, "They're a little gimmicky."

My mother said, "You know, Hilda, I think she's right."

I said, "Besides, a salad bar takes up the room of several tables, and tables equal revenue."

"Lots of time for these kinds of discussions," said my father.

"What's our next step?" asked Mr. Simone.

"I'll understand if you want to place the ad," I said.

"Why should they?" asked my mother.

"She's too modest for her own good," said my father.

"It's their restaurant," I said. "Maybe there's someone out there who would be their dream chef."

"More than you?" my mother cried, sweeping her hand above the leftovers, her eyes signaling that someone who can't close a deal should know when to shut her mouth.

Still, Mr. Simone smiled broadly and asked Mrs. Simone, "Hon? Any reason to keep looking?"

She shrugged. "If you're satisfied . . ."

There was a toast from their side, and one from ours. My father choked up, so my mother took over, explaining that the old softie knew someone would grab me up, but never this fast in a recession.

Finally, after two Sanka refills, the Simones said they had to run. They'd call me as soon as they found their space.

"In that case," my mother teased, "you'll be open for business before you have a name on the door."

"We can't wait," said Mr. Simone.

"We can't wait," echoed my father.

"Do you have our number?" asked my mother.

As soon as they were out the door, she whirled around. "You're your own worst enemy. Miss Equal Opportunity! They should spend another six months interviewing every *shmendrik* who ever flipped a burger?"

"She didn't do any harm," said my father. "Now the Simones know that she's not afraid of competition. They feel as if they got the best."

"You're a *shmendrik*, too," said my mother. "I'm surrounded by them."

We had heard it a dozen times before, the nice-guys-finish-last harangue. She stacked the dessert dishes, making a racket. "When are you going to learn that life is a series of compromises?" she asked me. "What do you think? That if you wait long enough, Locke-Ober's will come calling?"

"Enough, Audrey," said my father. "It all worked out."

She stamped her foot. "I want her to stop dreaming."

I said, "Gladly. Get me out of Café Shmendrik. I'll go back to real estate, or fruit. Or how about Vermont?"

"Honey—" said my father.

"Natalie, I didn't mean—" said my mother.

"Don't tell me what I want," I said.

$\mathcal{F}$ I F T E E N

$\mathcal{I}$ heard from no one, or so I thought. My parents didn't ask about my friends from the Inn, but talked of young men I should date from among their acquaintances' sons. I didn't see their chatter as a campaign; certainly didn't see it as a cover-up of something that would clear up my rash but aggravate family relations—namely, their failure to report that a male Berry had telephoned three times since I'd been home.

"No, no calls," was their blank, automatic answer—not messages forgotten, but deliberate lies. I had no precedent for this in my house. I had heard of crude and puritanical fathers who hung up on undesirable suitors, who revoked privileges from wild daughters. As close as my own street, Mr. Donabedian was famous for having brushed a non-Armenian admirer of his oldest daughter with his car.

But no closer, not inside my family. My father had always treated my teenage boyfriends hospitably and without suspicion—precisely the way Isadore Cohen had treated him—inviting them in for a man-to-man discourse on their part-time shelving jobs at Garb Drug or Franco's Market, or on the near-wins of Newton South's various teams.

"Nice guy, your dad," they always said as we walked to their cars. "He is," I'd agree.

But that was before boyfriends had to be taken seriously, before Danny O'Connor's mooning over Pammy metamorphosed into marriage, a state my father had not anticipated in anything but a far-off, misty way. Our thin walls made me privy to my parents' self-recrimination: They had underestimated Pammy's feelings for the boy. They had not taken Danny seriously as a suitor. They had not realized that a little grass-stained *pisher* would be putting fifteen bucks a week into a diamond-ring fund or that Pammy would enter college secretly engaged, never accepting proffered blind dates, never even attending a mixer at a Jewish fraternity. I heard them say, "Things will be different with the *klainer*"—the little one—me. They had discovered through one less than illustrious son-in-law that this was a dangerous age for a girl, an age when *sheygets* hangers-on turned into fiancés.

So when I received an unsigned postcard of the Inn, interior, dining-room view, saying only, "Wish you were here," and, "Did you get my messages?" I took it to my room and lay down with it, relief tainted only by the simultaneous discovery that, like everyone else, I hated my parents.

"What's with you?" my mother asked, arriving home to find me pacing the living room. I waited for my father to join us from the garage, then read, my voice shaking with anger, " *'Dear Natalie, Did you get my messages?'* "

"Who's that from?" asked my father.

I said it wasn't signed, but—

"Not signed?" he repeated, as if that were the transgression.

My mother put her hand out.

I held the card to my chest. "What do you have to look at? You know who it's from."

They busied themselves at the front closet, handing each other hangers and arranging their coats.

"Messages," I demanded. "Who took them?"

"I forgot," my father snapped. "Okay? You satisfied? Your old man forgot to tell you that a boy called."

"You forgot multiple times?"

"Once."

I slapped the postcard and read again, " '*Did you get my messages?*' plural?"

"You know your father can't take a message! Either he forgets altogether or he gets it wrong."

My father waved his arms. "The other phone was ringing! It was late. You were out."

I said, "I can't believe you'd lie to me."

"Forgetting to tell you about a *phone* message? That's what this is all about? That's the conspiracy?"

I said, "You knew I was waiting for a call."

He looked at my mother.

She twisted her lips before giving up, "The younger brother."

"Kris?"

"I believe he said Kris."

"When was this?"

My father said, "January? Then, maybe a week after that, he called back."

"And maybe a third time?"

He shrugged.

I said, "You managed to keep Mom up-to-date."

"I was right there," my mother said. "He probably thought I was going to give you the message, and I thought *he* was."

I said I was shocked. My own parents. Richard Nixon was one thing, but I never thought I'd see—

"Don't get on your high horse because of a secretarial slipup," my mother said.

"You lied! You purposely withheld information from me, and God only knows how many pieces of mail you intercepted."

"We don't like them," my father growled. "We don't like the parents and we don't like the sons."

"Eddie, please," said my mother, taking over. "Natalie, you too. Look, there's no harm done. You didn't get the messages. When your friend didn't hear from you, he wrote."

I flopped onto the couch and said, "I should have known I was too old to live at home."

"Old?" my father railed. "Old? I lived at home until I got married."

"So did I," my mother said.

I said what we didn't say in my house—"Yeah, until you had to get married."

"Natalie!" my father cried.

I said, "I'm moving out."

"Don't scratch," my mother said. "Your palms are going to be raw."

"Where will you go?" my father asked.

"I'll rent a room."

"When?"

"As soon as I find one."

"And pay for it how?" my mother asked.

"You paid for it. Audrey Marx Properties financed it. I saved every cent for a rainy day." I found my wallet, stuck the postcard in among the dollar bills, and walked to the front door.

"It's cold out there," my mother said.

I said I'd live; I'd be warm enough in the phone booth.

"Do you want the real estate page?" my mother asked.

I said, "You really think that? After all this, you think that's who I'm going to call?"

They didn't argue and they didn't say good-bye. I tugged my parka off its hanger and walked out the door.

"She can't call from here?" I heard my father say.

I could see lights on in every kitchen window on Irving Circle, and Mrs. Iacovello squinting into the dark on her neighborhood watch. When I reached my destination I remembered: It was from this spot by Purity Supreme's Goodwill collection box that I had phoned the fearsome Ingrid Berry on a cold winter's night twelve years before, without permission, coins clanging, mouth dry.

I dialed the number. When she answered, I asked for Kris.

"Is this Natalie?"

"Hello, Mrs. Berry."

"We were just talking about you today."

I waited, expecting what I got—a reference that was neither interesting nor flattering.

"Gretel and I were talking about that cake you made Kris for his birthday. Is that from one of our cookbooks?"

I said no, it was my recipe.

She asked if I shared recipes.

I said, "Look up any recipe for a chocolate ganache, and make a butter-cream frosting with a ripe banana mixed in."

"Ganache?" she repeated.

I spelled it, then asked if Kris was there.

She said, "I don't believe he is."

I waited a beat and asked how Nelson was doing.

"Nelson's in Rhode Island," his mother said. "He went back to school the Monday after New Year's."

I said I hoped he was doing okay. Please give him my regards. In the meantime, I was returning Kris's calls. Was there a better time to reach him?

Ingrid said it was hard to say. Tonight he was out with a friend. Tomorrow . . . something about an outing.

"Will you tell him I called?"

She didn't answer. I asked if she was still there.

"I probably shouldn't say anything," she began, but stopped. Her voice thawed slightly. "I don't want him getting hurt. That's all I wanted to say. I don't need another heartbroken child on my hands."

I must have answered, but all I've retained is a mental snapshot of that moment—me, stunned, at Purity Supreme, wondering if I had just heard Ingrid Berry asking a Marx for mercy.

$\mathcal{S}$ I X T E E N

$\mathcal{I}$ took the long route home and, in the manner of distressed daughters, went directly and noisily to my room. In minutes, there was a repentant knock on my door, my mother asking if we could talk.

I said, facedown on top of my taffeta comforter, I knew what she was going to say: " 'Your father and I want what's best for you. If we acted like Watergate conspirators—' "

"Natty, I never said you should live at home until you're married," she answered, conveniently off the mark. "That's what my generation did. You're not the kind of girl who wants to work in her mother's office all day and go home to her parents' house at night."

I got up and opened the door to find her holding a plate with a fried-egg sandwich on it. The egg had cooked up with lacy gold edges, and my mother had put it on toasted pumpernickel. As she pushed it toward me, chest-high, I could smell the white pepper.

I said, "You think this is all it takes? Room service?"

She asked what I was planning to do.

I said I didn't know yet, but there had been a serious infraction, the kind that caused permanent ruptures in a family. I said, "Not that I have anything like this in mind, but remember Linda Donabedian?"

My mother nodded.

"She eloped with that marine her father tried to run over."

My mother said that was true, but Linda Donabedian was a tart and a *meshugene*. I'd never run away with a boy I hardly knew.

I said I would have liked to have talked to Kris; that's all. Things were left awkward after the funeral, after he had been my chief ally at the Inn, and a very sweet one at that. I should have called him, because I was the one who left without saying a real good-bye. Had they considered his feelings for one second? Call after call after call into a void?

Still, she didn't take up the subject. Instead she asked, "What about an apartment? Do you want my help?"

I said, No, I'd find my own.

"Would you let Pammy help?"

I said, No, no Audrey Marx associate.

She took a step inside and closed the door. "What if I had a perfect listing?"

I sat down at my childhood desk and ate half the sandwich without comment.

"Does it need salt?"

I said, "No . . . what listing?"

"It's not a legal apartment—"

"Oh, great."

"That's the landlord's problem, not the tenant's. It's the third floor of a Victorian in Newton Highlands. It's only illegal because it doesn't have a separate exit, which is no big deal—you come down a back staircase and out through a back door. I don't even advertise it. Strictly word-of-mouth."

"How much?"

She whispered, "A hundred seventy-five a month, utilities included. Brand-new appliances."

I said I couldn't hear her.

She cocked her head in the direction of the door.

"Dad cares if you list illegal apartments?"

She shook her head.

"Dad doesn't want you aiding and abetting me?"

She said, "He thinks it'll take a good long while to find you something in your price range."

"So I'd give up and stay here?"

My mother smiled. "He'll adjust."

"What about the landlord?"

"Saul Zinler."

"A good guy?"

"It won't matter. He's never there. They're off," she said, flipping her hand toward my window and the wider world.

"Who's 'they'?"

"Saul and his girlfriend."

"Girlfriend? How old is this guy?"

"Late sixties, retired."

"And what's her story?"

"She's got money. And grown kids."

I chewed and swallowed the last bite of sandwich. "Sounds too good to be true."

My mother beamed. "I was saving it for the right tenant."

"You mean me?"

"I knew when you found a job, you'd want to be on your own. Besides, with you coming in late and Daddy leaving at the crack of dawn, no one here would get any sleep."

I opened my desk drawer and took out my savings passbook. Even if Chez Simone didn't open on schedule, I'd get by on my graduation checks and real estate wages. I asked how soon I could get into the place.

"Whenever you're ready. It doesn't need a thing." She looked too pleased with herself, so I said, "I suppose you think all is forgiven."

She walked over to my bookcase and aligned the edges of my Golden Books Encyclopedia. "Did you get him?" she asked.

"I left a message."

"With whom?"

"With his mother."

"Oy."

I said, "I can handle Ingrid."

"You think she'll tell him?"

"If I don't hear from him, I'll try again."

My mother turned around, crimped a handful of her hair, and let it spring back. "Natalie?"

I waited.

"Why not just leave things the way they are?"

"Which is how?"

It was the speech she came to deliver: "You're doing fine. Lots of exciting things happening. If you hadn't heard from him, you'd be looking forward to the restaurant opening, and you'd meet someone—everyone does—and you'd forget about this boy."

I said, "You don't know how I feel."

She took my plate and moved it to my night table. "Then tell me."

I said, "You lost that privilege."

"For how long?"

I said, "Indefinitely. Please turn out the overhead as you leave."

"It's not even eight o'clock."

"Then I'll go out."

"You just came back. What if he calls when you're out?"

I said he wouldn't.

"Where will you be?"

I shrugged. "Maybe I'll drive by the house in the Highlands."

"You won't see anything in the dark. I'll take you tomorrow."

"What about the landlord?"

"We don't need him. I have the keys."

"But he'd have to approve me, right?"

"Phfff. My daughter?"

I was starting to say, "Your *estranged* daughter," when the phone rang in the hall. My father answered on the second ring, brusquely I thought. His voice softened—Pammy.

"I'm in here!" my mother called.

Ignoring her, he answered in a code that told me Pammy had been briefed and was now checking to see if I'd returned alive.

"Does Pammy know Kris tried to call me?" I asked.

My mother began her defense of Pammy's awkward position, but I interrupted with a heretofore unexpressed accusation. "It's all her fault anyway," I snapped.

"*Her* fault?"

My father was still on the phone. I heard him ask if Danny's plow was up and running.

Precisely: his plow, his snowblower, his lawn mower, his ro-totiller, his high school diploma and no degree. Pammy had used up our family's mixed-marriage chit, even our liberal-dating chit. It was up to me to bring home the perfect Jewish son-in-law. I said, "You and Daddy had one church wedding. How could you hold your head up in Newton Centre if both daughters strayed?"

Instead of disputing my thesis, she spat out, "We couldn't have done a thing to stop that marriage!"

My father called, all pleasantness, "Natalie! Your sister wants to talk to you."

"I'm busy."

"She'll talk to her tomorrow," my mother said, and to me, "She's going to offer you her sleep sofa for the next few days, but I think after you see the apartment you'll want that option."

I said, "You're being suspiciously helpful."

My mother assumed an expression I'd seen her flash Pammy at the office, a girlfriends' pact implying, This is just between us; your father thinks I'm in here singing a different tune. "I never had a few years on my own," she whispered, "not even the two years in college. When I was your age I already had two babies. He doesn't think of that. He thinks I'm in here telling you that we know best. I'm going to say that you wouldn't budge; you're moving out and you wouldn't listen to me. Okay?"

"Just like that?"

She looked perplexed, "Just like what?"

"Is this your way of apologizing—taking my side against Daddy?"

She replied, no longer whispering, "I may be helping you find an apartment, but I'm with your father on the other matter."

"There is no other matter," I said. "You and Daddy took care of that."

She came closer, hooked my hair behind my ears, one side at a time. "Look. If you were saying, 'I'm madly in love with him,' that would be one thing, but you're not. You're waiting to see what it's going to turn into. What I'm saying is, If you can nip it in the bud, do it. Before you get in too deep. Even if you feel lousy in the short run, in the long run it's for the better. On all sides."

I said, "You're way ahead of yourself."

"Why even be friends with a boy from that family? You spent one week at that place, less than a week, you come home, you never mention him, and now you're pining for him?"

"I wanted to know he called. I'm not pining."

"And what? All of a sudden we're the enemy, because of a boy you're not pining for?"

"It's the principle of the thing, the cover-up. You lied to me and you lied to Kris—"

"I know who I'm dealing with! I know what kind of people they are and how they think. You don't." She raised her voice. "Not everyone grows up in Newton. My sisters and I got called a lot of names, by all kinds of kids—kids from nice families, kids whose fathers worked for my father."

I said, "What happened to you in Fitchburg in the nineteen thirties is not a good enough reason to lie about who calls me."

She was shaking her head, her eyes closed, but I persisted. "If you disapprove of someone just because he's Protestant, Lutheran, whatever he is, then *you're* prejudiced—"

"*I'm* prejudiced?" she yelled. "They don't want Jews at their hotel but they're going to welcome you with open arms? Because this isn't my problem; this isn't me worrying about another church wedding. This is me hoping that at least one of my daughters marries into a family who's thrilled to have her."

I tried to stop her, but she was ranting: "Wait until he gets angry at you and calls you a name. What do you think will be the first word that comes out of his mouth in anger? *Kike? Dirty Jew?*" She dodged me and strode over to my bureau, to my silver-framed photograph of my teenage great-aunt. "What do you think she'd say?" my mother asked fiercely, shaking the frame in my face. "Whose side do you think she'd be taking?"

"Put her down," I ordered.

She did, without rebuttal, as if she knew she'd gone too far.

I repositioned Nesha's frame in its hallowed spot. Knowing my mother was watching, chastened, I took the first step. I slid my trunk out from under my bed and unlatched it. It was stuffed with the house supply of gaudy afghans, crocheted by my Bubbe Marx in the colors she favored, without regard to my mother's decor. I dumped them out, then took one back, a child-size blanket in several shades of pink I had for a long time considered beautiful.

"What are you doing?" my mother asked.

"Packing."

"For where?"

"Israel," I said. "Miami Beach."

"Natalie—"

I said, "I want to hear you admit you were wrong."

She didn't move, and didn't speak until she said, "I found you an apartment, didn't I?"

"That's right. And a job. Several jobs. Not to mention inventing Pammy's entire career in real estate."

She liked being reminded of that, of her powers and her salesmanship, and I knew if I turned around I'd see a pinched, pleased smile. I also knew that tomorrow she would show me the apartment, buy me lunch, and later—with my father's truck transporting my few possessions and with all forgiven—they would together move me the half-mile to my new home.

$\mathcal{S}$ E V E N T E E N

$\mathcal{I}$ngrid didn't know—or wasn't saying—that her son's first stop was Newton, Massachusetts, and from there an even more tribal place. He found Irving Circle from a street atlas, rang our doorbell, saw signs of life in the Loftus house, rang *its* doorbell, and asked Shelley, who had cotton batting separating her toes for a pedicure, where Natalie Marx might be at this time of day.

"I'll call her mother," said Shelley. "You wait on the porch."

Reached at Audrey Marx Properties, my mother asked, "Who wants to know?"

Shelley put the phone down and returned to announce in its full *goyishe* glory, "Kristofer Berry."

"Send him over," my mother instructed.

Shelley offered to lead this Kristofer to Mrs. Marx's office if he waited a few minutes so she could put on something decent, but he declined.

Not ten minutes later he walked into Audrey Marx Properties wearing a down vest over a red chamois shirt. My mother shook his hand and asked, "Aren't you freezing like that?"

Kris told her no; he was from Vermont. She gestured toward the associate churning at her elbow: "My daughter Pamela."

"I was looking for your daughter Natalie," he said.

"Natalie," my mother announced grandly, "is no longer helping us out because she's accepted a start-up position in her own field, not far from Valle's."

Pammy pointed out that Kris wouldn't know what that meant.

"One-point-six miles from here. A nifty, nifty location. We've got our fingers crossed."

Kris asked if I was there now.

My mother glanced up at her *Better Homes and Gardens* wall clock. "My," she said. "What time did you leave Vermont to get here so early?"

"Eight, eight-thirty. It's not that far." He tried again: Might he call me at work?

My mother explained I was home, gearing up for my not quite up-and-running marvelous new opportunity.

"She wasn't there," he said.

"She's at her place," Pammy volunteered.

Kris said he wouldn't know; hadn't seen or talked to me since December.

"It just happened. *Just,*" my mother said. "She moved in last night."

He asked if he could make a call.

"No phone," she said.

Kris looked over my mother's head to the battery of phones. One rang on cue.

"The service will pick it up," said my mother.

"She means *Natalie* has no phone," said Pammy.

He asked for my address. My mother said, "It's hard to find."

He said all he needed was the address.

"I can take you there," my sister offered. "I'm showing a house at eleven that's two, three blocks from Natalie's."

Kris said later that they wore him down. Pammy was already in her coat, had collected her keys. "I'll run upstairs and give her a couple minutes' notice," she explained, "like I do when a seller's at home and I'm dropping by unannounced."

"If you insist," said Kris.

*O*ne Newton village away, I was bending at the waist, brushing my hair from the roots downward. Dressed in once-black corduroy jeans that had been mistakenly bleached and a simultaneously ruined black turtleneck, I had just shouldered my unmade Murphy bed up and into the wall. I heard running steps on my attic stairs at the same moment as Pammy's coy, "You have your first visitor."

I thought she meant only herself, so I yelled from underneath my hair, "Door's open"—prompting a lecture on the unlocked door and the trusting heart. I said, "*Okay*, enough, hello. Welcome to my new abode."

She shut the door behind her and hissed, "He's here. Kristofer. Downstairs. He came looking for you. He's adorable."

I shot up at the mention of his name, to the obvious delight of double agent O'Connor.

"He came to the office after going to the house first, but no one was there, so he went across the street and guess who helped him out? Shelley."

I led her to my door. "Thanks for bringing him. You can get back to work now."

When she didn't budge, I said, "If you're waiting for a tour, I'd prefer another time."

She put her hand on the doorknob, but turned back to me. "Aren't you going to change your clothes? Or at least make yourself up?"

I said, "*Bye*, Pamela. Send him up on your way out."

"He's nice," she said.

I walked her partway down my narrow stairs, held back until I heard brief good-byes and the back door bang behind her.

He didn't gallop up the stairs, and I didn't move. I took a few breaths to steady myself, then called his name.

"Can we talk down here?" he answered.

As soon as I walked across the kitchen threshold I understood that he was angry. His mouth and eyes had a downward cast to them, and his voice was combative. "I went to your house, but no one was there and a neighbor sent me to your mother's office."

"Pammy told me."

Neither one of us moved from our opposite sides of the Zinler kitchen. I tried, "It's nice to see you."

"I thought we were friends," he shot back. "I thought we'd be staying in touch."

"I thought so too."

"Your father said you were out for the evening, and always added something so I knew it was a date: 'She's at a movie. I assume they'll be going out for a muffin after—' "

I laughed at "muffin."

He said, "It's not funny, Natalie." He rattled a chair out from the square kitchen table and plunked himself down. "Is your father an idiot? Is he not capable of remembering a phone message?" He picked up the salt and pepper shakers—Kennedy and Khrushchev—and curled his hands around them as if they were cockpit controls.

I said, "I called the minute I got the postcard—the minute after I had it out with my parents. And I made up my mind that if your mother didn't give you the message—"

"She told me! Unlike your parents, she left me a note—'Natalie called at six-thirty while you were out. Call her tomorrow.' "

He jumped, or so it seemed, to an unrelated topic. "Did Nelson call you last night?"

I said maybe he tried my parents'—

"Of course he did! If I'd had another number, I would have tried it myself."

I asked calmly why Nelson would have called me.

Kris closed his eyes and sighed with the sheer fruitlessness of it all. "An idiotic idea I had. To go someplace. The three of us."

"Where?"

"Away. The Halcyon. A hotel in New York that a friend of his from Cornell runs." He shrugged: stupid.

"New York," I repeated. Neutral ground, and no parents coiled in the grass. Am I forgiven? I wondered. "Is it in Manhattan?" I asked.

Kris slouched in his seat, as if this were the delicate part that Nelson would have negotiated had he reached me. "Actually," he said, "it's in the Catskills."

"The Catskills," I repeated. "Is that where I come in?"

He waved that away. "All his friends from school work at hotels or run them. They majored in it. It was in the class notes, about Robin—'It is with great sadness' blah, blah, blah—and he got, like, a half-dozen invitations, some from people he doesn't even re-member."

"Is this a Jewish hotel by any chance?"

Kris said, "I don't know. What makes a hotel Jewish?"

"What's his friend's name?"

"Linette."

"Linette what?"

"Feldman."

I laughed. Kris said there was nothing funny about the name Feldman.

"It's just a coincidence? You two guys head off for a kosher hotel and you decide, after all this time, to swing by and get me?"

He repeated "after all this time" acidly. "Like I haven't tried? Like I wasn't the one who called every other day, and now show up to get a reading on this thing? And so what if I talked him into it? What's so bad about one brother enlisting another brother to rig up a weekend that might make one of us feel better?"

It was a signed confession, and one I should have accepted with grace. But I had inherited Audrey Cohen Marx's tendency to keep jabbing after the bell had rung. "Don't you think it's a little insult-ing?" I pushed on. "Like, 'Here's a place we could bring Natalie'?"

Kris stood up and, striving for a dramatic exit gesture, fastened the one open snap on his vest.

"Kris," I said.

He didn't look at me, but surveyed the room. "The last time we were alone?" he said. "In the kitchen? I had the impression—correct me if I'm wrong—that you and I were going to kiss."

I said, "That was my impression, too."

"But you took off."

"I know."

"You shook my hand in front of twenty people and drove off with your parents and I never heard from you again."

I was studying his face, having forgotten that his eyes were a light tortoiseshell brown and that there was a faint scar perpen-dicular to his upper lip. I saw a muscle twitch under one eye. "How mad are you?" I asked.

He said, his voice still hard, "It's negotiable." After hesitating, he sat down and folded his arms across his chest, not meeting my eyes.

"Want to take off your vest?"

He shook his head.

"Tea or coffee?"

He said, "No, thanks."

I said, "You're right. I did run out like a brat. I went home, I slept a lot. Watched TV. Then it was New Year's. Had Chinese takeout with my parents—sweet-and-sour chicken. Awful. Then it was Valentine's Day. My father brought me chocolate-covered cher-ries. I worked in my mother's office. Cooked them dinner most nights. They brought me breakfast in bed on my birthday—poached eggs. I developed a rash on my hands that the doctor said was actually in my head."

"Due to . . . ?"

"Stress."

"What kind of stress?"

"Personal," I said. "Emotional. Romantic."

He swallowed, still didn't look up.

"I saw a couple of doctors and they gave me creams." I held out my red hands. "See for yourself."

He unfolded his arms, examined my hands unhappily, as if they were gift gloves of the wrong size and color.

"Neurodermatitis," I continued. "The cream treats the symptoms, but I'm supposed to be working on the underlying cause."

He said, "I didn't break out in any rashes, but I could have."

I said, "If I had known, I would have called you back immediately."

He wasn't ready to call a truce, but he didn't take his hands away. Pipes carrying hot water knocked inside a wall. A radiator hissed. Finally Kris asked, "Why did you leave like that? How do you think it made me feel?"

I said I didn't know. I wasn't sure what had or hadn't happened on Christmas night. Maybe I had misunderstood; maybe I'd been standing under mistletoe and had misinterpreted his near-kiss. Because nothing was said afterward, was it? Not that night or in the morning.

"Because it was obvious—"

"The message I got was, You were welcome here, Natalie, until things got personal."

Kris said, "Bullshit. Not from me, you didn't. Not from Nelson, either, or my father, and certainly not from the Fifes."

I raised my eyebrows to elicit the unspoken name.

"It would be helpful," he said, "if you could differentiate between me and my mother."

I said I did. I knew from the first moment I arrived that he was my ally—

"Ally! Is that like buddy? Because we all know what that means."

I said, "Give me a break here. I'm thrilled to see you. Maybe I haven't said that yet." My hands were lying on his, lightly, clinically. I inched them forward to stroke the soft skin at his wrists.

He looked stumped, as if trying to decipher an impenetrable clue. "What does this mean?" he asked, staring at our hands.

I said, "I'll go with you."

There was the awkward matter of the extra night. Linette Feldman was expecting the Berry brothers for the weekend, and this was Thursday. One constraint, I explained, was that I was meeting my future boss at three at a restaurant-supply store.

"Can you put it off until next week?"

I said, "What is it that you do for a living, anyway?"

"Night manager. The Inn at Lake Devine."

"There's no such job."

He shrugged. "They feed me and don't rent out my bed, so I do what needs to be done. Nelson was supposed to be general manager someday, but that got screwed up when he went into teaching. So I'm the crown prince until they decide if Gretel's better suited to the family business."

"How is Gretel?" I asked.

We were on our second pink grapefruit, my only provision. He said, "She's the same." He sprinkled sugar from my landlord's bowl onto another half and asked, "What are your other constraints?"

I said, "Do you know if it's expensive?"

"Nelson is Linette's guest," he said, "and you'll be mine."

"Is this a date?" I asked.

He looked dismayed at having to revisit what had already been settled. I jumped in to explain I meant Nelson—Nelson and this Feldman friend. Was this invitation purely a professional courtesy?

"Nelson would say that . . ."

"But?"

"He's very lonely."

"And he likes her?"

"Sure." He smiled, which I took to mean, I know that's how you women view these things, that Nelson should be a little bit in love before he finds solace in Linette Feldman. My own reading brought on a new, troubling thought: that Nelson, under the easy-Jewish-girl doctrine, was going to the Catskills for a nonbinding fling.

I asked, "Is he ready to start dating again?"

"It's crossed my mind."

"Do you think it's crossed his?"

Kris said, "He'd never talk about another woman right now. We didn't discuss it in any detail except to say, 'I'll try to get Natalie to come. You and Linette can catch up.' "

"And that felt okay to him?"

"Guys don't discuss things," Kris said.

From Mr. Zinler's phone I called Hilda Simone to reschedule, and the Halcyon for particulars. "I'll give you Reservations," said the hotel operator. A new voice said, "This is Honey. May I help you?" Absolutely, she crowed. Rooms galore. When was I thinking of?

"Tonight."

"We have a three-day March Doldrums Weekend package."

I said, "Can we take it one night at a time?"

"You can't *not* love it here," she said. "I guarantee you'll be signing up for more."

I asked what their rates were.

"Forty-two to fifty-nine dollars a person, double occupancy."

I asked, "Do any rooms have two beds?"

"You name it, we've got it!"

I said, All right, we'd do that, the forty-two-dollar room, please. What did that include?

"Three delicious meals," said Honey. "Name?"

"Marx."

Kris had drifted back from studying my landlord's microwave oven, first on the block, and was paying careful attention.

"Mr. and Mrs.?" asked Honey.

Kris nodded to my raised eyebrows, not knowing what the question was. "Sure," I said.

"Have you been here before?"

I said no, and asked for directions from Boston, which she rattled off as if she commuted daily.

I put my hand over the receiver and said, "It takes four to four and a half hours."

Kris shrugged.

"We dress for dinner," Honey advised.

"Ties and jackets?"

"It's what we ask for, but truthfully? The maître d' can give your husband a tie. It happens all the time."

"He might need one," I said. "Thanks. We'll see you soon."

"You're all set, darling," said Honey. "You won't be sorry."

I packed a black dress, a purple dress, and a red flannel nightgown for sleeping one bed away from a man I'd still not kissed. Kris watched me from the Murphy bed, which he had pulled down, pushed back, and pulled down again as if analyzing its physics; watched me fold my nightgown, my chin anchoring it to my chest. When I looked up from the task, he was smiling.

"What?" I asked.

"Your nightgown. Good and sturdy."

"I froze at your hotel," I said. I packed my brown terry-cloth robe, a bulky sweater, a skirt, jeans, two turtleneck jerseys, and a half-dozen pairs of underwear in my overnight bag, having vowed during my Christmas vigil to overpack for all future trips.

"Toothbrush, toothpaste, all that stuff?" he asked.

"Got it. What about you?"

"Shaving kit's in the car."

He lifted my bulging bag like the experienced bellboy he was and asked if I could manage the rest. I said this was it, more or less. Just a pocketbook—I didn't say it was valise-size, with shells glued on straw, a gift I'd never used from my Florida grandmother; I'd be right behind him in a sec. When he was out the door, I looked around and tried to conjure up the sorriest hours in my Lake

Devine garret. I added a paperback novel, my tube of ointment, a can of sour drops, my only lace bikini underpants, my purse-size vial of Je Reviens, and a pair of rag-wool socks.

Kris was gunning the blue VW Lake Devine bus. I walked to the passenger door and climbed in, squashing my straw bag to fit around my feet.

"Got everything?" he asked wryly.

I said, "We'll find out," adding, "Can't be too different from the Inn at Lake Devine, right?"

He glanced over, then returned his eyes to the rearview mirror. "Was that a trick question?"

I said, "More like a joke."

"The joke being?"

"The joke is that nothing could be further from the Inn at Lake Devine than a place in the Catskills owned by the Feldman family."

He made a strangled sound. "Do you think there are any other subjects two people can discuss besides you're Jewish and I'm not?"

I said, "Apparently not."

"And why is that?"

I said, after searching for a weighty enough phrase, "Because of your family's civil rights record."

He finally backed down the driveway and braked at the end. "Oh yeah?" he replied, smiling. "Would you care to be more specific?"

I said, "The one outlined in a 1962 letter, signed by Ingrid Berry, saying, '*Gentiles only.*' "

He turned, startled.

I said, "I didn't *think* you knew."

"Your parents told you this?"

I said I had seen the letter with my own eyes, and it was unmistakable—the green sketch on the pebbly white stationery. I asked him the question I had asked myself several times over Christmas with each kind and enfolding act performed by a Berry son. "Even if you had seen that letter, would it have meant any-thing? As a kid, would you have known what *Gentile* meant?"

He stared straight ahead and said, almost inaudibly, "I don't know."

I said, "C'mon. You wouldn't have known. Let's get going."

He said, "You came with the Fifes, even after getting a letter like that?"

"I had to see it for myself."

He backed the bus into the street, now swearing softly.

I asked after a few blocks, "Did you ever see the movie *Titanic?*" Kris said no.

"Clifton Webb plays this rich guy who can't get a ticket because they're booked solid. He goes over to a line of immigrants waiting to board, flashes his wallet, and offers one guy a fortune to take his place in steerage. The guy says to his wife in broken English, 'I take another boat. I meet you in America.' As soon as they're on open water, Clifton Webb comes upstairs, easy as you please. A steward says, 'You're not allowed up here,' and Clifton Webb, in these beau-tiful clothes, says regally, 'I'll try to behave myself,' and walks right past him."

"Did he get caught?" Kris asked.

"Of course not. He was this upper-crust guy married to Barbara Stanwyck and she had a stateroom, so he was all set."

"Until they hit the iceberg."

"True. But the part that stayed with me was his gliding up the stairs and past the rope barrier, and how cool he was."

Kris said, "So?"

"I wanted to see what went on at a place that didn't let Jews in." I motioned *go;* the light had turned green.

He drove absentmindedly, creeping, then speeding. I asked if he wanted me to drive, and he said, "No. Sorry. Am I doing that badly?"

I read the next three steps from Honey's directions in Honey's voice, concluding with, "You're all set, dawling."

Kris smiled gratefully. Thinking we had moved on, he said, "We should be there by five-thirty."

Another minute went by before I asked, "In all these years, you never noticed there weren't any Jews at your hotel?"

Kris said, "I didn't! I'm sorry, but I didn't know. Unlike you, I don't know what religion people are from fifty yards away. I'll take full responsibility for the letter, okay? You can sue me as soon as we get to the Catskills."

"I don't blame you," I said. "I don't even blame your father. He was unbelievably kind to me when I was there."

"Just my mother."

"She sent the letter. I'm assuming she wrote it and meant it."

Kris said, "She never talked about it."

"You never heard your mother say anything anti-Semitic?"

"Look," said Kris. "I've heard stuff from people that would make you sick, stuff they say when they assume there're no Jews around. Which happens to be the case pretty much of the time in Gilbert, Vermont. My mother has said a lot of things that I wouldn't care to repeat, not all of them anti-Semitic."

I tried to cajole some offensive phrases out of him, but he wouldn't budge. He turned on the radio and drummed on the steering wheel to tune me out. After a few minutes I said, "Mass Pike coming up."

"You haven't changed your mind about this weekend? Even though we've been fighting since the second I arrived?"

"Fighting?" I said. "This isn't fighting. This is a stimulating discussion."

He swore softly, and for a moment I thought it was road-related—trouble merging into the right-hand lane. I checked over my right shoulder, and heard him ask, "Then why do I feel like son of Hitler?"

"Hardly," I scoffed, Miss Magnanimous. "I told you I'm not blaming you for what your mother says or does. I can differentiate."

He made the turn off Route 128, then said, " 'Not blaming you' is like a million miles from what I was hoping to accomplish by coming down here, Natalie. I wasn't looking for clearance on being a bigot."

It was, I knew, another declaration. As we pulled up to the toll-booth I put my rashy left hand on his. He must have been waiting for the first sign of affection or conciliation, because it was then, with the window open and the turnpike employee holding out our ticket, that Kris said, "Natalie, what if I'm in love with you?"

"With me?" I said. "Really?"

The car behind us honked. I barked, "Boston driver!"

"Ticket," said the toll taker.

"I'm waiting for directions," Kris told him, taking the ticket, and to me: "Something concrete. Something that would reassure a guy in agony."

I said, "Go. It's okay. I mean, how can I think with this racket be-hind us?"

The bus bucked and almost stalled coming out of neutral, but it recovered and we were off.

$\mathcal{E}$ IGHTEEN

$\mathcal{I}$ realized, as soon as we crossed into Sullivan County and saw the first splashy billboard, that the correct name of our destination was the Halseeyon. A two-lane highway and Honey's directions took us to Halseeyon Way, a long, baronial driveway bordered by privet hedges.

Kris zoomed up to the main building as if it were his regular shuttle loop. A taxi driver stood smoking by his cab, and a blond woman in a fur stole was arriving, but there were no uniformed greeters. "I'll let you out, and I'll park down by those buildings that look like barracks."

I said I'd check us in.

He said, "Wait for me. I know a few tricks."

I carried my straw bag into the largest lobby I'd ever seen, wall-papered in red and offering more sofas and chairs than ten dentists' waiting rooms could hold. The vast hall telescoped into lobby additions, decorated in the wallpaper cousins of the original flocked red.

At every corridor intersection, a cluster of mock street signs pointed to destinations: the outdoor pool, the indoor pool, the upper lobby, the lower lobby, the ice rink, the clubhouse, the bar, the coffee shop, the main dining room, the children's dining room,

"Boutique Alley," and the synagogue. I retraced my footsteps, not wanting Kris to register alone. He was already at the front desk when I returned, standing in front of a grandmotherly woman in a tailored gray suit, one of three idle reservation clerks. He waited for me, then announced, "Mr. and Mrs. Berry."

I said, "I put it under Marx."

He nudged me, meaning, Follow my lead.

The woman looked through her records, and back at us over her half-glasses. "Barry?" she asked.

"Berry."

Another search. Kris turned to me and said, "Hon? You made them under Berry didn't you?"

I cleared my throat and said, "Could I have made the reservations under Marx?"

The woman said, "Which is it?"

Kris announced, trying hard to look abashed, "Well, the thing is—she *was* a Marx at the time she made the reservation."

I could see delight dawning across the woman's features. "You two just got married! She made the reservation under her maiden name!"

Kris beamed.

I murmured, "What was I thinking?"

"Wedding nerves," said the woman. She studied the room assignment, then tore it up, shaking her head. "This won't do."

I knew what wouldn't do—separate beds. She turned around to see what cubbyholes still held keys, and emitted an "aachh" of pleasure when she saw what must have been her first choice. "This is more like it," she said.

I said, leaning across the counter toward our benefactress, "We're on a budget."

"What did we quote you?"

"Forty-two per person, American Plan."

She smiled and stuck her pencil through the curls above her ear. "Do you know who I am?"

I said, "Are you the manage—"

"I'm Estelle *Feldman*, the owner's mother. And I'm telling you that when honeymooners come here, they get the honeymoon suite. I don't care what their budget is or what they reserve over the telephone."

I said, "Really, it isn't necessary. I wouldn't feel right."

"You are too generous," my pseudohusband told Mrs. Feldman. "I don't know what to say."

"Not another word! You take your lovely bride upstairs and see what you think, and you tell your friends that the Halseeyon is not just for old fogies." With that she slapped the bell. "No bride and groom stay in a twin room if the honeymoon suite is empty, and that's that."

A bellman scuttled over; a dollar bill changed palms smoothly as Kris said, "Don't bother. I've got it."

"You can't do anything for these two!" Mrs. Feldman proclaimed. She handed us a pink legal-size syllabus with the heading "Daily Activities," and pointed a knobby right finger over her left shoulder. "Left past the newsstand, elevator's on your right, top floor. Dinner's at seven, even for honeymooners."

"Really, thanks so much," said Kris. "You're a doll."

"Thanks, Mrs. Feldman," I added.

If it weren't for the fact that we were there at the invitation, once removed, of a Feldman, I would have congratulated Kris on his prank. "Are you crazy?" I whispered when we'd walked a safe distance from the desk. "Now we're going to have to keep up an act."

The elevator doors opened and a short man in a black tuxedo hurried off. "See you later, kids," he said, without stopping.

We stepped aboard. Kris said, "It's called an upgrade. Hotels do it all the time, even ours. Besides, it's a matter of pride. I'd be afraid to tell my mother I paid the rack rate."

I said, "Like you're going to tell your mother you shared a honeymoon suite with me."

He tried to squeeze my shoulders in a one-armed hug, but I told him he'd crush the corsage that my maid of honor had pinned on my going-away outfit. *Hon.*

"C'mon," he said.

I said, "Do you upgrade every Tom, Dick, and Harry who sashays up to your desk with a honeymoon story?"

Kris said, "Okay, we got more than I was angling for. I thought maybe a larger room with a nicer view. Or a complimentary bottle of wine at dinner." He thumbed the button repeatedly, then asked, "Are you mad about the lie or about me assuming too much?"

I said, "What happens when we meet Linette? Do we let her in on your little joke?"

He pretended to be absorbed in the numbers flashing above the door. When PENTH lit up, a chime sounded, and we stepped onto a hallway with brown faux-marble wallpaper and plum carpeting. At the end of the hall was Room 1000, which had silver bells stenciled above the number and an ugly brass knocker. We stepped into a pitch-black room. The light of a pink-bulbed chandelier revealed white satin walls and a floor carpeted in a polar-bear shag. It was no suite, just a standard double with a theme—plastic roses, plastic champagne glasses, and a round, ruffled bed as big as a sand trap.

Kris said, "Never get excited about an upgrade before you see it."

I said, "There's no room to walk around."

We tossed our bags onto the bed. Kris checked his watch. "Dinner's in forty-five minutes, right? I'll take my shower, or you could go first. Or I could take a walk while you got dressed."

I said, "We're like an arranged marriage from the old country. Never been alone until the wedding night."

Kris took off his down vest and went to the closet. "Bedwise?" I heard from inside. "Just because we got the giant marriage model doesn't mean I'm going to roll over to your side. Unless you want me to."

I said we didn't have to decide anything now. We'd eat, maybe dance—I read from the pink schedule—" 'to the music of the Sonny Cirrell Orchestra with Songstress Toni Falcone.' "

Kris walked back to the bed and offered me one of two wooden hangers he'd wrestled from their detachable hooks.

"Thanks," I said.

"Do you like to dance?"

I said I did.

"You think it's just ballroom dancing?"

I said we had our choice—ballroom dancing in the Red Sea Room or disco dancing in the Blue Lagoon. I looked up from the schedule. "Or maybe we'd want to turn in early."

"No pressure," he said.

I unzipped my suitcase and took out my short black dress, then tossed my black special-occasion bra, bikini underpants, and panty hose onto the shiny white bedspread. Kris looked away.

I said, "Are we bashful?"

"Hotel policy," he said. "You avert your eyes and back up to the door to await your tip."

"Who says?"

"My mother—when certain female guests, whose husbands don't come up until the weekend, unpack their unmentionables in front of the bellboy."

"You're kidding," I said. "Such a thing actually happens at the Lutheran Lodge?"

He said, "I'm not kidding."

"To you?"

"Even to me."

I asked why he said that—"Even to me"?

He shrugged. "I'm a distant second. But that's okay."

"You think you're a distant second in what way?"

"I meant growing up. Nelson was the handsome one and the object of all the guest crushes. But it's okay. I shouldn't be talking like this—as if Nelson hasn't been through hell."

I said, "Not to be argumentative or anything, but Nelson had the lifeguard advantage."

"While I did laundry and watched Gretel for fifty cents an hour."

I walked a pile of my underwear to the dresser and put it in the top drawer. I said, "Nelson is a great guy, and I'm sure his students are all in love with him—but he's the obvious choice. Like Paul McCartney. But the truth is, women eventually realize that George and John, who were right under our noses the whole time, are more sublime."

"Is that true?"

I turned around. "I was a ninth-grade girl once. I thought Nelson was the greatest. Robin and I both did."

"Are you leading up to something like 'But then I grew up and met you, and suddenly I realized Nelson was just a pretty boy with a Red Cross patch sewed on his trunks'?"

I said, "Exactly."

He smiled.

I asked, "How come I don't remember you from that summer?"

He hesitated, then puffed out his cheeks.

A fragment of an image flashed—a fat boy with a round, sweaty face. He must have seen his clue register, because he said, "That was me—Spanky."

I asked if he remembered me from back then.

"I've tried to." He shrugged. "Apparently I've blocked out my fat phase."

"You remember Robin, though?"

"The Fifes came every summer."

I sat down, so we were side by side on the edge of the bed. Thinking of him, once chubby and possibly tormented, the imagined second fiddle to a blandly handsome brother, I said instead, "Poor Robin."

"God," he said. "What a winter."

"How are the Fifes?"

"Lousy, I'm sure."

"Are the boys back on their feet?"

"Not quite."

"Anything ever develop between Gretel and Chip?"

"Gretel thinks so."

I said, "Does she know I spilled the beans?"

"Absolutely not."

"She did flash me that warning look when she escorted Chip up to his room."

"And then you and I were alone."

"For at least ten minutes," I said.

Kris dropped onto his back and put a pillow over his face. "That moment? When my mother burst in? I wanted to kill her."

I liked that anti-Ingrid sentiment, so I countered with something charitable: "You can't blame her for walking into her own kitchen. It wasn't like she barged into your bedroom."

"Yes it was! You had your arms around me, and I was so happy, even with the funeral ahead of us. Then it was over in a split second, and you were gone for good."

I lowered myself down beside him, propping myself up on one elbow. "*For good?* Aren't you being a little melodramatic?"

He lifted the pillow as if tipping a hat, flashing the smile that had conquered Mrs. Feldman.

I said, "No hurry or anything, but I'm a little tired of hearing about this kiss."

*W*e were led to a round table, where the Seidlers, Reenie and Harry of Staten Island, and the Mizitskys, Marilyn and Al of Queens, were already seated and energetically buttering rolls. So happy to make our acquaintance—Natalie and . . . *Chris*, is it?

"With a *k*," he said, pumping the men's hands across the relish tray.

"Who are you with?" asked Marilyn.

"Miss Marx," said Kris.

"What group, I meant."

"No group. Just escaping for a couple of days."

"What about you?" I asked.

"Eleven ninety-nine," said Al.

Before I could ask, his wife offered, "Health-care workers."

"You're doctors?" asked Kris.

"Doctors!" Al scoffed.

"We represent the health-care *workers*," said Harry, his mouth full of curled carrot. "Almost everyone here this week is Eleven ninety-nine."

"You two kids," said Reenie, whose red dress shimmered with fish-scale sequins. "Are you married?"

"We're friends," I said.

Kris leaned sideways until our shoulders bumped.

"Okay, good friends," I amended.

"Your first time here?" asked Marilyn.

I said it was, and we'd chosen the Halseeyon for a reason: the Feldmans' daughter, Linette—

"What do you do?" Harry asked Kris.

"Wait," said his wife. "What reason? Who's Linette?"

"The daughter," said Marilyn. "The one in the office we spoke to about the facecloths."

"What do you do?" repeated the husbands.

Kris smiled. "I'm in the family business."

"What kind of business?" asked Harry.

"Hotel."

"No kidding? What hotel?"

"The Inn at Lake Devine in Vermont."

"How big?" asked Al.

"Forty-two guest rooms and four cabins."

"Small."

"Can you make a living from a place that size?" asked Harry. "If you don't mind my asking."

"We get by," said Kris.

"Do you get big names up there?" asked Reenie.

I could see Kris mentally scanning the mailing list. "She means entertainers," I said.

"We're not set up for that," said Kris. "We're on a beautiful lake, so we have swimming, boating—"

"How's the food?" asked Marilyn.

"Hearty."

"Kosher?"

Kris said, "No."

"Vermont," Reenie reminded her.

A waiter, dressed in black pants and a short black jacket, appeared with six small tomato juices and mimeographed menus. I noticed the first item was "Melon Cup" or "Choice of Your Favorite Juice." I asked what the melon was this time of year.

"The little balls," he said.

"I'll have that," said Kris.

The waiter darted into the kitchen and returned immediately with six Melon Cups.

"What's good, Victor?" Harry asked.

"Everything."

"What's too good to pass up?"

"The roast beef. The capon. The turkey. The flanken."

"I'll have the roast beef and the turkey," said Harry.

"Same," said his friend.

"For the ladies?"

"Is the flanken fatty?" asked Reenie.

"Get it," said her husband. "You can taste it. Get the chicken, too."

"I'll have the chicken," she told the waiter. "No flanken."

"Me too," said Marilyn. "Just the capon."

"I'll have the roast beef, rare," Kris said.

"Well done for me," said Harry.

"Same," said Al.

I asked what the flounder was stuffed with. Victor rattled off, "They take crackers, melted margarine, garlic powder, bell pepper, parsley—"

"Fine," I said.

"Natalie's a chef," Kris told them.

"Can you bring us more pickles?" asked Al, handing over the relish tray.

"Just the roast beef?" Victor asked Kris.

He looked at the menu. "Can I get . . . let's see . . . a baked potato?"

"It comes with potayda kugel," said the waiter.

"You'll like that," I said.

"He means, Do you want another main course?" said Marilyn.

"Is that the practice?"

The waiter said, "Nothing surprises me—one, two, halfa dozen—"

"I'll start with one," said Kris.

"You do catering?" Marilyn asked me.

I said, No, I was a restaurant chef.

"A *French* chef," Kris added.

I said, "I trained with a French chef."

"In France?"

"In Newton, Mass."

"Natalie can tell whether boiling water's been salted just by sniffing the steam," said Kris.

"I know Newton," said Harry. "My kid went to college with a kid from Newton."

"What's your job at the hotel?" Al asked Kris.

"Night manager; jack-of-all-trades."

"Are your service employees organized?" asked Harry.

"We don't have many."

"How many?"

"Depends on the season."

"Probably exempt," Al said to Harry.

"We love your dress," said Reenie. "At your age you can wear black."

"And fitted," said Marilyn, who was concealed under a chocolate-and-cream awning-striped caftan.

"He likes it too," said Reenie, winking at Kris, who winked at me.

"We have a daughter who's dating a non-Jewish fellow," said Harry.

"Harry—" scolded his wife.

"He's a nice enough boy, but he's a Roman Catholic."

"They're only eighteen years of age, though," said Reenie.

"Too young!" said Al.

"No, I meant eighteen is good. These things don't last when they start that young."

"Not that we're prejudiced," said Harry. "I've spent my whole adult life fighting that kind of crap at the bargaining table."

"They're not interested—" his wife said.

"They don't mind! Do you mind my discussing this with you?" Kris and I said no.

"Your folks go along with this?" Harry asked me.

"Our folks," I began. "It's a little unusual—"

"They've seen us unhappy," said Kris solemnly, "and they want us to be happy."

Marilyn pinched the back of my hand. "I see what you see in him."

"Why were you unhappy?" asked her friend.

I began with Robin, but had only gotten as far as our reunion at Pappagallo when I was stopped by the sight of our waiter race-walking toward us with a Hula-Hoop–size tray held above his head. "Is this ours already?" I asked our tablemates.

"They have everything prepared," said Reenie. "Right there for the taking."

"Hope he remembered the pickles," said Al.

When the tray was lowered to a nearby server, I counted nine silver-domed entrées, which turned out to be everyone's order plus a flanken for the table.

"Ice water?" asked a busboy.

"Is a beer possible?" Kris asked.

Barely possible, the busboy's expression seemed to say. "I'll send the cocktail waitress over."

Harry leaned across the table to ask Kris, "Are you having a drink with dinner?"

"A beer."

"You think they have beer?"

"I'm sure they do."

"I sometimes have a beer with a frankfurter," said Harry.

"Try it," said his wife. "You're on vacation."

"I will if you will," said Al.

We watched a first-rate magic act in the Blue Lagoon, then followed the crowd to the Red Sea Ballroom, where a spangled Toni Falcone charged up to the mike, elbows pumping, and let loose. Every few songs, she'd note an anniversary or birthday, reading from a slip of paper stored coyly in her bra.

I worried that we'd be next, a hot tip from the front desk, the impostor honeymooners. Toni announced there were new grandparents in the room . . . their name, their borough, their grandson's name and weight, then, to my relief, she crumpled her crib sheet. I whispered to Kris, "I think we can relax—" which was cut off by the band striking up "Hello, Young Lovers."

Toni sang directly to us at our chrome toadstool table, arms outstretched, fingers flexing. Neither of us moved a muscle. She stamped her spike-heeled, ankle-strapped foot and cried, "C'mon, you two! Get up and dance." I shook my head, which had been enough to decline the magician's call minutes earlier. But Kris knew there was no getting away. He took my hand and we walked into the spotlight. Reenie and Marilyn clapped ecstatically.

We danced primly at first, then closer and closer. Wrinkled, bespectacled faces studied us and mentally pinched our cheeks. And then, because it was the Catskills, where you give the audience what it wants, Kris twirled me once in a pirouette, then clamped me to him in Latin-ballroom fashion. "Aren't they darling, ladies and gentlemen?" Toni purred. When we returned to unremarkable footwork, she grew restless; she put out a call to "everyone still in love to come up and join the happy couple." Dozens of old-marrieds did, a few great fox-trotters among them, relieving us of the spotlight. Toni and the band moved on to a shmaltzy "It's All in the Game."

I said into Kris's collar, "Is anyone watching now?"

"No one."

I tightened my left arm around him and sighed.

"What?" he whispered.

"Just this," I said. "You."

We continued to dance on the now-packed floor, the perfect excuse for our barely moving. I remember thinking how wonderful he smelled; how I liked the texture of his wool jacket; how warm and solid his hand was; that I'd steal the hotel soap and buy a Mathis album, which led to the realization that either a show tune or a corny oldie would be our song. I said, "Thank you for hunting me down in Newton," and kissed the spot where his earlobe met his jaw.

Soon he whispered, "Are you tired?"

I said I didn't want to let go, if that's what he meant.

He said, "It's getting a little dangerous."

"I could stop nuzzling you."

"Actually," he said, "I wouldn't mind being alone."

"Me too."

It was a medley: "It's All in the Game," segued into "Wonderful, Wonderful." A ripple of applause drew a "Thank you, you're *too* kind; Sonny Cirrell, ladies and gentlemen."

"Let's make our move," said Kris.

If we thought we were slipping away unnoticed, we were wrong. At the door we heard Reenie or Marilyn call, "See you at breakfast!" And from the stage, through the amplifiers, out the speakers—a husky, loaded "Sweet dreams, you two."

NINETEEN

We weren't so far removed from dormitory life and childhood beds that a locked, private room didn't seem like the best real estate on earth. I used the bathroom first, then, from the doorway, watched him remove his tie, jacket, shirt, and T-shirt; saw for the first time his swirl of chest hair, his freckled shoulders, his extremely affecting collarbone. He walked over to where I stood transfixed, ran his hands up and down my arms in soothing fashion, and—assuming modesty had paralyzed me—said, "Everything's totally up to you."

I took my shoes off, one at a time. My panty hose. I don't remember the actual act of unhooking, unzipping, and removing my dress, but we must have, because I do recall a slip phase, horizontal on the shiny bedspread, some acrobatic rolling, and the unwrapping of his purchase from the Halseeyon's all-night pharmacy. I know we must have pulled the bedspread down and fallen asleep at some point, because we woke under the covers, smiling, even though it was 8:30 A.M. and the phone was ringing.

"Breakfast only goes till nine, kids," advised someone who sounded like Honey. "We didn't want you to miss it."

Groggy, I asked, "How much time?"

"Half-hour. But as long as you get there under the wire, they'll take care of you."

I pulled on jeans and my bulky Irish sweater, brushed my hair into a ponytail, then sat on the flat edge of the pink bathtub to watch Kris's shoulder blades and the indentation of his waist while he shaved. I said, "What did we tell those people at our table? That we were friends?"

"I think they got the picture," said Kris.

"Didn't we get introduced at some point as actual newlyweds?"

"*Young lovers*, I believe, was the musical term."

I aired the thought I'd had while dancing—that one of Toni's tunes could end up being our song.

"I like that," he said. "I like that you're thinking ahead."

"Ahead"—life beyond the Halseeyon—brought forth a vision of my mother yoo-hooing up the stairs from Saul Zinler's kitchen, having used her master key to see if I had died in my sleep, or worse.

I mumbled, "She'll figure it out."

He wiped foam off his face with a pink towel. "Who?"

"My mother. I told her: 'I'm an adult. I make my own decisions.' "

"Right. You've got your own life and your own garret."

He sat down next to me as I heard my mother phoning my father, the neighbors, the Inn at Lake Devine, and, without a doubt, the Newton police. "You could call them," he said. "Tell them you're safe. And in good hands."

I smiled. He took my face in his hands and kissed me, his skin still warm and spiced from shaving, a morning-after kiss that started sweetly, then intensified.

And as I gripped the edge of the slippery tub, I was thinking, This man, this dear man—imagine—is Ingrid Berry's son.

"We're so proud," cried Marilyn and Reenie when we sat down. "Everyone saw the show last night, all our friends. They knew you were from our table. They think you look like sister and brother. How did you sleep? We asked them to call your room; we didn't want you to miss breakfast . . . oh, look—isn't that the Feldman girl?"

From the surprise and pleasure on Kris's face, I knew it had to be Nelson's friend approaching, but whatever I had expected in a Catskills hotel heiress, this wasn't it. Her tight black leather jumper over a tie-dyed body stocking startled me, and her high-heeled clogs made me smile. She was short and wiry, with a teenager's freckled face and frizzy, cider-colored hair. "Hey!" she was saying, picking up speed. "Hey, Kris Berry!" When she came closer, I saw that the black leather was man-made; another step and I saw that her left hand was weighed down by the largest emerald-cut diamond ever mounted within four prongs.

"Linette," Kris was saying. "I want you to meet Natalie Marx."

Linette beamed and squeezed my hand.

"How'd you know we were here?" Kris asked.

"Word got back to me," she said.

"I did a little fancy footwork at the front desk," said Kris.

"No problem, kiddo." She gestured around the vast, teeming dining room. "We're practically empty."

Victor the waiter was at our elbows and on his best behavior, smiling unctuously. "Folks? Can I get you appetizers, hottahcold cereal, halfagrapefruit?"

"Appetizers?" I repeated. He handed me the breakfast menu and pointed to a list of various pickled and smoked fish, and every fruit that had ever been dried, stewed, or buried in sour cream. "Canned figs," I said. "I haven't had canned figs since I was a kid. My father used to put evaporated milk on his."

"Can you join us?" Kris asked Linette.

None of the rapt and fed onlookers offered to give up his or her front-row seat. "We're the Seidlers and the Mizitskys," said Reenie. "We met you earlier in the week."

"Of course," said Linette. "You're with Eleven ninety-nine. I spoke with Housekeeping. We're thrilled to have you. Did you get whatever it was you didn't have?"

"Before we got back to our rooms!" said Marilyn.

"You're a miracle worker," said Reenie.

"I wish all my problems were that easy to solve." A busboy, unbidden, brought a chair. Victor returned with a cup, saucer, and a small stainless-steel teapot. As she bobbed the teabag, Linette turned to Kris and asked, "How is he doing?"

He shook his head. "It hasn't been that long."

"What was her name?"

"Robin Fife."

"Was she wonderful?" Linette asked, eyes shining. "Were they madly in love?"

"I guess so," said Kris, flinching. "Sure."

"Where'd she go to school?"

"UConn," said Kris.

"Connecticut College," I corrected.

"Beautiful?"

"Tall and blond," I said. "Very sweet and kind. The all-American girl."

"Are we talking about the brother's fiancée?" Reenie asked.

"She was killed on her wedding day, on her way to the church," Linette supplied.

"More or less," said Kris.

"*Oy Gotenyu*," someone murmured.

"He and I were friends at Cornell," said Linette.

"But you never met Robin?" I asked her.

Linette said she hadn't. There was no Robin back then.

"Actually," said Kris, "he's known her since we were kids. Her parents have been coming to the Inn for ages."

I turned to the older couples and said, to flatter our host and upgrader, "Linette was one of the first of his college friends to call Kris's brother. She thought it would be good for him to get away."

"No big deal," said Linette. "Who wouldn't?"

Victor was back with several small glasses of juice and my canned figs, asking about eggs. I said, "Lox, eggs, and onions, please. And a toasted bagel."

"I'll . . . try . . ." Kris said, scanning the list of two dozen possibilities, ". . . a jelly omelette with a side order of belgian waffles. And what's in the breadbasket?"

Victor said, "You name it." He plucked the menus out of our hands, careful to produce a smile for the boss's daughter. "Anything else from the grill? French toast? Griddle cakes, latkes, blintzes?"

"Bring them an order of blueberry," Linette said.

"How are her parents doing?" Reenie asked Kris.

"Not too good."

"Was it the saddest, most heart-wrenching funeral in the entire world?" Linette asked.

Kris said, "It was extremely sad."

"The saddest," I said.

"Were you there?"

I found myself, out of loyalty to genteel Robin, who would never have interrogated anyone about anything, describing the bereaved recessional of Nelson as pallbearer.

Linette splashed water into a glass and handed it to me. "I'm asking now," she confided, "because I wouldn't bring any of this up in front of Nelson."

"You never recover from something like this," Marilyn declared.

Her husband said, "How do you know? People recover from plenty."

Kris said, "I think work helps, and time."

"And friends," I added.

"How old is your brother?" asked Harry.

"He'll be twenty-seven in May," said Kris.

"Young," said Harry. "By thirty he'll be married with a couple of kids."

"Is that your father?" I asked Linette.

"Who?"

I pointed to a freckled bald man, wearing a white HALSEEYON golf shirt and brown trousers. She shook her head at whatever he was telegraphing.

"Father and general manager," said Harry.

"I try to ignore him," said Linette.

"We met your grandmother last night," said Kris.

"She upgraded us," I said.

Kris laughed.

Linette said, "She screws everything up doing that."

"She couldn't have been nicer," I said.

"She's supposed to be retired, but she doesn't know what that means."

"What about you?" I asked. "Will you be staying on after you get married?"

"Oh," said Linette. She looked down at her hand, but didn't raise it from her lap.

"Is that an *engagement* ring?" asked Kris.

Reenie and Marilyn repeated his question in a kind of coo, as if to say only a male of the innocent Vermont variety could fail to grasp the meaning of such a rock.

"Of course it's an engagement ring," said Linette. "Think I'd wear this as *jewelry*?"

"Was it a surprise?" I asked.

She said, without a hint of nostalgia or sentiment, "Yeah," followed by, "I wonder if Victor got the order in before the grill closed."

"It's taking an awfully long time," said Marilyn.

"They could at least have brought her the bagel," said Reenie.

Neither Linette, Kris, nor I seconded her observation. We sipped our coffees and tea without comment, as if to say, We've included you in this conversation thus far out of courtesy, but we've had enough.

Someone among them got the message. They gathered up their pocketbooks and newspapers and unlit cigars and said good-bye, unoffended. Their easy goodwill made me instantly contrite. I said, "We're staying another night, so we'll see you later?"

"We're looking forward to it," said Marilyn. She stopped to touch Linette's shoulder, confided to her that I was a French chef like Julia Child, then said, "*Mazel tov*, whoever he is."

As soon as they were five steps away—all wearing bell-bottoms of various lengths—Kris asked, "Who's the lucky guy?"

"No one you know," said Linette.

"When's the wedding?" Kris asked.

"Undecided," she said.

"How long has it been official?" asked Kris.

Linette unpinned and repinned her polka-dotted barrette into the same clump of unruly hair. "We got engaged Thanksgiving before last."

Kris asked for a name.

"Joel . . . Taub. He's a graduate student."

"What's he studying?"

Linette called, "Vinny! Go get Victor. These people have waited ten minutes for their eggs." She turned back to us and said, "Sorry."

Kris said, No problem; we were still full from dinner.

I repeated his question: The field of her intended?

Linette said, "He's at Hebrew Union College in Cincinnati."

"Rabbi," I translated.

"No kidding," said Kris.

I asked, "How does one take up with a rabbi?"

She smiled. "He wasn't a rabbi when we met."

"What was he?" I asked.

"A cabana boy."

"Isn't that interesting," said Kris. "Cabana boy. Did you hire him?"

Linette turned to me. "Is he asking because that's what his mother does? Takes up with her employees?"

I laughed.

Kris said, "First of all, we barely have any employees. Second of all, my mother would never dream of taking up with anyone." He waited a beat and added wryly, "Even my father."

"Really?" I asked.

"Who the hell knows," he said.

"Have you met his mother?" I asked Linette.

"I've had the pleasure," she said.

"His father's a sweetie," I said.

"The boys take after their father," Linette threw out with some authority.

Kris rolled his eyes, changed the subject. "Where does your boyfriend do his . . . rabbiing?"

"He's graduating this June and he's spending next year at Berkeley as an assistant chaplain."

"Berkeley's supposed to be great," said Kris.

Linette shrugged, as if she'd heard its praises sung too many times from too many champions of Berkeley.

"How often do you get to see him?" I asked.

"That's a problem. He's in school all week, and I can't travel on Saturdays."

I said I never thought of that—the problems of a long-distance romance with an Orthodox Jew.

Linette said, "He's not Orthodox; we are—" which was the moment Victor arrived, perspiring and apologizing, balancing an embarrassing number of plates up and down his arms.

Linette's father called her name. She rose, touched Kris's arm, and said, "Nelson'll be fine. Nothing happens here from sundown Friday till sundown Saturday, so we'll ease him in."

I asked if she'd give me a tour of the kitchen later.

"I wanted her to be our chef, but she hates my mother," Kris said cheerfully.

I thought I caught something in Linette's reaction, a slight lift of her hairline, as if it were a subject that deserved further exploration. "If I'm not at my desk, dial '0,'" she advised. "I always have a walkie-talkie with me. . . . Natalie, we'll talk some more. Defi-

nitely count on a kitchen tour. Kris, call me when your brother ar-
rives." She took the small stainless-steel pitcher of maple syrup out
of his hand. "Please get Mr. Berry some of ours," she said to Victor.

She walked back to the Feldman table, recognizable by its telephone centerpiece, and sat down next to her father. I saw him ask
a question; witnessed the telling of a pleasant lie that made him
beam at us.

Kris, pulling his jelly omelette platter into position, said, "I'm figuring Nelson will get here around six-thirty."

I asked him if he had known Linette during her college days.

"I met her a couple of times," he said. "Once on a toboggan in
Ithaca at some winter-carnival thing. And once at our place."

"Lake Devine?"

"A bunch of his friends came for a weekend. The hotel crowd."

"When did he switch majors?"

"He didn't. He took an extra year for a master's and a defer-
ment."

I tasted my eggs; noted that the onions hadn't been sautéed in
advance. "Were they ever boyfriend and girlfriend?"

"I doubt it."

"Just buddies?"

"Sure," said Kris. "Why?"

"No reason," I said.

"I'm catching on to the fact that she couldn't have dated him
even if she wanted to," Kris said, between bites of a blintz.

"Because of the religion thing?"

"That's right," said Kris. He smiled, his teeth bluish. "Your favorite subject."

"Was she invited to Nelson's wedding?"

"Doubt it," said Kris.

"It sounds like they lost touch after college."

"That happens," he said. "Especially when you become engaged
to other people." At that moment, I caught Mr. Feldman studying
us. I smiled and he waved back happily.

Kris said, "He must be thrilled she's marrying a rabbi."

I said under my breath, "Even if he's Reform and penniless?"

Kris's eyes widened over the rim of his juice glass.

"Trust me: Her family paid for the ring. Rich people don't work as cabana boys. Anyone headed for Berkeley wouldn't support diamond mining in South Africa, and only a Reform rabbi would take a job as a chaplain there."

"How do you know all this?" he asked.

"I know these people." I poked around his breadbasket and came up with a prune muffin, underbaked, all the while watching Linette. She was on the phone, fingering the ends of her frizzy hair. Clearly, she was giving someone orders, repeating two syllables that were undoubtedly "Berry."

"What's so interesting?" Kris asked.

"Linette. On the phone. It's about us."

She hung up, caught my eye, nodded sternly.

I pointed to my bulky sweater—*me?*

She nodded again.

"Clue me in," Kris said.

"It's all set, a second night in the honeymoon suite."

Kris asked, "Think Nelson will mind?"

"Mind what?"

"Sleeping alone, no roommate."

I touched his face and said, "Too bad."

$\mathcal{T}$ W E N T Y

$\mathcal{L}$inette sat beneath a blowup of a stony woman with sharp cheekbones who was ladling soup to boarders.

"Sad, isn't it?" she said, watching me study the grainy mural. "Just being in the mountains was considered vacation." She twisted around in her desk chair and looked at the wall above her. "Did you ever see a grimmer bunch?"

I asked when it was taken and whether they were relatives.

"We think nineteen fifteen." She stood up and pointed to a child seated on a man's lap. "That's my father, and we think he was two or three."

"Who's the cook?"

"His grandmother."

"What was it called?"

"Nothing formal—Tilly Feldman's place in the mountains, or however you say that in Yiddish."

"Is it still standing?" I asked.

Linette pointed out the window. "There, the white house by the first tee, improved and immortalized."

I asked what it was used for now.

"Us," she said. "Home of the famous Feldmans."

"When did it become the Halseeyon?"

She groaned and said, "I hate this part." She reached for an open pack of Virginia Slims and knocked one out. "The answer is: when Hal Feldman took over."

"Seriously? Hal?"

"It's true, my father"—she pointed above her head—"baby Heinick. He took over during the Depression and named it after himself." She lit the cigarette that had been bobbing between her lips. "And he's continuing the family tradition of not retiring until he's dead."

I said I assumed she would take over for her dad sooner rather than later, and that she had been sent to Cornell with that in mind.

"They all *plan* to retire. Estelle's allegedly retired. My dad will retire—let's see, he's sixty-two . . ." She hit a few buttons on her adding machine, then cranked its arm. "Roughly? In thirty years?" She laughed, and repositioned herself, one leg bent underneath her. "What about you? Someone said chef."

I said, "About to be."

"You are or you're not?"

"I have a job beginning May first."

"Where?"

"Outside Boston."

"At?"

I hesitated. "Chez Simone."

"And who's Simone?"

"Hilda Simone, restaurant dreamer."

"How so?"

"She thinks it'll be like having friends over for dinner every night."

She rolled her eyes. "Spare me."

I said, "Well, on the bright side, she recognizes that she knows nothing, so she's promised me a free hand."

Linette forced smoke out of one corner of her mouth. "Here, there *is* no free hand. We tell cooks when we hire them, 'People have been coming here since they were kids, and now they're coming back with their own kids. They expect pickled tomatoes on the table and sponge cake for dessert. If you need to make quiche, call it a cheese pie. And if you need to make Lobster Newburg, you'd better go somewhere else."

I said, smiling, "How would you know about Lobster Newburg?"

"I know," she said, kicking a second desk chair on wheels into position for me, "because I've read menus in the big wide world."

"But not tasted it."

"Lobster? Nooo."

"And that's fine?"

"I don't know what you mean," she said.

I said, "I guess I meant are you ever frustrated by the constraints of a kosher resort?"

"Kosher resort or kosher kitchen? Because the resort part isn't that different."

I said, "I'm sure you're right."

"What seems odd to you?"

I said quickly, "Nothing."

"Does it embarrass you in front of Kris"—she picked up and waved the day's ditto master—"the kasha and the derma?"

I said, "Kris? He loves it!"

"You don't think he's uncomfortable being the only *goy* in the place?"

I said, thinking of Toni Falcone and Mad Mulligan the magician, "First of all, he's not. Second of all, he wouldn't notice if he were."

"That's because he's used to being in the majority," Linette said. "He doesn't know the meaning of *fish out of water*. Nelson was the same way."

I asked, "Was Nelson ever here?"

"Once. There were a bunch of us from Cornell, and we called it a field trip. My father put us all up in the barracks, gave tours of the kitchen, the butcher shop, the pantries. Fed us. Said things like, 'This round roll is what we call a bagel. We eat it with cream cheese and a delicacy we call lox.' 'These skullcaps? The things that look like beanies? Our people cover their heads in *shul*, which is our word for church.' " Linette smirked.

"When was this?"

"Fall of our senior year." Her phone rang. She signaled time-out and took the call: No, she didn't hire the summer counselors . . . okay, she would talk to the *mother* of a summer counselor. . . . "Yes, we certainly do have curfews and supervision . . . certainly there are separate quarters for boys and girls . . . absolutely, hot showers. . . . You're very welcome. Call me anytime during the summer if you're worried about your daughter, which you shouldn't be. We're one big family up here." She hung up and said for my amusement, "Oh, and one more thing, Mrs. Sussman: Be sure Heidi packs her birth control pills."

I laughed. "A lot of that going on?"

"What d'you think? Forty college kids, not to mention horny waiters and lonely wives whose husbands stay in the city."

She scribbled a note on one of a half-dozen clipboards hanging on the wall behind her.

"You were telling me about Nelson's visit," I prompted.

"That was it," she said. "One three-day weekend in low season."

"Kris told me you once went to Lake Devine."

"Once. Also a field trip." She began pulling on the ends of her hair, scraping a few strands at a time between her fingernails.

I asked when that was.

"Summer of 'sixty-eight—which I know offhand because I remember watching the Chicago convention on their shleppy TV and feeling like I was the only Democrat in the rec room."

"You probably were."

"Didn't Kris fill you in? He was there and—what's her name?— Shirley Temple."

"Gretel."

"*Gretel.*" She shook her head. "That says it all, doesn't it? . . . What'd she turn out like?"

"Like her mother."

Linette shuddered, a theatrical tremor that made me laugh.

"What's Joel's mother like?" I asked.

"Cynthia? A hippie pediatrician—long gray braid, socks and sandals. Bakes her own bread."

I smiled. "And what's Joel like?"

She turned around a picture frame so it faced me. It was Linette and a young man, both laughing hard, their arms around each other's waist. He was wearing aviator glasses, a beige poplin suit, and a wide tie in a tropical-foliage print. Linette was wearing a garden-party frock of white eyelet over shocking-pink taffeta, sashed at the waist and puffed at the sleeves.

"Nice-looking," I said.

She took a deep drag on her Virginia Slim. "For a rabbi, you mean?"

I protested—no, by any standard.

She took the frame back and said, "This was us at his sister's wedding."

"Did Joel perform the ceremony?"

"He wasn't ordained yet. He did the blessings in Hebrew, which was nice, because otherwise it was a civil ceremony—they're practically Quakers; they can't believe they produced a rabbi. Also, he lectured on the historical significance of breaking the glass." She crossed and uncrossed her eyes. "His pedantic streak. They'll love him at Berkeley."

Knowing her high threshold for cross-examination, I asked, "So? Are you madly in love?"

"Of course!"

"In a long-distance kind of way?"

"That can't be helped."

"How often do you talk to him?"

"Often," she murmured.

I asked, "Did you have a boyfriend before Joel, in college?"

"Sure."

"Not Nelson, though."

She'd been losing interest, glancing at pink phone slips on her desk, but I had brought her back. "You know what this is all about? You're anxious about Nelson—maybe about his making the drive, or about his state of mind—and you're displacing that anxiety by asking me weird questions. But coming here is just what he needs—to have a little . . . well, *fun* is too strong a word after what he's been through; maybe *change of scenery*. That's all—a little swim, a little *shvitz*, a little bingo. We'll wine him and dine him and maybe even get him on the dance floor by Saturday night—why shouldn't he?—and he'll fall into bed exhausted."

"Maybe," I said.

"He used to love to dance."

I asked if rabbis danced.

"Some do. Some even dance with women." She shimmied her chair forward, so that her rib cage was pressed against the edge of her desk, and asked me solemnly, "Are your parents *frum*?"

"Are they from where?"

"*Frum*. Religious."

"Oh," I said. "In their own way. Why?"

"You're seeing Kris."

I tried to reconstruct his graceful answer of the night before. "On one hand, they did what they could to derail things," I said. "On the other hand, they don't even know about him."

"Would your parents disown you if you ended up together?" she asked, another of what I was coming to recognize as her trademark intense yet premature questions.

I said, "This is the nineteen seventies. Priests marry nuns. Heiresses marry their tutors. My sister married Danny O'Connor."

"Did he convert?"

"Hardly. They were married in the biggest Catholic church in Newton."

"Wow," she said. "Did your parents go?"

I cheated, editing out the months of railing. "They went, and they walked her down the aisle."

"Wow," she said again. She picked up the phone suddenly and dialed three numbers. "I'm calling our captain," she confided, as if we'd never strayed from the subject of my cooking career. "Would you like the tour now?"

I said, "Sure."

"Kris too?"

"Maybe. He was playing Pong in the game room last time I saw him."

A voice crackled on the line. "Arn? Linette. I'm sending a guest for a tour"—she winked at me—"the insider's tour. She's a chef in Boston . . . thanks . . . as soon as she can walk from here to there." She hung up and said, "It's huge, two floors, a butcher shop, a bakery. We bake all our own bread and pastries."

I said, "Great. Will I see you later?"

Linette began collecting the pink telephone slips again, effectively dismissing me. "We have Shabbat dinner at home. I'd invite Nelson to join us, but I think he'd be more comfortable with you and Kris. And my father would ask him a thousand questions."

"Which is the last thing he needs," I said.

"I'll sneak over at some point, just to say hello." And repeating the morning's watchword: "We'll ease him in."

$\mathcal{K}$ris wasn't playing bingo or billiards, pinball or Pong; nor was he swimming in the indoor pool. I called the room and our line was busy, so I went upstairs. He was off the phone by the time I got there, looking preoccupied, as if he would pace the room if only there were floor space. He had been trying to reach Nelson at school, he said, but had missed him. The secretary told Kris that his brother had cut out after sixth period—with full permission, of course. Any time Mr. Berry needed off was fine with the office, she told him. They were very, very fond of him and they all felt just sick about his fiancée.

"Why were you trying to reach Nelson?" I asked.

He went into the bathroom, shut the door, peed, flushed. "It'll be fine, don't you think?" he called over running water.

"What will?"

He opened the door. "The weekend."

"Why were you calling him at school?"

He answered, sounding surprised that it wasn't obvious: "Linette."

"What about her?"

Kris said, "Maybe, when she invited him, Nelson got the idea that her situation was different than it is."

"Do you know for a fact that she didn't tell him she was engaged?"

"I know for a fact," he said.

$\mathcal{W}$e met him on the front steps, where we had begun our vigil at six P.M. Kris greeted Nelson as soon as the car door opened by saying, "Velcome to the Ketskills."

Nelson, in a tweed jacket and khakis, put his arm around Kris's neck, feigning brotherly love, but dragging him down to perform a hard noogy. Kris's muffled cry of "It's Shabbat, asshole" got him released.

"Hi, Natalie," said Nelson, kissing me on the cheek. "You and my brother back on speaking terms?"

I said, "We're the mascots of the Halseeyon. Everybody clucks when we walk by."

"Dinner's in, like, sixty seconds," Kris said, taking his brother's garment bag.

"Let me check in," said Nelson.

The substitute Sabbath clerk, a Mr. Spinney, greeted us solemnly. He said, all modulated tones, "Mr. Berry will be staying in Sunset Cottage."

"Where's that?" Kris asked.

"It's one of our outbuildings."

"The barracks," I explained.

"As a guest of the family," said the clerk.

"Is Miss Feldman around?" Nelson asked him.

"Not Friday evenings," he said. "It's their Sabbath."

"Did she leave me a message?"

The clerk made a cursory check of a few spots where a rare message might be left for an occupant of the barracks.

I volunteered that Linette had to eat with her parents, apparently in private.

Kris said, "Aren't there any rooms in the main building?"

The clerk said blandly, "Miss Feldman left instructions for Sunset Cottage."

"Is it even *open* this time of year?" I asked.

He smiled superciliously. "We have keys."

"Is it heated?"

"Of course. And there's an underground passageway so Mr. Berry can get there without going outdoors."

Nelson said, "Never mind. I'm sure it's fine." And to Kris, "Can't be any worse than the bunks at home."

Nelson smiled as he accepted the key being dangled in front of him. "I stayed there once, years ago," he told the clerk.

"Enjoy your stay," said the clerk.

"I think I might," said Nelson.

TWENTY-ONE

The Mizitskys and the Seidlers had been replaced by two pious brothers in matching eyeglasses, Avi and Ira Lupow, who seemed mortified to have an unmarried woman and two *sheygetses* without yarmulkes at their Shabbat table.

"What brings you to the mountains?" Kris asked the brothers, who were low over their soup and not noting our arrival.

A minute later, Nelson tried, "Good soup?"

They looked up, puzzled.

Kris asked, "Do you speak English?"

One of them said, "Yuh."

Kris asked where they were from and was told, "West Hartford."

"I'm from Vermont," said Kris. "My brother teaches in Rhode Island, and Miss Marx here is from outside Boston."

Nelson whipped his napkin into place, picked up his soup spoon, and said, "You guys can clear something up for me, which is essentially this: If you live in Connecticut, what team do you follow—the Sox or the Mets?"

The brothers recoiled. "We're Yankee fans," they sputtered, spoons abandoned at the bottom of their bowls. "New York Yankees."

"Both of you?" Nelson asked.

The brothers nodded vehemently.

"And is that because you think they're a better team than, say, the Sox? With better pitching?"

We were off and running, through the fish course, the fowl course, the brisket-and-potato course, the honey-cake-and-compote course, and blessings over each. My role was limited conversationally by the Lupow brothers' pretending I wasn't there. I addressed my baseball remarks, such as they were, to Kris or Nelson.

A good hour later, over tea, Nelson returned to his opening gambit: "What brought you two to the mountains in March?"

"A reunion," they said.

"Really!" said Nelson. "Of what?"

"Our summer camp."

"On Shabbat?" I asked.

Ira and Avi both regarded me as glumly as they could without making eye contact. One tore a piece of challah from the centerpiece and chewed it with what looked like disgust.

"Not everyone attending is as observant as you are," I interpreted, "but you wanted to come anyway, and it was okay because it's a kosher resort so you knew you could keep the Sabbath?"

"Yes," one of them hissed.

Kris asked, "So, are you two kosher and all that, like, all the time?"

Nelson said, "I think we can assume so."

"What's on tap, reunion-wise?" Kris asked.

"Services," said one of the Lupows, "and Oneg Shabbat and a dance tomorrow night."

"What was the name of your summer camp?" I asked.

"Applegate," they said in Nelson's direction.

"So it must have been a co-ed camp if they're having a dance," I said.

"Across the lake. Miriam. The sister camp."

"Is it a joint reunion?" asked Nelson.

The brothers said, "Yuh."

"Why did you pick the Halseeyon?" asked Kris.

The brothers shrugged.

"They must've given you a decent group rate," Kris said.

"Lower than a group rate," said one.

"How did that work out?" Kris asked.

"The owner," said another.

"What about the owner?" asked Nelson.

"His daughter," said one.

"Linette?" I asked.

"Went to Camp Miriam," said the other.

$\mathcal{W}$e skipped services and drove to a townie bar in downtown Monticello. Kris and Nelson ordered beers; I had, after several cups of Manischewitz Concord Grape with dinner, a glass of Tab. We hadn't discussed Linette in front of the Lupow brothers, and Nelson didn't seem to be grasping Shabbat etiquette. "I feel a little weird," he said. "Like, she invites me here and we run out on her. Maybe she's looking for me."

I nudged Kris's foot under the table.

"Nels?" he said, his voice a note higher than usual. "Did Linette tell you she was getting married?"

Nelson swallowed, but his face gave nothing away. "No kidding," he said. "Who's the guy?"

"A rabbi," I said.

"Well," he said. "A rabbi. Sounds serious."

"Kris was worried that you might not have come if you'd known that."

"Why?"

"You know—I came with Natalie. You and Linette would make four. We'd hang around together and have some fun."

"Dance," I said.

"And you think that's out of the question?"

Kris and I must have been wearing twin apologetic expressions, because Nelson said, "Hey, look. I got out of Providence, which I needed to do. And I get to see Natalie under happier circumstances than last time." He punched Kris's upper arm. "And I get to see my brother back among the living." He raised his glass, and we raised ours, with less gusto.

Nelson said, "I see a jukebox."

Kris said, "I've been here too long. I was actually thinking, Better not play music on Shabbat."

Nelson stood up and fished quarters out of his pocket. He spent a long time flipping through the jukebox's offerings, deep in what looked like bleak contemplation. When he rejoined us, he asked, "So what do you know about this rabbi?"

"Hardly anything," I said.

"A few details," said Kris.

"Does he have a name?" Nelson asked.

"Joel," I said.

"When's the wedding?"

"*Mañana*," said Kris.

"Does she have a ring?"

"Like this," said Kris, indicating a rectangle the size of a pocket lighter.

"When did they meet?"

"Unclear," said Kris.

I said, "I guess you two lost track of each other after college."

Nelson looked expectantly toward the silent jukebox.

"What'd you pick?" Kris asked.

"Elton John and Roberta Flack." In seconds, we heard, as if it were a parody of Sonny Cirrell, the opening notes of the theme from *Love Story*.

Kris said, "You bozo."

"It's a mistake," Nelson protested. "I must've hit the wrong buttons."

Kris eyed the half-dozen locals and muttered, "We're gonna get beat up."

A man in a dark green leisure suit walked by us, leading a tough cookie in a nurse's uniform onto the dance floor.

Nelson said, "Go ahead, you two."

We said, No, not if he wasn't.

Nelson said, "In that case, Natalie, may I?"

The song was difficult to dance to; it called for slow, skating steps that felt ridiculous. I said, "We can sit this one out if you want to."

He said, "I was hoping we'd have a chance to talk."

"Sure," I said lightly. "About what?"

"Stuff."

"Such as?"

"Things good with Kris?"

"Very good." I was conscious of his hand holding mine, his chin not quite grazing my hair, and I thought, If I were back at the lake and fourteen again and someone had said, "One day you'll dance with Nelson Berry to a theme song from a movie called *Love Story*," I would have been thrilled.

"Has Linette mentioned me at all?" Nelson asked.

"A couple dozen times."

"Concerning . . . ?"

"Robin. And how you're doing."

"And you said . . . ?"

"Essentially, that you were okay, not great. I told her Robin was sweet and beautiful, and that she was the happiest bride-to-be I've ever seen."

After a long few moments he asked hoarsely, "Do you think that's true?"

"I know it."

The song played on painfully. I glanced over at Kris, who was wearing the sweetly anxious look of a guy who was letting his older, reputedly more charming brother dance with his girl.

"Aren't all brides-to-be happy?" Nelson asked.

I said, "Some are happier than others."

He shrugged. "I haven't known that many."

"I'm thinking of your buddy Linette." Nelson waited, didn't prompt me. After a minute I said, "I get the idea that she's not madly in love with this guy."

"Why?"

"She doesn't see him very often, and when she talks about him . . . I don't know. I didn't really get a sense of why she's marrying the guy."

"People don't always wear their heart on their sleeve."

"I think Linette would . . . and I'm fairly certain that sleeve would be attached to a hideous outfit."

Nelson laughed, and said fondly, "Doesn't she have the *worst* taste in clothes?"

I thought of Robin's classic, starched, all-cotton clothes, her long, straight hair, the Pappagallos on her feet, and the tasteful diamond solitaire on her hand. In danger of saying emphatically, "The *worst*, the polar opposite of Robin's," I murmured, "Just an impression about her as reluctant bride-to-be. Just something in her eyes, and what she didn't say about Joel."

"People expect me to act a certain way and say things that will reassure them that I'm incapacitated by grief."

I protested that it was just the opposite: People wanted signs that he was okay.

"I'm not okay," he said, "but I have to keep putting one foot in front of the other."

"I know that."

"One reason I wanted to come up here was to be around strangers who wouldn't be giving me the poor-Nelson look I see everywhere else."

"Then you came to the right place. I can't imagine a look of pity on Linette's face. I think she'll expect you to do the limbo at the camp reunion."

Nelson laughed, then said he was going to give Linette a call and tell her where she could find us.

"They don't answer their phone."

"Ever?"

"Friday night's a big deal," I said. "Observant Jews don't answer the phone or turn on a light. Did you ride the elevator? It stops on every floor so no one has to press a button."

"I knew her in college, remember? Friday night was no different from any other night."

I said, "You're saying she isn't observant?"

"What she is," said Nelson, "is an obedient daughter."

The song ended, finally, and we went back to Kris, who was trying hard to look unworried.

I said, "I was telling Nelson about our various conversations with Linette."

Kris said, "She and Natalie hit it off."

"More importantly," Nelson said, "I understand you two are hitting it off."

I wanted to keep up my end of the banter, but it seemed the right moment to make a declaration in front of the brother who had always won the hearts of the guests. I said, "I understand I have you to thank for all of this."

"All of what?"

"Accepting Linette's invitation. Coming here this weekend—"

"This glorious weekend, she means," said Kris.

I said, "Let's not exaggerate; it's only been a glorious twenty-four hours."

Nelson patted his brother's cheek approvingly.

Kris said, "You're in an awfully good mood for someone who was—" He stopped, then said, "Downgraded to the barracks."

"Am I?"

I said, "I noticed that, too."

"You guys worry too much." He executed the fake stretch and yawn of a bad actor, checked his watch, and asked, "Want to go? I might as well turn in early."

"Did you bring a book?" Kris asked him, a manager of lodgings without TVs, and now a guilty brother who had a woman. "Want to stop and pick up a couple of magazines?"

"Let's just get back," said Nelson.

I touched Nelson's arm. "Has it been a complete flop so far?"

"Not at all." He stood up, looking oddly untroubled. In parallel gestures, he and Kris took dollar bills out of their wallets and put them under their glass mugs.

"She'll show up at breakfast," said Kris, "which is when she came looking for us."

Nelson pushed his chair in and said, "I know you thought this weekend was going to be one big double date, but it ain't gonna happen, folks. And that's fine. I'm going to dance at her wedding."

"Whenever that is," I said.

Nelson said, "Tell you what: If we don't run into each other before the camp reunion, then I'll make a big entrance. I'll crash the party and demand one dance for old times' sake."

"When you were nothing but pals," I said.

"You've never crashed a party in your life," said Kris.

Nelson said, "I'm your older brother. I was crashing parties before you were born."

"Oh yeah? Name one."

"This one, Jack," Nelson said.

We left him at the entrance to a damp, dim passageway, its vinyl wallpaper peeling. Watching him, the Ivy League math teacher in his pressed khakis, recede into the camp counselors' tunnel, I harrumphed, "Some change of scenery she's offering. It breaks my heart."

"I offered to talk to Estelle," said Kris. He found my hand and kissed it.

"Go to bed," Nelson yelled back.

TWENTY-TWO

Inasmuch as a dining hall full of pious Jews on Shabbes could create a buzz, there was one at breakfast, and Nelson was its subject.

"Your brother!" cried Avi and Ira, more animated than they'd been when discussing Don Larsen's perfect game. "Did you hear what happened last night? At the pool? He jumped in and saved someone!"

"The indoor pool," said a woman at the next table.

"After services," said Ira, or Avi.

"Who'd he save?" Kris asked.

"An elderly woman," said the other brother.

"A cantor's wife—"

"From Pennsylvania," said another stranger.

"Fully dressed, with heels and a big heavy pocketbook," said someone else.

"He *is* a professional lifeguard," said Kris.

"They should have a lifeguard on duty here, regardless," said the woman one table over.

"Is she okay?" I asked.

"She was more scared than anything else," said a man with a goatee, who was passing by our table.

"Nelson jumped in?" I asked.

"Spread-eagle. With all his clothes on."

"I wasn't there," said a Lupow brother, "but I heard he jumped in without even taking his shoes off."

"He got her out of the pool in a matter of seconds," said the other.

"She was no little slip of a thing, either," said the man with the goatee.

"A big individual," added the woman by his side.

"Who doesn't swim," said a Lupow.

"She's from outside Philadelphia," said Victor, arriving with many juices and a vat of canned figs.

"Her husband doesn't swim, either," said the first woman.

"Where's your brother now?" Victor asked.

"Must be sleeping," said Kris.

"He deserves it," another piped up.

"He desoives breakfast in *bed*," said an old man. "On a silver tray."

"With a medal," said Victor.

"It'll probably make the papers," said Ira, or Avi.

"What's his name again?" someone asked.

"Nelson Berry," Kris said. "He's my brother."

"He's a teacher," said Victor.

"A swimming teacher?"

"Mathematics," said Victor.

"He was so modest," said a pretty woman with a perfect flip to her wig. "He said it was instinctive."

"We were there," said her husband. "He flew into the water, never giving a thought to his own safety."

"He's a very experienced lifeguard," I said.

"At the Inn at Lake Devine," plugged Kris.

"What was she doing by the pool?" I asked.

"Just walking by! Oneg Shabbat was in the Coney Island Room. She lost her balance."

"Her pressure," I heard.

"Her sugar."

"Her inner ear."

"It would have been *some* lawsuit," said a bald man in pinstripes, "if a guest of this hotel had drowned on her way to Oneg Shabbat."

"She was lucky Nelson was there," I said.

"Hal Feldman is the lucky one," said the well-dressed man.

𝒩elson, pressing a pillow over his face, denied the heroics. "I couldn't help myself," he groaned. "All those years—I didn't even think. I saw her go in, and I went flying like a jerk, shoes and all. They're ruined. It wasn't even over her head."

"Everybody's talking about you," I said. "They're saying you saved her life."

"Someone screamed," he said, "and next thing I knew . . ." He pantomimed a plane taking off.

"We brought you a danish and a muffin," said Kris.

I looked around the austere barracks and saw nothing but a toiletry kit that was exactly like Kris's. "Where's your stuff?" I asked.

He sat up and arranged the raggedy white thermal blanket at his waist. Same chest-hair swirls as his brother, I noticed. "In the laundry," he said.

I asked if his suit was ruined.

"They should buy you a new one," said Kris.

"That was discussed," said Nelson.

"With whom?"

"With the grateful management," he said.

"With Linette?" I asked.

Nelson said, with a teacher's wide-eyed irony, "That's right, Natalie. I discussed it with Linette."

"She saw you fish out the cantor's wife?"

"Wait," said Kris. "Did she, like, just happen to be there?"

"It was after services."

"You went to services?"

"We talked after I got back from town."

"You called her?" asked Kris.

Nelson gestured around the room. "Do you see a phone?"

We saw six sets of bunk beds and twelve unpainted pine bureaus with initials gouged into every surface.

"She just showed up?" I asked.

Nelson finished the danish and peeled the paper from the muffin. He said finally, "She came over to say hello and to pay her respects."

"And?" said Kris.

"And nothing. We had a lot to catch up on. . . . You didn't bring coffee, did you?"

I said, "No, sorry. Did she look the same?"

"Her hair's a little more out of control. She used to iron it."

"She came here to talk?" asked Kris, "when there's ten lobbies upstairs and a couple of hundred couches?"

"First of all, what is the big deal? Second of all, she's engaged to be married."

"But—" Kris tried.

"So was I until very recently."

"We know—" I began.

"I'd appreciate it if you two could accept that we're just friends. It'll make things a lot easier for everyone concerned if you drop it."

"I'm sorry," I said.

"How'd you get from here to the swimming pool?" asked Kris.

Having temporarily forgotten that spectacle, Nelson groaned anew. "We were hungry, and they have some kind of reception after the services, so we went up for some brownies."

"Then the fat lady slipped," said Kris.

"And the rest is Halseeyon history," I said. "How Nelson Berry became the savior of the Jews."

"Without even trying," said Nelson.

"Without even converting," I said.

*A*lthough Hal Feldman had gone directly to sleep after *shul*, he heard from Minna Gitlow personally about the nice young man who helped her out of the pool and went back in for her purse. She had forgotten his name but would like to buy him a box of hand-kerchiefs or some almond bark.

"You leave that to me," said Mr. Feldman.

After sundown on Saturday, before the semiformal camp dance, there was a ceremony in the main dining room. The cantor-husband of the near casualty sang "God Bless America." Mr. Feld-man introduced "my daughter, the real boss, who needs no introduction," garnering applause for Linette, in a long skirt that looked patched together from faded quilts, and a cowgirl blouse. "The man we're honoring tonight is going to say it was nothing," she began. "He's going to insist Mrs. Gitlow wasn't in serious dan-ger, but that isn't the point. He acted without regard to his dignity, his clothes, his shoes, or his watch. And while he will probably never forgive me, we couldn't let his act go unrecognized.

"I've known Nelson Berry since the first day of classes, nineteen sixty-six, at Cornell University," she told the assembly, winning ap-plause for that alone. "I know that the simple act of jumping fully clothed into cold water is true to his character. He is an unselfish young man, who left the world of business to become a teacher, and I am very proud to call him friend."

Nelson came forward, head down, wearing a borrowed corduroy jacket and managing to appear both pleased and mortified.

From a black leatherette box, Linette took a silver whistle hang-ing on a blue grosgrain ribbon. "As soon as the jeweler opens on Monday, he will engrave 'For Nelson Berry with gratitude, from the Feldman Family, March 21, 1975. The Halseeyon,' " she said. They faced each other, smiled fondly. She slipped the ribbon over his head and, in un-Olympic tradition, kissed Nelson firmly on the lips. I nudged Kris, who nudged me back. I looked at Mr. Feldman, who had no reaction other than an emcee's delight. Linette ges-tured toward the microphone: a few words, please, to your adoring public.

Like a pro, Nelson let the ovation subside. "I teach math, so even though I have to stand up in front of an audience every day, I never have to come up with anything witty or profound," he began, to audible cooing. "I was only acting on autopilot, and let's face it: I ignored the first rule of waterfront safety, the thing that's drummed into you from the first day, which is: Reach, Throw, Row, Go. So if you're going to thank anyone, thank the Red Cross, who certified me in junior and senior lifesaving. Or thank my parents, who employed me as a lifeguard for a dozen summers." He paused, checked with Linette, then added winningly, "I might as well plug my family's establishment, the Inn at Lake Devine, in Gilbert, Vermont, with apologies to Mr. Feldman. I mean, it's not in the same league with the Halseeyon, but please take a ride up to see us during foliage season, and tell them that Nelson sent you."

Linette started the applause. Waiters rocketed out of the kitchen doors with pitchers of coffee as pastry chefs marched to the buffet table, each a trustee of one cake, one pie, one torte.

"They're gorgeous," I whispered. "How do you make baked alaska without ice cream?"

"Let's find out," said Kris.

The maître d' was chanting as he directed traffic: "Exactly the same at both tables, ladies and gentlemen. Two tables, no waiting." Kris yelled for Nelson to join us in line. He shook a few hands on his way over, and sagged when he got there, as if to say, Not much longer now.

"Nice job," I said, handing him a plate.

"Strudel?" asked the first server.

Ahead of Nelson, a woman in a blue lace dress, with hair the smoky gray of cat fur, turned to speak. "What's the name of your hotel again?" she asked.

"The Inn at Lake Devine."

"Is that near Rutland?"

"Very close. Do you know Rutland?"

"I have cousins there," she said. She held her plate out to the chef overseeing the Linzertorte. "Is it a white hotel with a big porch and a lawn that goes down to the water?"

"That's us," said Nelson.

She paused before asking, "And how long has your family owned it?"

"All my life," Nelson said, with the polish of a spelling bee finalist. "And my grandparents before that."

"My cousins told me about you," said the woman, minus the smile of a satisfied customer.

"Baklava?" barked a chef, meaning, Move along, lady.

"Hope you'll drop by next time you're visiting your cousins," Nelson tried.

"German apple schmarren?" asked the next server.

"I think not," said the woman.

The Justices Brandeis and Frankfurter Conference Room had been transformed, in senior-prom fashion, into Camp Applegate's moonlit paddock. An abridged Sonny Cirrell's Orchestra, wearing tuxedos and cowboy hats, played teen love songs with a summer theme—The Beach Boys, The Carpenters, The Serendipity Singers, Jan and Dean, Paul and Paula, Chad and Jeremy—alternating sets with a fiddler. Kris and I sat out the square dancing, but were coaxed off our bale of hay for the mandatory shoe dance. A blue-eyed, bearded man whose name tag said BOBBY ROTHBERG, '59–'67 picked my purple suede pump from the pile and claimed me for a dance, which lasted only until Kris cut in smoothly and unapologetically. Nelson, I noticed, pounced on Linette's red snakeskin boot, pretending to be surprised at who was wearing its mate.

As the band played "See You in September," I watched them carefully. Linette's arms circled Nelson's neck; his fingers locked behind her waist. I saw Linette smiling at Nelson and Nelson smiling back. I saw Nelson mouthing the words to the song. I saw that his hands rested one centimeter below the boundary of pure friendship; and when the music ended, they didn't let go.

$\mathcal{T}$WENTY-THREE

$\mathcal{M}$y mother screeched her relief into the phone. I said, "I refuse to believe you were seriously worried about me."

"I wasn't," she said, taking gulps of air, "but your father was frantic."

"I'm fine," I told her. "Now we're going up to the Inn for a night or two."

There was a knotty silence on her end.

"Mom?"

"You're getting to be quite the Gypsy."

"Some people's children travel to different continents, let alone different states. They take jobs on the Alaska pipeline. And their parents don't consider it a betrayal. They encourage it."

"What states have you been to?" she asked.

"Just New York. The Catskills."

"Oh." She sounded relieved.

I told her I'd be back.

"Your phone is in," she said. "Do you want the number?"

I said, "You have it memorized?"

"Excuse me. I jotted it down, if that's allowed."

"I won't be calling there," I said.

She paused. "You might want to give it to people. Your friends."

I said, "Okay, shoot."

"Are you in love with this boy?"

I said, not quite truthfully, "I don't know."

$\mathcal{A}$s a mutinous daughter myself, I would have agreed to be Linette's beard, to hear her admissions and protect her confidences, but she wasn't asking that of me. I stood obediently at her side, improvising, as she fashioned a story for her skeptical father and unwell mother in the kitchen of the Feldman homestead, where the doilied, antimacassared look of Tilly's regime coexisted with the chromes and turquoises of the moment.

"Don't you work?" Mr. Feldman asked me.

I said, "I'm an executive chef. Currently—"

"Monday's her day off," Linette supplied.

"Aren't you the new bride? Married to the brother of the . . . what's his name?" He pantomimed something vague—part ruined sport jacket, part dog paddle.

"Not *her*, Pop," said Linette easily. "That was someone else. This is Natalie, from the reunion."

"What are you going to do in Boston?" asked Dolly Feldman in a thin, bedridden voice. She was eating breakfast in brown silk Chinese pajamas, a clear tube running from prongs in her nostrils to a flesh-colored, humming tank.

"See some other friends from camp," her daughter said.

"And college," I added.

"Did you go to Cornell too?"

"Not as an undergrad," I said.

"Maybe you'll look for a dress," said her mother.

"She's too busy running around to plan a wedding," Mr. Feldman grunted.

Linette said, "I plan plenty of weddings. Too many."

"When was the last time you took a few days off?" I asked, Best Supporting Actress.

Linette was standing behind her mother. She put her hands—

ringless, I noticed—on Dolly's bony shoulders and proclaimed, "This is a *resort*, Natalie. People who are lucky enough to live at a resort never have to leave. Our lives are an endless holiday."

"I want your number in case we need to reach you," said Dolly, holding her mandarin collar against an imagined draft.

"I'll be back tomorrow, Ma. Tuesday at the latest."

"Where in Boston?" asked Dolly.

"Newton."

"Do you live at home?"

"Of course," Linette answered for me.

"Take something. Everybody likes coffee cake."

"Already thought of that," said Linette.

"Nice meeting you both," I said.

"Likewise," said Dolly wanly.

"Come back when you can use the outdoor pools," said Mr. Feldman.

For appearance's sake—and just for a short first leg—we divided up, boys in one car, girls in the other.

I said, "I guess you couldn't just tell your parents that you were going to Vermont."

"They're vague," she said, "but not completely out of it. The hotel part registered during Nelson's remarks last night."

"And that wouldn't be kosher—visiting the hotel of your old friend?"

"I'm engaged," she said simply.

I turned down the music to ask, "Where's your ring?"

"I don't wear it all the time."

The guys passed us in the VW bus, honking and grinning. We waved and signaled, Yes, we know; passenger swap coming up.

"When don't you wear it?" I asked.

"I leave it in the vault when I'm dressed like this, or when I'm negotiating with a vendor or an employee union, or when I'm going to a place where I think people will judge me by a big, ostentatious diamond ring—people who vacation in a small Yankee inn with no frills, no midnight buffets—"

"And no Jews."

"Exactly."

"You noticed?"

"I guessed."

"Because?"

"The place, the guests, the feel of it . . . something in her eyes."

"Mrs. Berry's?"

Linette widened her eyes and smiled Ingrid's unblinking, slightly deranged smile.

"Screw her," I said. "This is nineteen seventy-five."

Linette intoned with perfect pomposity, "Our Israelite brethren are welcome anywhere in our fair land."

We both laughed. With no outsiders in the car, and our passage assured, we could.

*I*ngrid, dressed in camel-hair trousers and a matching Perry Como cardigan, said only, "Welcome," in the same rote way she greeted all guests, as if the word itself did the job. Linette was reintroduced from 1968, recast in her most favorable Cornell light: hotelier, classmate, and thoughtful pal who had extended a hand as soon as she read about Robin in *The Alumni News.*

"Of course I remember you," said Ingrid, many degrees more charming for Linette, rich girl and Halseeyon scion, than for me. I was greeted coolly with, "You're looking well, Natalie. We have a new cook. Did Kris tell you? She has a degree in nutrition, and so far—" Ingrid crossed her fingers and wagged them prayerfully.

"Kris didn't tell me," I said.

"Kris didn't realize she was anything but a stop-gap measure," said Kris, his tone reproachful.

"She's very much at home in this kind of setting," said Ingrid.

"A nursing-home kitchen is not a hotel dining room," said Kris. "I wish you had talked to me about this."

Ingrid's round face was a portrait of unexpressed annoyance. Who do you think you are that I would consult you about a personnel matter? I read in her eyes. Above them, a microscopic arching of her brow was the unspoken corollary: When was I supposed to consult you? As you were commandeering my company vehicle to God-knows-where with misguided romantic ambitions?

I asked Ingrid how the guests liked the new cook.

"March is quiet," she said.

"Any complaints?"

"No more than usual."

"What about compliments?"

Linette spoke up for the first time. "How many entrées do you offer at dinner?"

"Two," said Ingrid, the number ending in a purse of the lips.

"Two?" Linette repeated, as if Ingrid had said, "Zero."

"We've always done it that way. No one's ever gone hungry."

Kris volunteered that at the Halseeyon there were six or eight full-fledged offerings and—get this, Ma—you could order as many as you wanted. You could get all of them—take one bite, try the next.

Ingrid smiled her tight, superior smile. "The Catskills are known for that. Our guests don't come here expecting every meal to be a feast, the way New Yorkers do. It's not the raison d'être of their vacations."

Linette remarked, in a voice full of counterfeit wonder, "Ya know, I've heard of that."

"Me too," I said.

"I've read about it in the literature," she added.

"What literature?" asked Ingrid.

"Hotel management—food customs and preferences, broken down by region and ethnicity. Jews, Italians, and Lebanese love to eat. The French do too, but not over here. They hate margarine and sliced white bread."

"Ouch," said Kris.

I listened to Linette addressing Ingrid in a breezy, almost imperceptibly disdainful way, which I now wanted to adopt. "Haven't you found that to be true, Natalie?" Linette was asking. "That the average American diner has a less sophisticated palate than the average French peasant?"

I said, Yes, *absolument*. Inspired, I turned to Ingrid. "I've always thought you could use a little *zalts un fefer* in your meal planning."

"I beg your pardon?" asked Ingrid.

"Literally? 'Salt and pepper.' "

"But," Linette amplified, "when grandmothers say it, it's disparaging, as in 'No excitement, no personality.' " She and I nodded: Total agreement; excellent translation, by the way.

Nelson had been standing slightly apart, flipping through mail that looked, from its hand-addressed square envelopes, to be stockpiled sympathy cards. Finally, he asked, "Where's Dad?"

"Kris"—Ingrid actually snapped her fingers—"go find your father."

"Where is he?"

"In the woods," she answered, as if such a thing were obvious and annoying.

"Where?"

"He saw some mushrooms he wanted. Out back. Yell. He'll hear you."

"I'll go with you," I said.

We cut through the kitchen. At the spot where we had once wiped dishes and hidden from mourners, two women in hair nets were pounding cube steaks. Kris made a quick left into the pantry, me in tow, and found a familiar linoleum-topped counter to maneuver me against.

"What if they come in?" I asked, my lips on his.

"Ten seconds," he murmured.

It was sweet and almost bashful, as if it were that lost kiss; as if we hadn't just spent three nights in a huge round bed, sleeping in a knot, exhausted from what we had both confessed was sexual gusto of an overdue, unquenchable, and highly compatible variety.

I whispered, "What about tonight?"

"What *about* tonight?"

"The sleeping arrangements?"

Kris said, "You're talking to the night manager."

We stayed that way for another minute. I said, "I feel something."

Kris closed his eyes and said with a grimace, "Okay. I'm thinking about ice fishing." He jiggled each leg in turn and did a few shallow knee bends. "I'm ready," he said. I checked and said, "You're fine." I couldn't resist—one more kiss to a soft stretch of neck.

"No more," he said. "Not until I can do something about it."

I touched only his hair, lifting one hank that was across his forehead. "I'm crazy about you," I said.

*M*r. Berry, with a sad, chewed-up, feminine-looking basket at his side and a trowel in his hand, was gingerly prying a clump of small brown mushrooms from the base of an overturned stump. "Why, look who's here," he said with a shy grin, rising and exposing wet knees on his shabby corduroys. He looked past his son to put his arms around me for a hug. Over his shoulder, I smiled at Kris, who shrugged as if to say, Who knows?

"We were sent to fetch you," I said.

"Nelson brought Linette," said Kris.

"Linette?" said Mr. Berry.

"Feldman. From Cornell."

I knew that without me present Mr. Berry would have said— benignly enough, merely for identification—"The Jewish girl?" but said instead, "Of course."

"We were up at her family's place in the Catskills."

"Busman's holiday," I said.

"Did you all come together?"

"I stopped in Newton to get Natalie—remember Linette called

here looking for Nelson?—and I tried to convince him that a change of scenery would do him good."

"Did you succeed?"

I answered first, playing against Mr. Berry's unswerving innocence. "Kris? Would you call our trip to the Catskills a success?"

He replied, "Dad. All I can say is—yes, it was a success. Beyond my fondest hopes." He turned to me. "Is that what you were going to say, Nat?"

I said, "God, was it a success."

"What happened?" said Mr. Berry, nodding his sweetly befuddled encouragement.

"I don't think you want all the details," said Kris. He touched his father's shoulder, signaling him to lead the way on the path. "They'll be wondering what took us so long," he said, with a quick, private adjustment to make me laugh.

"*T*his was the night they got engaged," Ingrid was saying, passing a snapshot to Linette. She dipped into a shoe box and selected another photo. "This is the engagement party at the Fifes' house in Farmington. . . . This is our Gretel. With Robin." She looked away quickly in phony, stoic silence as the three of us came through the kitchen door into the meeting room.

"She offered," Linette said helplessly, a photo in each hand.

"Let's put those away now," Mr. Berry said gently. "It's much too soon."

"Do you remember our Gretel?" Ingrid asked Linette.

"Of course I do. Blond ringlets and saucer eyes."

"I'm not usually emotional," Ingrid said, "but this is the first time I've seen Nelson since New Year's, so it makes it that much fresher."

"Why look at pictures if they're going to upset you?" Nelson asked impatiently. He walked over to the hot plate, a new addition to the bar, and poured an inch of overcooked black coffee into a discolored mug.

"Maybe we shouldn't have descended without warning," Kris said. "Although I didn't think it was necessary—a Sunday in March."

Linette helped herself to coffee, and offered it all around.

"We're spending the night," said Nelson. "I'm taking a sick day tomorrow."

Kris said, "And Natalie might stay for a couple of days."

"Have you found work?" Ingrid asked me.

"As a matter of fact, I have."

"I see," said Ingrid. Then, after a pause, "Are you on holiday?"

"I start soon."

"Not only does she have a job," said Kris, "but she'll be running the show."

Ingrid wasn't interested. She turned to Linette. "I assume you work for your family's hotel chain?"

"Chain?" She laughed. "No chain; one big white elephant with two eighteen-hole golf courses, but it's all one joint."

"You're confusing the Feldmans with the Hiltons," said Nelson.

"I thought—" Ingrid began. "Must have been another classmate."

Linette said, in her now-familiar born-yesterday voice, "You wouldn't be confusing me with Jodie Levine, by any chance? She was in our program. Her father owned a bunch of HoJo's."

"No," said Ingrid firmly.

"That happens," said Linette. She shot me a wry look that said, Among the *goyim*.

Mr. Berry announced, in dotty-aunt fashion, "We're getting listed in a guidebook that A.A. puts out."

Kris laughed.

Ingrid spat out, "Triple-A. Not A.A."

"What do they say about us?" Kris asked.

"We won't know until it's published, but I imagine flattering things, or we wouldn't be listed."

"Maybe it'll help," said Kris.

I could see the business bulb flashing above Linette's head. "What's March like?" she inquired chummily.

"Depends on the snow," said Kris.

"Forty, fifty percent occupancy?"

Ingrid said, "The thaw came early this year."

"Thirty percent," said Kris.

I asked, "Any chance the double with the yellow-chintz head-board is free?"

Ingrid straightened her spine. She looked at me as if I had asked her for the deed to her hotel.

"I'll check," said Kris, walking over to the cubbyholes behind the registration desk. "Empty!" he called, waving the key.

Ingrid barely reacted.

Mr. Berry said, "Let your mother figure out the sleeping arrangements. That's her domain."

Linette murmured something to Nelson.

Nelson said, "If the room's empty, what's to figure out?"

*D*inner was a choice between Swiss steak and a roasted leg of spring chicken. Salad was a surgical wedge of iceberg lettuce dribbled with orange dressing. There was no excitement in the room: People cut their meat with a slow intersection of knife and fork and chewed as if counting bites. Unpardonably, there were instant mashed potatoes and frozen mixed vegetables, with their telltale crinkle cuts. I waited until dessert was served—Indian pudding or Floating Island—before saying, "Frankly, Ingrid—and I know you didn't ask for my opinion—this new cook has no feel for food."

She broke off a pale piece of Parker House roll and chewed it prissily. "At least this is well balanced and nicely presented."

Linette, in a plaid jumper that looked like a parochial-school uniform, said, "I have to agree with Natalie, Mrs. Berry. She's talking about a whole lot more than presentation. Nothing is more important at a hotel than the food."

"Look around," I said quietly.

"Where?" said the Berrys.

"No one looks happy. It's the look of patients eating hospital food."

Ingrid looked to her flesh and blood, begging silently for help. *Was* this hospital fare? Were her patrons unhappy? *Is* nothing more important at a hotel than its food?

"Can Mrs. Crowley do any better?" I asked. "I mean, is she more creative than this, but she thinks this is what you want?"

"Is it really bad?" asked Mr. Berry.

I heard the word *shmendrik* in my mother's voice but dismissed it out of loyalty.

"Dad," said Kris. "*Instant* mashed potatoes?"

"I don't discuss these kinds of decisions in public, ever," said Ingrid, leaving teeth marks in each word.

"You're right," said Linette. "Absolutely." She took a spoonful of Indian pudding, having been assured by Ingrid that it wasn't made with lard. "At least one table should be smiling."

"Maybe while Natalie's here she could give Mrs. Crowley some tips," said Mr. Berry.

Under her breath, trying to smile, Ingrid hissed, "I said *later.*"

We sipped our tea and weak coffee. "What's on tap for tonight?" asked Linette.

"Steve and Eydie," said Nelson, at the same moment Kris said, "Simon Says."

"Nelson," murmured Ingrid, after another boisterous round of Catskills jokes. "May I speak with you privately?"

"Just say it, Ma."

Ingrid placed her cup carefully in its saucer and did an eyeball sweep of the room. "We have returning guests. They know the family; many know the Fifes. They know that you're in mourning."

"So he's not supposed to be out in public, enjoying himself?" Kris demanded. "When does Emily Post say he can laugh again?"

"That's not what Mother's saying," said Mr. Berry.

"It doesn't look right," Ingrid whispered.

Linette asked, "Is it because Nelson's here with a woman and it looks like he's on a date?"

Nelson said, "I wasn't married. I'm not a widower."

"Nelson and I are friends, Mrs. Berry," said Linette.

Ingrid blinked hard and said, "*I* know that. It never occurred to me that you were anything but friends."

Kris looked at me, seeking permission, I thought, to work us into a declaration. I signaled, Don't.

"I have no patience for this," said Nelson.

"Why would that never have occurred to you, Mom?" Kris asked. "What is it about Linette that made you rule her out, categorically?"

I thought of saying, "Isn't it a moot point? Linette is engaged to Joel Taub. She has a ring. Just tell her that." But I waited, wondering what was next and how he'd word the showdown: You don't like Jews. You never did. One Jew girlfriend in this family is enough.

"Let her be," her husband said. "She's had a terrible week."

With only that much mercy shown her, Ingrid said, "Linette and"—she hesitated, as if she'd forgotten my name— ". . . *Natalie* are welcome here, whatever the reason."

"Thank you," I said.

"Thanks," said Linette.

"The guests can go to hell," Nelson sputtered.

Ingrid stood, but never raised her voice. "I'm saying good night. I can't seem to say or do anything right as far as my children are concerned, so I'm leaving you to your . . . party."

We watched her make the rounds of the dining hall, placing her hand lightly on the backs of guests' chairs, saying a few gracious words in her pinched fashion, and disappearing out the front door.

Linette finally lit a cigarette, inhaled, and exhaled as if on an overdue break from an exhausting job.

Mr. Berry asked, "Was that necessary?"

"Yes," Kris said.

Our gray-nylon-uniformed waitress appeared and asked if she should clear Mrs. Berry's place.

"Do you know what I was getting at?" Kris asked his father as soon as the waitress had left. "Did you grasp the fact that I was referring to Linette being Jewish?"

"I thought that might have been—"

"And to your habit of turning Jews away before there were laws against it?"

Mr. Berry looked down at his plate, then up at me. "We've had many families of the Jewish faith through the years . . . lovely people."

"Not my people," I said. "It was only by chance that I slipped in."

"You took Jews starting when?" asked Linette.

"I never—" Mr. Berry tried, stopped, tried again: "I didn't make the rules. I didn't even register guests—that was her domain."

"You never noticed there weren't any Jews around? You never got a call from the Anti-Defamation League?" Linette asked.

"I never answered the phones. I worked outside. Not just the grounds, but the outbuildings and the waterfront. I did all the painting myself, and grooming the trails, and all the upkeep on the dock. Of course, the boys helped when they were home, but I had plenty to do without answering a phone or mailing a letter. We weren't so big that we could say yes to everyone."

"Is that what Mrs. Berry told you? That you were small so you could pick and choose whomever you wanted?"

"She said it was our home."

"So?" said Kris. "What's that supposed to mean?"

"I thought it meant that we could hold our rooms for the same people year after year, because they were like family . . . like the Fifes."

"He doesn't get it," said Nelson.

"It's not that complicated," said Linette. She turned to Mr. Berry. "A hotel is not a home. It's a business. You can't turn people away because of race or religion or anything like that."

"We weren't the only ones," he said.

"No kidding," said Linette. "Why do you think we had to start our own hotels?"

I was on my feet by now, plotting my getaway through the scraping of plates. No one responded until I heard a plaintive, "Natalie?"

"What's she supposed to say, Dad?" asked Kris. "All is forgiven?"

"Maybe I could tell her I'm sorry," said Mr. Berry.

I answered him, knowing I was disappointing Linette: "Remember how you sent me that book about mushrooms and you wrote, 'Keep it until you come back'? That's not what an anti-Semite says to a little Jewish girl. That's how I knew I was welcome."

He released the whimper he'd been stifling.

"Jesus," said Nelson. "Not in the dining room."

Kris hurried away and returned in thirty seconds with a glass. "Brandy," he said.

"Bring the bottle," said Nelson.

We tried to resuscitate Mr. Berry. We told him stories about what goes on in big, splashy hotels on the American Plan—dancing, music, and magic every night. He listened, even asked questions about their grounds, their perennials, their flowering shrubs; but I could see he was embarrassed and distressed. After only a few sips of brandy, he announced he was going to bed, adding anxiously, "You're still planning to spend the night?"

"We are," I said.

"You're all set? Kris, you'll give Natalie that room she wanted?"

"Sure."

"And you boys will stay in the Inn tonight?" he asked sweetly, absent any subtext other than "Mother and I need the little house to ourselves."

I felt Kris's stockinged foot slide onto mine under the table. We nodded solemnly.

"Good night, then," said Mr. Berry.

TWENTY-FOUR

When Linette and I sauntered down to breakfast, trying to look like girlfriends who had giggled into the night rather than like outside agitators, no one at the family table took note. Clearly, there was a conference in progress—that is, until Ingrid saw us and clammed up.

"Everyone's going to find out sooner or later," Nelson said.

"What are we going to find out?" asked Linette, her curly hair bound into two sprouting pigtails by mismatched novelties.

"Family matters," said Ingrid.

"No problem," said Linette, taking the empty chair between Nelson and his mother. "Good morning," she said to him. "Sleep okay?"

"Off and on," he said.

I sat down between Kris and Mr. Berry, and touched Kris's knee underneath the table, which elicited only a blink.

Linette consulted the chalkboard, then asked Ingrid if everything was cooked on the same grill.

Ingrid said, "I don't understand."

"Like, eggs and home fries and pancakes *with* the bacon?"

"Oh," said Ingrid. "I see what you mean."

"Yes," I said. "They are."

"You can make a special request," said Ingrid. "Or you could ask for your eggs poached or boiled in the shell."

"We're very accommodating," added Kris, still unsmiling.

I assumed Ingrid had asked who had slept where and that Kris had refused to sugarcoat his answer. We drank coffee and worked at our grapefruit halves; didn't speak, except to note that eight inches of snow had fallen on Mount Mansfield—too bad the trails around Gilbert got only rain.

My eggs, ordered over-easy, arrived with hard yolks and a scoop of cottage potatoes. "They can redo the eggs," Kris offered, but I demurred.

"Is everything okay?" Linette finally asked the silent table.

The boys looked to the issuer of the gag order.

"Mother," said Mr. Berry. "Don't you think we can talk freely in front of these girls?"

Ingrid, furious, bounced a triangle of toast back to her plate, the worst display of temper I had seen since she caught me in the kitchen about to kiss her son. She shot up, knocking her chair back on one leg, which Nelson caught and righted, but not before his mother rushed away.

Guests looked over, then away. Mr. Berry said softly to me and Linette, "It's not your visit. Please believe me. She has a lot on her mind."

Nelson finally spoke, impatiently, and with an economy of style no doubt polished in parent-teacher conferences.

"Gretel's pregnant," he said.

I looked to Kris for confirmation. He nodded.

"She'll be getting married, of course," said Mr. Berry.

"When?" I asked.

"As soon as possible," said Kris. "The baby's due in September."

"How old is Gretel?" Linette asked.

"Twenty," I said.

"Nineteen," said Nelson.

"Nineteen can work out," I said. "My mother was nineteen."

"It's going to be a small affair," said Mr. Berry, "but even so . . ."

"Who's the father?" asked Linette.

"A nice boy," allowed Mr. Berry. "From a good family."

"He's a jerk," Kris burst out. "A zero."

"Why do you say that?" asked Mr. Berry.

"It's Chip Fife," said Nelson.

I told Linette the whole distasteful story—the midnight rendezvous at the end of my bed, the Grecian goddess getup, the fact that I had offended Gretel when I'd asked if she was using birth control. I was secretly delighted that she'd been caught in her solace-and-companionship lie, but couldn't voice my satisfaction in front of the family. The news depressed Kris for several reasons, beginning with his antipathy for the groom—apparently lean, tall Chip had been the worst guest tormentor during Kris's fat phase—and ending, simply, with Gretel, who for all her failings and airs, was still his baby sister.

Nelson was also dismayed, but for a reason more internal than brotherly: The Fifes would forever be the grandparents of his niece or nephew, hovering on the edges of his life.

"*Mekhutonim* after all," Kris confirmed joylessly.

"Why so glum?" Linette asked the boys. We had the meeting room to ourselves, along with a bottle of scotch that Kris had smuggled from the bar. Linette was marching in place and doing jumping jacks, her daily routine, in a raggedy warm-up outfit. "Sounds to me like Gretel got exactly what she wanted."

Oh yeah? they said. Chip Fife? That upstanding citizen? Like she knows how many girls he tried to screw in our boathouse?

"Don't all guys do that?" asked Linette. "Didn't you guys?"

"*Here?*" said Nelson.

"Us?" said Kris.

"They're being protective," I explained to Linette. "We don't know about this because we don't have brothers."

"I can't handle the Fifes," said Nelson. "Especially here, for a wedding."

"Maybe they'll elope," said Linette.

"*Gretel?*" Kris said. "Who still plays with her bride dolls?"

"He's right," said Nelson. "She'll want an extravaganza. And don't forget our mother will be taking great pains to disguise the fact that it's a shotgun wedding."

"Look," Linette said, now rubbing energetically between Nelson's shoulder blades. "You don't have to *go* to their stupid wedding and see the Fifes sobbing. Gretel's got another brother. Kris will go, right? And be an usher. And if anyone asks, he'll say, 'Well, you understand. This is a little rough on Nelson.' "

I couldn't help myself. I added, " 'He's very sensitive about mourners fucking in the back of the church during a funeral.' "

Linette looked at me, bit her lip. We all looked at Nelson. There was a shine to his eyes that could have gone either way, and some indecipherable emotion pulled at the corners of his mouth.

We stared, poised to do what we had to do. One choked note escaped.

"Go ahead, Jack," Kris said gently. "Laugh."

𝓛inette and I went down to the water alone and sat on the bird-stained dock in bleached canvas chairs. The morning rain had stopped, but a mist had settled between the mountains and us, obscuring views of anything except the shore. Linette said she was leaving; she didn't think it was right to stay at a once-restricted hotel and break bread with the chief offender, no matter what our being there said about her change in policy.

I asked, "What difference would leaving make? She'll never draw the inference that your leaving is a protest."

"She'll draw the inference just fine if I spell it out for her."

I told her I'd been coming here ever since I knew it existed, first in my imagination and eventually in the flesh. I said, "I guess I'm of the temperament that it's better to muscle my way to the lunch counter than stage a silent walkout."

"You're of the temperament," she countered, "to forgive and forget."

I said, "I walked out once before, and it was a mistake."

"Because of Kris, you mean."

"I mean, what counts is between me and Kris, not me and Ingrid, not me and my parents."

"That's not true," she said. "It never was. And if you think it is . . ." She shook her head—pity for my woeful misapprehension of history.

I waited a few beats; found moth-eaten mittens in Kris's borrowed parka and put them on. I moved my chair an inch closer to her and said, "Okay, hypothetically—and don't bullshit me: Let's say you weren't engaged to Joel, or to anyone, but were a free woman. You're twenty-six years old. You meet a wonderful man and fall in love. He isn't Jewish. You keep it a secret as long as you can and then you tell your parents. What happens, after the obvious?"

"What happens? They go nuts. They wail, they call the *rebbe*. My father says he'll never be able to see me again; they'll have to cover the mirrors, tear their clothes, sit *shiva*, which must be why God gave him four daughters—so he'd have three left after I rip out his heart and spit into the chest cavity. Et cetera. My mother would drop dead, literally. She'd have nitroglycerine under her tongue right now if she knew what you were selling."

I asked what she thought I was selling besides freedom of association.

"A romance with your boyfriend's brother."

"Is that so far-fetched?"

"Has he said anything to you?"

"Nelson has the same response that you have to all of my theories: 'We're just friends.' "

"We *are* friends," she said softly. "That really is true."

I asked, after a careful silence, "How ill is your mother?"

"Very."

"And she wants to see you settled."

"What she wants," said Linette, "is to have one more production—one more champagne fountain and one more night with Peter Duchin's orchestra."

"Is that what you want?"

"I'm trying to decide."

I stood up and said, "I have to get something. Save my seat." I cut across the lawn to the kitchen entrance, retrieved the house keys from my room—still undisturbed by a chambermaid—and returned to the dock. The larger silver one, I explained, is for Mr. Zinler's back door and the brass one unlocks the room at the top of the stairs.

"What for?"

"More time. Another night."

Without the argument I expected, she took the keys. She stared straight ahead at the fogged-in shore, releasing and reclamping her largest barrette. "Single or double?" I heard her murmur.

"Double. A Murphy bed. There's clean sheets in a cardboard box somewhere."

She continued to stare in what I thought was uncharacteristic, dreamy fashion, until she asked, "Any off-street parking?"

I knew it was as near as she would come to confiding in me, so I said only, "Yes, plenty," swallowing my urge to advise that Providence, at sunup, would only take an hour.

"I'll probably rent a car after Nelson drops me off."

I added, "It's not just selfishness on my part. I'd be rooting for the rabbi if I thought you loved him."

Linette put the keys in her coat pocket. "You'll tell me how to get there," she said.

$\mathcal{B}$efore Nelson and Linette left, they walked over to the little white house to say good-bye. Still red-eyed from breakfast, Ingrid delivered something like a speech, which Linette thought had the sons' fingerprints all over it. "I hope you know that I never meant to hurt anyone's feelings," Ingrid began.

"Do you mean me in particular," Linette cut in, "or Jews in general? Because you didn't hurt *my* feelings. On the other hand, I can't speak for all the Cohens and Goldbergs you turned away."

Ingrid appealed to Nelson, a look that said, There's no delicacy left in this world. What purpose has this served other than to humiliate me once again? Now you fix it.

When he only stared back, she said rotely, "I appreciate your being such a good friend to Nelson. You're always welcome at the Inn. All of my children's friends are. Anyone who wants to stay here is."

"Just like you're always welcome at our little *kokh-aleyn* in the mountains"—Linette threw back without translation.

"Things will work out for Gretel," Linette continued cheerfully. "She obviously loves this guy, right? Even if he is a jerk. And a baby is good for a hotel."

Nelson picked up their suitcases and led the way gingerly to the door.

"You'll be back for the wedding," his mother said.

"Don't ask me to," he replied.

TWENTY-FIVE

Because it was Mr. Berry and not Ingrid who introduced me in the kitchen as Kris's little friend who had some ideas about pepping up the menu, Mrs. Crowley barely looked up. She went about her business, grating cheese for the next day's Welsh rarebit and reconstituting various powders into liquids. "Ever make cakes from scratch?" I asked, as if it were a new trend I'd read about. "Ever try mixing a good oil and a nice vinegar for a salad dressing? I could whisk up a couple of quarts and leave them with you."

Kris passed through the kitchen every few minutes as he unpacked a liquor delivery, and asked if we two chefs were having a nice time.

"We're talking recipes," I lied.

"I don't have the help to do anything fancy," said Mrs. Crowley, her upper arms shaking from the friction of desiccated cheese against metal.

"Maybe I can help," I said. "What needs to be done for tonight?"

"All done," she said, tight-lipped.

"What are we having?" Kris asked.

"Hot turkey sandwiches and Italian lasagna."

Kris and I exchanged looks down the length of her chipped, white enamel work table. I continued to watch her as if I were interested in her craftsmanship. "It's nice that you take the trouble to grate fresh cheese," I said.

"I don't throw anything out," she said.

"I could make a meat sauce for you, if that would help. For the lasagna."

"That's Natalie," Kris explained. "She thinks cooking is entertainment."

Mrs. Crowley harrumphed as if to say, She would. "Sauce is made." She pointed her chin toward the pantry, home of jumbo cans and gallon jars.

"You know what?" I tried again. "What if I made one extra dish, just to entertain myself? A third option."

"Like what?" she said.

"Mind if I poke around?"

I opened the cooler and saw bricks of margarine, milk crates, egg crates, slabs of bacon, sides of salt pork, a fifty-pound bag of Spanish onions, the requisite bus buckets and stainless-steel pans, cabbages, potatoes, carrots. I asked, trying not to sound judgmental, "Mrs. Crowley? Do you have any other vegetables?"

"Such as?"

I didn't dare pronounce the first five that defiantly crossed my mind—Belgian endive, watercress, *haricots verts*, celery root, artichokes—so I said, "Maybe spinach? Or broccoli?"

"In the freezer," she said primly, as if anyone who called herself a cook should know where vegetables came from.

I opened the freezer and poked around among the plastic sacks of lima beans, brussels sprouts, broccoli spears, chopped spinach, rutabaga, crinkle-cut carrots, crinkle-cut french fries, corn Niblets, peas, pearl onions, and mixed vegetables. "You certainly have a great selection," I said.

She allowed a vain smile. "I have a B.S. in nutrition."

Underneath the sacks, I spotted small clear bags of something not packaged by Birds Eye—flat, stiff strips of something mousy brown. I took out one packet, examined it, recognized its contents. "Mushrooms!" I said.

"Oh," said Mrs. Crowley. "Those are his."

"Can we use them?"

"I sauté them for him first," she said, in a tone that implied, He can't even do that much.

"He usually labels them," said Kris, turning over a plastic bag. "Here we go: 'Honey mushrooms, 10/74, behind Loon Cottage.' "

"What about a nice mushroom bisque?" I asked.

Mrs. Crowley said, "This crowd doesn't go much for mushrooms."

"What if I made a mushroom lasagna? We could write on the chalkboard, 'Lasagna, red or white.' "

Kris was looking dubious: Why bother?

"Nothing too exotic," I promised. "Noodles, cream, Parmesan, ricotta, mozzarella. I season the mushrooms with lemon, salt, and pepper, and make a béchamel—"

"Fine," she snapped.

I said, "Not because you need a third entrée. Just because I'm in the mood. I haven't cooked in weeks—and you know how that gets."

"It's how she relaxes," said Kris.

"I don't have those cheeses," said the cook.

"No problem," said Kris. "I'm going out anyway."

"Honey mushrooms," I said, flapping the plastic bags at him. "I even like their name."

I called mine Lasagna Bianco con Funghi, and, if I say so myself, it was stunning. I resautéed the mushrooms in butter to disguise the taste of cheap margarine, and because Kris brought me farmer's cheese instead of ricotta, the ingredients combined to taste miraculously of blintzes. The top layer caramelized to a finish reminiscent of toasted marshmallows, so that even Mrs. Crowley smiled when I brought it forth and set it down next to hers.

Fortunately, it was a slow Monday. Eight guests selected Italian Lasagna with Meat. Fifteen chose Hot Turkey Sandwich and Dressing with Gravy, Peas, and Cranberry Sauce. Luckily or unluckily, only two diners that Monday night—Natalie Marx and Kristofer Berry—chose the gourmet option.

We ate our squares of creamy white lasagna, pronounced them delicious, drank wine, had a brick each of Neapolitan ice cream, had coffee, felt great, played one game of Nok-Hockey and two games of Ping-Pong in the game room, said conspicuous good nights in front of witnesses, went to our allegedly separate rooms, rendezvoused two hours later at midnight, fell into each other's arms, kissed each other's faces and necks and other exposed stretches of hot skin as our clothes came off, and made love as quietly as we could manage in the face of our urgency and ardor. We had a short, drowsy postcoital conversation, in which we speculated on the likely locations of Nelson and Linette, and discussed our plans to leave the next day, together. Soon afterward, Kris tiptoed down the back stairway, out the delivery entrance, and down the path to the little white house.

At or about three A.M., I was seized by the worst stomach pains of my life. Soon after, Kris's vomiting and groaning woke the Berrys, who suspected food poisoning. Remembering we had eaten identical meals, they rushed over to find me groaning, unable to leave the bathroom, weak, delirious, and begging for water. They called an ambulance and their doctor, who called Poison Control, who located a mushroom expert in the botany department at UVM, who predicted we would—if we survived the acute phase and the honeymoon phase, which was the fingerprint of this poisoning—slip into a coma and die.

Ingrid called my parents. My brother-in-law, the only steady hand, was enlisted to drive the hysterical Marxes north to the community hospital, where we would become doomed medical celebrities. My mother wailed, begged for magic serums, antidotes, transfusions, operations, specialists, and modern medicine. Why couldn't I be airlifted to Children's; no, Beth Israel; to Mass General; to Peter Bent Brigham; to anywhere outside this godforsaken town, with its two G.P.s and no medical schools?—code, for "I want a Jewish doctor."

The mycologist, a bald, smoothly round, and pale man, who looked like a mushroom himself, came the next day and stayed. It was he who played detective, dissecting and analyzing my casserole, examining the remaining unused Baggie, which he personally rescued from the Dumpster after Mrs. Crowley had purged the freezer, her last act before quitting. It was he who found the single Autumn Skullcap—*Galerina autumnalis*—among the harmless *Armillaria mellea;* he who dressed down the already distraught Mr. Berry, ordering him to avoid all little brown mushrooms, because this is what happens when the picker has not carefully examined each and every spore.

The Vermont expert brought in out-of-state experts, who hovered behind the doctors as they caucused in our separate ICU rooms, moving in to interview the victim-chef, read our charts, muse over test results, feel for coldness of the skin, peer into our jaundiced eyes, lobby for tests of the vital organs that were expected to fail. "If recovery occurs," I heard them begin, just outside my door and my semiconsciousness. One loudmouth explained in a hallway caucus that autopsies in these cases reveal necrosis of the liver and kidney. His voice carried to my parents, who thought it was the announcement of my death. Their cries boomeranged back down the hall to my bed, and pitched me to my first upright position and my first coherent calls for help.

There was nothing the four parents could do but wait and watch and refuse each other's overtures, everyone hating and blaming whomever their gaze fell upon across the uncarpeted waiting room. Most of all they fell on hapless Mr. Berry, who had, as the Board of Health saw it, gathered the toxic Autumn Skullcaps along with the beautiful brown Honey Mushrooms from the same mossy log. Half-delirious, I thought our parents and the doctors were lying to me, swearing Kris was alive, while he, down the hall, was daily trying to trick them into admitting I was dead. "Did you go to Natalie's funeral?" he asked his parents.

"Natalie is *alive*," they would say to each of his questions. "Why don't you believe us?"

"Prove it," he would say.

One night, late, the nicest nurse in the world, a huge muscle man with a gray buzz cut and SEMPER FI tattooed on a bicep, carried me—in two johnnies—and my IV pole to the door of Kris's room.

"See," he said. "Okay? Do you believe me now?"

I said, "How do I know he's not in a coma?"

"Look at the tray. He ate two turkey dinners."

I said, "Please, Hank."

He carried me across the threshold. "Kris?" I whispered.

"Hey! Berryboy," said Hank, louder.

Kris opened his eyes.

I said, "Are you alive?"

He said, "I am if you are."

I cried, "It's all my fault. I never returned your father's book."

He said, looking like a prisoner of war, but sounding like himself, "Baloney!"

I cried into Hank's thick neck, thrilled, knowing that a dying man would utter something more poetic.

"Can't she walk?" Kris asked Hank.

Hank groaned, pretending to be annoyed, and put me down gently.

I said, "You wouldn't give us a minute?"

He said, "One minute. But sit in that chair."

"How about on the bed?"

"When are they letting us out?" Kris asked him.

"You're wasting your valuable time," said Hank. "I'd be smooching by now if it was me."

I tried to sit on the edge of his bed, and when I couldn't manage the hop, I fell to my knees. "I thought they were lying," I sobbed.

"About what?"

"About you."

I felt his hand smoothing my hair. "The Polaroid didn't help?" he asked.

I wiped my face on his sheet and looked up. I said, "I was scared and delirious. I thought it was a setup, a snapshot they took before you died."

"Smiling? Giving the peace sign?"

I whimpered.

"The notes didn't do it, either?"

I said, "They weren't notarized. I only had my father's word."

He smiled, and his eyes shimmered. "You must really love me," he said.

Eventually, they let us watch TV and take meals together, and once, with Hank standing guard, we had an illegal fifteen minutes in the shower. My parents' generalized fury at all things Berry softened as they paced with Ingrid and Karl, waiting—first, for their children to die, and then for them to come back.

They returned to Newton after a three-week vigil, after the doctors announced the danger past, and the famous mycologist said we'd simply ingested too few specimens to die. Everyone kissed and meant it—Ingrid and Eddie, Audrey and Karl, Gretel, doctors, nurses, orderlies, phlebotomists, Hank.

"I'll visit her every day and call you," Ingrid promised Audrey.

"Collect," said my mother.

"If you insist," said Ingrid.

"You're not taking Natalie home with you?" Kris asked when my parents went in to say good-bye.

They said, No, not this time. No.

"If the Inn doesn't reopen, I won't have a job," he said.

My mother held up a hand to shush him, imperiously, like the chairman of a congressional committee. "I used to think that was important," she said. "Now I'm only interested in things like life and death."

"I never understood what you did there anyway," my father said.

$\mathcal{T}$he cost to the Berrys was the hotel. "Poisonings at the Inn at Lake Devine" went forth from Green Mountain Medical Center and the Vermont Department of Public Health to the streets of Gilbert, to provisioners, to rival innkeepers, to travel agents, to tourists, to subscribers of mycology newsletters, to leaf-peepers, to stringers, to wire services.

Ingrid and Karl had to hold their heads up in Gilbert, had to endure further humiliations, such as hiring an outside caterer and hall for Gretel's wedding reception. The Inn was also cited for mouse droppings in a pantry drawer and a failure to post an EMPLOYEES MUST WASH HANDS sign in the downstairs lav—transgressions that would never have made the papers but for Mr. Berry's picking little brown mushrooms containing deadly amanitins and my baking them into a near-fatal pie.

We knew that our tiny hospital wedding—with no relatives in attendance, Hank as witness, cake from the cafeteria, flowers from Maternity, and officiating by the mayor, who, unavoidably, had issued the executive order to close the Inn—while not the unwelcome news it once would have been, was the silver lining that would remind the public about the cloud over the hotel.

"Is she pregnant, too?" my mother-in-law of one hour asked when Kris called to tell her our news.

He said, "Let's start this conversation over: I announce to you, in a tone suggesting that your most floundering and least favorite child has returned from the dead to find true love. What does a mother say to that?"

I could hear her grousing syllables crackling over the wires.

"For *love*, Ma," he said impatiently. "I love Natalie, and she loves me, and when you feel this strongly, you get married."

Blotches started on his neck and rose to his face. "Yeah, well . . . life is short, isn't it? Some of us learned that this winter."

I signaled, It's okay. It doesn't matter. Say good-bye.

Exasperated, he ran his bony fingers through his dark brown hair, thrilling me with the sight of the gold ring on his bachelor hand. I didn't ask him to repeat Ingrid's outburst or condemn it. Inside my own wedding band were the words that counted, a surprise he'd dictated over this same hospital phone to the local jeweler: *Kris & Natalie ≈ Semper Fi*—all the blessings I needed from a Berry.

We were discharged together, twenty-seven days after the poisonings, and, while Kris technically had a home to go back to, it no longer functioned as an inn.

My mother had kept up my rent on the attic apartment, so Kris and I returned there, to part-time jobs at Marx Fruit and Audrey Marx Properties, respectively, and postponed our honeymoon for the foreseeable future. A check was waiting—five hundred dollars for "consultations rendered" from Mr. Simone. They had read about my mishap and miraculous recovery in the *Boston Herald*, he wrote on his firm's letterhead. He and Hilda wished me every success in future endeavors, but, there being no formalized agreement with the future Chez Simone, the deal—such as it was—was off.

"They don't want the mushroom murderess on their payroll," I said.

"You didn't want that stupid job anyway."

"I'm a pariah."

"It'll pass," he said.

" 'NEWTON GIRL BRINGS DOWN THE HOUSE OF BERRY.' "

"Not on purpose," said the true-blue Kris.

I resigned myself to a future in real estate, telling myself that few people return from the dead to achieve both professional and personal happiness. Back at my old desk, I took messages, and wrote classified ads; I photographed the interiors and exteriors of houses with my mother's Polaroid, and then, like an extra-credit project, mounted them on poster board for display in the agency's dusty front windows. I was particularly unconvincing at sales, which I did only at the unlicensed, telephone level. If a caller asked about the cozy ranch on the dynamic street, I would picture its cramped rooms and the traffic whizzing by. Distaste for the property would creep into my voice. My mother tried to educate me in the ways of real estate diplomacy, explaining that one person's bad taste was another person's dream decor, so I should not spit in anyone's water, because I might have to drink it.

I hated it still. I hated the buyers and the sellers, the competition and the co-brokers, the dress-up clothes required for desk work, the clerks in the courthouse, and the typesetters in Classified. When I confessed to my mother that I didn't think I could ever be fulfilled in real estate, she said, "I know."

She paid for me to see a therapist, who pointed out that I couldn't undo the poisonings by staying out of kitchens. For homework she asked me to write a list of life-affirming things that could happen at a future restaurant of mine. Grudgingly, and not until I was seated in her waiting room the following week, did I scribble: "marriage proposals," "wedding receptions," "anniversary & birthday parties," "bar and bat mitzvahs," "job offers," "mergers," "deals," and "misc. celebrations."

I should cook toward that goal, the therapist said, waving my lackluster list: for love and for personal happiness—my own and my future patrons'.

I asked, "What if I make another mistake? I know someone who put peanut butter into her chili, and a customer died of an allergic reaction not an hour later."

"And where is that cook today?" she asked smartly. "In a penitentiary?"

"No."

"Why not?"

I admitted what my friend the unindicted chef had learned the hard way: A horrible mistake is not a crime. The customer takes his chances, the restaurant's attorney had said, when he orders a mélange like chili. Case law regarding fish bones in chowder and a choking plaintiff backed him up.

She asked if I was staying out of kitchens because I was genuinely afraid of poisoning more people, or if I was sentencing myself to life behind the bars of Audrey Marx Properties for my imagined crime.

I said I hadn't seen it in quite that way.

"Do you find anything fulfilling in the work your mother and sister do?"

I said without a second's reflection, "Not a thing."

$\mathcal{I}$ read my short, gaping résumé to Kris as he scrambled eggs for dinner.

"What's the big hurry?" he asked. "We're doing okay. I don't want to deliver baskets for the rest of my life, but it's only temporary." He pointed out that I was not back to my fighting weight, and as long as I was still fading in the afternoons, it was best to have the flexibility offered by working for family.

"What if this never passes?" I asked.

He knew I meant my fear of food, not the fatigue. He said, "Doctors lose patients and go back into the O.R. Drivers hit pedestrians and get back behind the wheel. Firefighters reenter burning buildings. Liz Taylor and Richard Burton are heading back down the aisle. You'll cook again."

TWENTY SEVEN

Distraught over our condition, Linette had enlisted Mr. Feldman and his minions to pray for us. More than one bison-size flower arrangement had arrived at the hospital from "Your friends at the Halseeyon," followed—when we had been upgraded from serious to fair—by enough *rugalekh* to feed the town of Gilbert.

"Who's that boy who calls here after he thinks we're asleep?" her father finally asked.

"Nelson?" Linette said, managing to convey the sheer nerve and wrongheadedness of such a question. "He's calling with medical bulletins. He's just a friend."

"I was young once," said her father, "no matter what kind of a shnook you take me for. You haven't been the same since that boy jumped in the pool."

"Natalie and Kris may die," she told him.

"I'm watching you," he warned.

When we didn't die, when my parents survived the news of my mixed, civil marriage and the world didn't end, Linette found the courage to call Joel. He listened with unusual, almost suspect, equanimity and said, "Let me think this over. There's someone I should confer with here. I'll call you Sunday."

"I'm sorry," said Linette. "I never meant to drag this thing out. I didn't know my own mind."

"I'm not exactly stunned," said Joel.

He didn't wait until Sunday, but called her back that same night. "Here's what you do," he advised. "Tell them it's my decision."

"Why?"

Joel said, "Tell them I had doubts about your commitment to marrying a rabbi and to being a *rebbetzen*. Tell them I was concerned about the differences in our backgrounds and our values, and in the end I felt it was wrong to uproot you and ask you to give up the hotel."

"Is this true?"

"Tell them that," he said. "It'll make it easier if they hate me instead of you."

"What a great guy," I said later, marveling at his civility.

"Please," Linette sneered. "He's *shtupping* someone in Cincinnati."

$\mathcal{H}$e didn't sit *shiva* or formally disown her, but Mr. Feldman stopped speaking to Linette as soon as she began collecting corrugated boxes and talking nonsense about a change of scenery. Out of nowhere, he grumbled, she's interested in Providence. "Who moves to Rhode Island?" he wanted to know.

Linette countered that Providence had much to recommend it: It had ocean, it had Brown, it had history, it had hotels in case she wanted to keep her fingers in that pot. It had been seven years since graduation, and he knew what that meant, didn't he? A sabbatical. She would audit courses at the Rhode Island School of Design and at Johnson & Wales, where disciplines would accrue to the eventual benefit of the Halseeyon. Hal Feldman believed none of it. There was a boy at the heart of this—in Providence of all places. The wrong kind of boy, he was certain, despite Linette's denials.

He said cunningly, "It would be one thing if I thought you had a friend or two there, but leaving your family to go live among strangers . . ."

"I have friends there," she said.

"That boy," he pounced. "The *shmegege* who jumped in the pool."

"You gave him a medal. You called him a great humanitarian."

"I treated him like a headliner," Hal retorted, "and the *gonef* helps himself to my daughter."

"He saved a soul. You said that in front of witnesses; you quoted the Talmud; you announced that his name was inscribed in the Book of Life."

"You think Minna Gitlow needed saving in four feet of water?" her father yelled, his complexion deepening to a purplish red. "I was looking to make a gesture, to liven things up. I'm no rabbi."

"It's irrelevant. My taking a leave of absence has nothing to do with Nelson Berry or Minna Gitlow."

"You'll be back," he shouted. "You're not walking out on the Halseeyon. I'm semiretired. And you're engaged to someone else."

"Daddy," said Linette. "It was Joel's decision to break up. I need to get away so there aren't the constant reminders."

"She's lying," he told his friends around the pinochle table.

"You've got four daughters," they counseled. "Did you think every one of them was going to take up with someone you approve of?"

Young people . . . It's different today . . . My niece, my nephew; my own daughter, my own son, his friends said.

"Achhh," said Mr. Feldman.

*M*y mother seized the opportunity to contact the Feldman family, writing a thank-you note for flowers and baked goods on my behalf, introducing herself as practically *mekhutonim*. "You must miss Linette terribly," she wrote. "We saw her yesterday, when she stopped by my place of business to visit my daughter Natalie. What a lively and intelligent girl you raised. She is broadening her horizons in Providence, but as a parent I know what a hole this leaves in your heart. P.S. The Inn at Lake Devine is on the market."

Her note and business card arrived a month after Linette's departure, at a time when Hal Feldman was feeling unfamiliar sensations. What had seemed in the heat of the moment a father's prerogative—to scream things he didn't mean at his daughter's back and to throw away his little red-haired baby with the bathwater—now discomfited him. While conceding nothing on the boy, he did admit one night, after a particularly satisfying dinner of lima beans, sweet potatoes, and carrots simmered all day with brisket, that the thought of bringing her back into the business sooner rather than later wasn't the worst idea he'd ever had, especially given Linette's talents and, God forbid, her prospects with a Gentile schoolteacher.

He told his wife and mother what he was thinking: a hotel for Linette to cut her teeth on; a small, classy inn with no overhead to speak of—they were asking *bubkes* for it—in that state with the foliage, not New Hampshire, the other one—cows, maple syrup, Calvin Coolidge: Vermont. Far enough from Providence to wear down the *sheygets*, far enough from home to make her think she was on her own. Someone give her a call.

"*You* give her a call," said his wife and mother both.

 Stubbornly, in the face of their poorly disguised affection, and, more often than not, no answer when we phoned Linette's apartment, Nelson and Linette continued to call their love affair a friendship. At odd moments I believed them, but mostly I felt that I knew the truth: They were in love, had been in love for longer than even they acknowledged to each other, but for reasons of religion and ascension and superstition—both had been engaged with full ceremony to people they never married—neither wanted to advertise or formalize their union. Linette's truth, as I understood it, was that as long as her parents were alive, she would be the daughter who went to business; the modern one, who didn't live at home, who didn't need a ring, a wedding, or china, or silver. A presentable, amiable companion like Nelson would do very nicely on those occasions when a woman wanted to be seen with a man.

$\mathcal{I}$ approached food slowly, coaxing artless dishes like roast chicken and broiled chops from my narrow apartment stove. I moved on to stewing and braising, and even to creamy mélanges that required layering in glass casseroles. Finally, in an arithmetic progression of ingredients, I made an elaborate Moroccan couscous with lamb—kosher lamb, actually, because Linette was coming for dinner, our first dinner party in Mr. Zinler's attic, on our telephone-cable spool table.

She and Nelson brought not only wine, and cannoli from their favorite bakery, but gift-wrapped knives, a wedding present that made me burst into tears for its generosity, its aptness, and for the faith it implied: top-of-the-line German high-carbon-steel works of art—a six-inch chef's knife, an eight-inch chef's knife, a paring knife, a boning knife, a slicing knife, plus a steel for sharpening and a magnetic bar for storage. The card read, "Your biggest fan, Nelson."

"How did you know?" I asked.

"Everyone needs knives," Linette said, "and I figured a chef needs them more than most people."

"Pammy wanted to give me a kitchen shower, but I declined," I said, marveling at their feel, the weight of the blade against the mass of the handle.

"Robin had a bridal shower," Nelson said quietly, "but I think all she got was lingerie."

"I had one," Linette said brightly.

"Oh really?" asked Nelson, eyebrows arched. "What would that have been? A hair gizmo shower? Or a dingy-cotton-underpants shower?"

Linette stuck out her tongue at him, and he returned it.

"Do you have to return shower gifts after an engagement is broken?" I asked, hoping to elicit more private jokes, more displays of affection.

"Nah," said Linette. "It was so long ago, I don't remember what I did with them. Except a popcorn popper. I took that with me." She turned to Nelson. "And the electric blanket, now that I think of it."

Kris stabbed a leftover piece of lamb on my plate and, just before popping it in his mouth, asked, "Are there dual controls on this blanket? If I may cut through the bullshit."

"What bullshit?" Linette asked.

He mimicked in falsetto, "We're good friends, my pal Nelson and I. Notice that the wedding present is from him alone, because we're not a couple. We're so clever that nobody has caught on."

"Are you really angry?" Linette asked.

Kris said, "I get the part about your parents—a sick mother and a hothead father. But Natalie and I don't need a song and dance. It's insulting."

"It's not like you can't trust us," I said.

"And it's not like Nat and I are the couple of the year."

Nelson cleared his throat and said solemnly, after studying our faces, "If it works out—Mr. Feldman's offer on the Inn—I'm taking a leave of absence from school."

"As what?" I asked.

He smiled. "Manager-in-training. See if I still have it."

Kris prompted with twirls of a finger. *And?*

"To see if he's cut out for the hotel life," said Linette.

"With—?"

"Me," said Linette.

"My cupcake," Nelson said.

"So what was the big secret?" Kris demanded.

"My parents," said Linette. "Your parents. The Fifes. Five thousand years of Jewish law."

"The Fifes?" I repeated.

"It hasn't been so long, and you know Nelson—always wants to do the *menschy* thing."

"And where will you hide him when your father visits?" I asked.

Linette was shaking her head emphatically, curls flapping from a cinched geyser of hair on her crown. "He won't leave my mother overnight, he won't eat non-kosher food, and he won't stay in a *pitsel* hotel with no golf course."

"How's this acquisition going to get you back in the fold?" I asked.

"It'll be in the family," said Linette. "If he can't have me at the next desk, he'll settle for me managing a satellite location."

"What if it's a complete disaster?" Kris asked. "What if you can't undo the damage and no one comes?"

"They'll come," said Linette. "I'll see to it."

"It might take time," said Nelson.

"And if they still don't come," Linette said, "he can always sell."

"Or book a couple of headliners," said Kris.

I knew enough to ask if her father's offer had been presented in writing, with a binder, and Linette said, "Of course."

"Have they accepted?"

"They will. There's been no takers," Linette confided. "Not one other offer tendered."

"Are they furious?" I asked.

"Not exactly," said Nelson.

Linette held out her wineglass. "It's America, remember? If the Berrys don't want Hal Feldman's money, they can send him away."

TWENTY-EIGHT

Gretel became Mrs. Donald Fife, Jr., at the Dogteam Tavern in early May. Kris was an usher, and I was nothing official, although my pink moiré sheath and dyed-to-match high heels had served as my bridesmaid outfit at my sister's wedding. Rosy and plump but not obviously pregnant, Gretel wore her mother's satin wedding dress and 1940s pageboy to great effect. I was sure her fashion decision was purely one of fit and cut, but I still gave her credit for wearing an old-fashioned dress that would not remind anyone of Robin's. The Bobolinks, Middlebury's a cappella group, sang "One Hand, One Heart," which I found an ironic and sad choice, in view of the single-ring ceremony and the smirk on Chip's face from start to finish.

The Fife sons were sober enough to perform their groom and best-man duties but drunk enough to infuriate Kris, who demanded a caucus in the men's room. Immediately afterward, a chastened Chip held his child bride close for two slow dances. Gretel looked pleased with her husband, snuggling against him, her wide gold wedding band on display. In marked contrast to his wife's blissful smile, Chip mugged for his friends, as if an unpopular girl had snagged him for a ladies' choice.

At the head table, Kris asked me, smoking the only cigar I'd ever known him to light, "Is it as clear to everyone else as it is to me?"

I said, "You can't always tell. Maybe when they're alone, he's different."

"He's twenty-six years old," said Kris. "He shoots hoops every night in his driveway. He's going to an amusement park for his honeymoon."

I said, "Look at her. She's beaming. And you know they're going to have their picture taken with Goofy and Pluto, which will become their Christmas card."

He stubbed out his cigar and kissed me. At the other end of the head table, as if we had reminded him of a duty yet to be performed, Mr. Fife tapped his champagne glass with a knife until the guests took note. I steeled myself for the inevitable eulogy to the near wedding of Robin and Nelson and the near union of these two families. Instead, he toasted Kris and me, taking credit for our meeting as children and finding each other again as adults, to the muted applause of the mildly bored spectators.

Eventually Gretel, in her peach-linen ensemble and black straw boater, lobbed tea roses into the brood of Bobolinks, none of whom, I noticed, had been asked to dance by a single former fraternity brother of the groom. On impulse, I kissed Gretel, who surprised me with the intensity of the hug she returned.

Kris and I left shortly after Chip's Mustang honked its way out of sight, crepe paper flying and hubcaps clanging. By way of goodbyes, I complimented Ingrid on her ice-blue raw-silk outfit and the fruit cup, the london broil, the wild-rice pilaf, the green beans almondine, the mimosa salad, the lemon wedding cake, and the champagne punch. "Excellent choices," I told her.

"Thank you, Natalie," she said, and offered me her cheek.

My parents gave us a wedding check I didn't think they could afford, and—when Linette created our jobs at the Inn—the title to my mother's car, which she claimed did not have enough leg room for clients. We received an enormous carton, parcel post, from my in-laws shortly after Gretel's wedding. Nestled in newspaper confetti were a pressed-glass punch bowl and twenty-three dainty cups. The card said, "Kris, you probably recognize this from many happy occasions. It is a family heirloom, one we didn't want to auction along with the rest of the contents. Please think of us when you use it. (Scoops of sherbet floating on top are a nice decorative touch.) With our best wishes, Mother and Dad."

$\mathcal{G}$retel gave birth to Berry, quite adorable, in September, on schedule, on the very day Squeaky Fromme aimed a pistol at President Ford. Because she looked like Chip, lean rather than round, baby Berry also looked like her Aunt Robin, or maybe it was wishful thinking on all our parts. To my astonishment, Kris and I were asked to be her godparents. Gretel explained in less than flattering fashion that of the three brother-candidates, Jeff had no interest in or aptitude for babies; Nelson—well, who knew when he'd ever be back to normal; which left Kris, who had been a decent enough brother, and even had a wife to help.

As godparents by default, we tried a little too hard when visiting, offering to change diapers and to negotiate Berry's unwieldy navy-blue English perambulator around the neighborhood. Often it would be Mr. Fife accompanying me, pushing the carriage proudly, calling out to neighbors as they raked leaves and washed cars, "Come see our new little girl. Come meet my granddaughter." He'd introduce me as the baby's aunt, his daughter-in-law's brother's wife, then would always add, quietly if inaccurately, "Natalie was a dear friend of our Robin's." As he and I would move dolefully on to the next house, I'd cheer him slightly by saying, "I think you're her favorite. She coos and smiles a lot more when you're pushing the carriage. It must be your voice." On solo walks, he serenaded her the whole time—Rodgers and Hammerstein, mostly, or early Peter, Paul, and Mary. Before long, he noticed a sound coming from inside the carriage—a toneless, steady, one-note hum: tiny Berry trying to sing.

. . .

$\mathcal{A}$s soon as their granddaughter was christened and the papers were passed, Karl and Ingrid moved to Florida. They claimed it was what they had always dreamed of—to live in a condo, free of responsibility, no guests, no employees. They kept up their subscription to the Gilbert *Independent*, and sent the occasional clipping and help-wanted ad, which they thought might interest Kris. Once in a while, Ingrid would report some social tidbit by telephone, dropping a Jewish surname so I'd understand that she had won friends around the swimming pool by mentioning the heritage of her second son's wife.

She tried golf and tennis, and somewhere within those circles found a crowd and a purpose. Her Christmas card was a photograph of her new prides and joy—two adult miniature schnauzers with papers and long names. Training and showing her ready-made champions not only kept her busy but suited her, temperamentally and socially. "She likes the other owners as much as she likes the dogs," reported Karl. "Her boys have won two second-place ribbons so far, and she's not-so-secretly hoping for Best of Breed in Tampa."

Mr. Berry wrote to us every week, telling us more than we wanted to know about his new garden—his lemon, lime, and date trees; his hibiscus and gardenia bushes; his orchids, bougainvillea, and birds-of-paradise, none of which, he bragged, would survive Vermont winters. "I'm thinking of a part-time job," he eventually wrote. "Maybe as a volunteer guide. Looking into the Everglades, or helping out at the Thomas A. Edison and Henry Ford winter home in Fort Myers a couple days a week. It's an arboretum, and, as you know, I'm pretty handy with the flora and the fauna."

$\mathcal{L}$inette and I recommended, and Kris and Nelson agreed, that the former owners' name should not be printed on any promotional materials, and that the word *mushroom* must never appear on the menu—in any form, in any dish, in any language. We wanted the appearance of a new management, a new kitchen, a new spirit. Linette said, "What we want to achieve is the sense that the old Inn burned to the ground and we started over fresh, not risen from the ashes; no ghosts, no leftover monogrammed plates and towels; no matchbooks, no vans still registered to the old regime."

Kris said, Okay, then; two could play this game. For his part: no bingo, no Simon Says, no Polynesian nights, no shuffleboard, no boiled meat, no non-dairy coffee creamer, no Harry of Harry's Hairpieces fitting toupees in the lobby.

Nelson insisted on one concession to his dignity and to his years in the classroom—that his branch of the Halcyon, on his lake, be spelled correctly. He also asked one day, well into the renovations, if we could relocate instead of junk the old porch sign, perhaps hang it indoors on an inconspicuous wall, like folk art; like a memorial plaque.

"Absolutely not," said Linette. "We're severing that tie."

"The matriarchy is dead; long live the matriarchy," intoned Kris, paintbrush in hand. The four of us were turning the big gray dining room to a soft yellow with a glossy white trim that afternoon.

Linette said, "But you know what we can do? In terms of an archive? Those old photos of guests in the Adirondack chairs and the men in knickers playing croquet? We'll frame them and make a grouping in the office—those, and that adorable one of you two holding Gretel on the dock, in matching outfits, scowling into the sun."

"Any photo, in other words," said Nelson, "that doesn't identify the place."

"No?" said Linette airily. "Not a good idea?"

"Sounds cute to me," I said. "As long as we're not sweeping too much under the rug."

"You know what else we could do?" Linette continued. "We *could* keep that sign out front—it's got a nice shape and it's in good condition—and just paint *The Halcyon* on top of it in the new colors and the new typeface."

I said, "I like that. It would still be there—'The Inn at Lake Devine, established nineteen twenty-two'—and you two would know it was underneath, its maiden name, so to speak, even if no one could see it."

"What would be the point of that?" asked Nelson.

"Like an undercoat," I said. "A primer."

Nelson said to Kris, "Do you notice how they patronize us?"

Kris said, "They think we're shlemiels."

Linette said, "Really, think about it: We agreed it's not good business to remind people of what was here . . . as much as we hate to be unsentimental about the birthplace of our loved ones."

Nelson went to work. He dipped his brush into yellow paint and began writing THE INN AT LAKE DEVINE across the old gray wall. Kris caught on after the first few letters and joined in. Their graffiti contest raged from there: BERRY BROS., PROP . . . CHRISTIANS WELCOME . . . FOR A GOOD TIME CALL NATALIE @ EXT. 07 . . . And the one that left them hanging off each other: HOME OF THE LITTLE BROWN MUSHROOM.

To amuse only myself, I wrote discreetly in one corner, "Long Live Chez Natalie." I painted a bulging, anatomically correct heart around it, an arrow through it, an aorta ascending, various arteries, four chambers in a cross-section, and a set of initials in each.

Kris saw it, nudged Nelson, and in two strokes it was gone.

Linette and I smiled—at the boys, at each other, in general. Good sports and gracious winners, we collapsed the ladders and declared the workday done.

ACKNOWLEDGMENTS

I wouldn't have started or finished this book without the support of the following exceptional people: Mameve Medwed and Stacy Schiff, my first readers, safety nets, and inexhaustible friends; my editor, Deborah Futter, who made me feel that revisions were gifts from me to her, and inspired them in the most doting, constructive, and good-humored way; Ginger Barber and every blessed person at the Virginia Barber Literary Agency; Madeleine Blais, who claimed, when I called, that she had always wanted to go to the Catskills; Ben Austin, Nick Katzenbach, and Justine Katzenbach for their company and contributions to that trip; Bob Austin, the model for my dear fictional husbands; Pat McDonagh, who taught me everything I know about mushrooms; Caroline Leavitt, who got well and back to her computer; and my mother, Julia Lipman, who remembered after thirty-five years the exact wording of the letter from the hotel on the lake.

ABOUT THE TYPE

This book was set in Berling. Designed in 1951 by Karl Erik Forsberg for the Typefoundry Berlingska Stilgjuteri AB in Lund, Sweden, it was released the same year in foundry type by H. Berthold AG. A classic old-face design, its generous proportions and inclined serifs make it highly legible.